KATERI

FROM THE
DEEP

SECRETS LURK BENEATH

Content compiled for publication by Richard Mayers
of *Burton Mayers Books*.
Cover design by Richard Mayers

First published by Burton Mayers Books 2022.
All rights reserved.

A CIP catalogue record for this book is available from
the British Library

ISBN: 1-8383459-4-5
ISBN-13: 978-1-8383459-4-5

Typeset in **Adobe Garamond**

www.BurtonMayersBooks.com

A writer wouldn't be anywhere without their support team. I want to thank my family and friends for their love and support. To my partner, Kenny for being there for me.

Thank you to Richard Mayers for taking a chance on this story.

My wonderful beta readers, Michelle Cook and Sarah Davis, and also to Gavin Gardiner; your feedback, suggestions, ideas and well wishes have really turned this story around.

To Ric O'Barry and your team, thank you for making The Cove. This novel wouldn't exist if it wasn't for your documentary.

And... to you my dear reader,

thank you for being on this journey with me.

The time will come when men such as I will look upon the murder of animals as they now look on the murder of men.

-Leonardo da Vinci

For my parents,

Paula Antonia Maria Edwards

and

Philip Charles Edwards.

If it wasn't for the introduction to the world of creativity
through your choice of music, movies and so much more -
I wouldn't be doing this.

Thank you.

I love you.

Prologue

Ian Copton decides to head out on his boat, Serenity. After the fallout from today's demonstration, his job had been cut short due to a potential danger. The authorities never said anything about the amount of rubbish protestors left behind. It was a sure way to drive anyone holidaying in Drake Cove to demand their money back. But this is the world nowadays. Emotions are more important than rationality and steel hard facts.

"A load of bullshit," he whispers, dangling the rod over the edge.

Ian waits for several minutes until he senses a pull before reeling in the line. Pierced by the sharp hook, the fish flaps helplessly. He clasps his hand around its head, rips the hook free and drops it into the bucket by his foot. Ian repeats this several times until Serenity shakes, violently.

Ian reluctantly resumes his fishing, hurling the line back into the water, muttering swear words under his breath. If it wasn't for his choice of career, people wouldn't be able to eat fish at all unless they fetched it from the sea themselves. The consumers didn't have to get up at the crack of dawn, heave a heavy net and come home stinking of fish guts.

There's a sudden pull on the fishing line. Ian frowns, trying to yank the rod, twisting the coil, but he can't shift it. He must've hooked a pretty big one. He uses his full weight to pull the line in but it doesn't budge. Then

Serenity shakes again. The line goes slack.

Fuming, Ian peers over the side with his flashlight and sees something. His blood runs cold as his brain explodes with hectic possibilities. Before he can process some sort of strategy, it springs out from the water, seizing his fishing rod, dragging him overboard.

The ice-cold water munches at his limbs and he kicks out at the figure, his palm tightening around the handle of the rod. He hears an angry squeal when the rod splits in two. Then a pain erupts in his chest.

Ian breathes out, water races into his lungs like a tidal wave, suffocating him. He remembers seaweed circling his head and a pair of large, piercing eyes glaring back before the darkness finally engulfs him.

Herb Clarke kicks several coffee cups across the sand, mumbling about the mess. Alone time with his thoughts and the fresh sea air always got his creative juices flowing. His current worry is marketing his book shop whilst coordinating everything else. He hadn't grown up in the social media age until his niece showed him the mechanics. Now, he's all over it, taking pretty decorative pictures, hoping the attractive graphics would inspire any literature loving customers to empty their pockets. His niece mentioned something, a popular social media platform the younger generation lapped up like milkshakes. But he'd read enough scathing stories to know it wasn't for him. How would it generate sufficient interest to sell books? What could he do to stand out?

Herb continues with his walk until he sees a murky frame lying on the sand. He squints, trying to get a closer look, thinking it's a heap of black bin liners. Then he notices...the outline of an arm, and leg.

"Oh my God," he utters, jogging over when he realises it's the body of a man. It's someone he knows too.

"Ian?" Herb asks.

The man's clothes have darkened from the water. His golden hair has whitened and it clings to his grey skin. Herb touches his shoulder, turning the man to find a metallic spike lodged in his chest. Ian's eyes bulge out of his head. The fishing line is lashed around his neck, penetrating his skin. The hook is embedded in his face, right down to the bone. The repulsive smell of dead flesh hits Herb's stomach.

The police station's only a half an hour walk away, ten if he drives but he can't leave the body. Herb's shaky fingers jab at his phone screen, missing the correct numbers now and then as he makes the call. When someone answers on the other end, Herb has to carefully piece his words together like a puzzle.

1

My head feels ten times too big when the alarm rattles. The sound's like a drill burrowing into my ear. My back's sticking to the bedsheet, it's a fucking oven in here. I blink through the fog, the whiskey bottle stares back at me, half of its contents drained. A shameful reminder.

My phone buzzes and I reach for it, seeing the blurry letters of a text message. I have to wait a couple of seconds for my eyes to adjust:

Work cancelled. Again. Come to the office anyway. Got something to tell you.

It's from my boss, Michael Blocksidge.

I reply:

Hope it's nothing bad. Got to drop Em off at Herb's and I'll be right there.

I have a quick shower and haul on my clothes. My daughter's sitting at the kitchen table with bright blue buds lodged in her ears. The music is screeching. What is it with young people, do they not care about losing their hearing?

Apparently, times have changed. Everything's available from the click of a button or the swipe of a screen. Emily would have to be surgically removed from her phone. When we used to go on holiday, I insisted she turn the damned thing off or at least put it on airplane mode so we could have some proper father and daughter time. Eventually, it'd transform into an argument and end up in me losing the battle.

My wife was better at dealing with those conflicts. She

was a better parent too. We had Emily pretty young. We met in school, in the same year. We were married at nineteen and pregnant at twenty-one. In the contemporary world, we'd be classified as old fashioned.

I'm so glad I had a childhood without the influence of the internet and everything else. There was no such thing as iPads, apps and whatever the kids are into now. Mobiles were just getting popular when I was a teenager, back when its only function was to call and text. And play that Snake game. I miss those days.

Our cat, Keira is sitting like a loaf by her empty bowl, waiting for her breakfast. She glares at me with her luminous green eyes. I empty a wet pouch and it splats into her bowl. She nudges my hand when I scratch the top of her fuzzy head.

"You look terrible," Emily says.

"And a good morning to you too Em," I chuckle, marching over to the kettle.

She waves my travel mug. "I've already made coffee."

"You didn't need to."

Em shrugs. "It's fine. I don't mind. Plus, I'm better at making it anyway."

I observe my fourteen-year-old. Her white nails dance across the keys of her little laptop, PC thing. She has a strong feline gaze with cropped caramel blonde hair, inherited from her mother, cut just above her chin, emphasising her lovely oval face. She used to have it long and sweeping down her back, then after her mother…well, Em chopped it all off.

I sip my coffee. "What are you writing?"

"My blog," she answers.

"Blog?"

She looks at me like I'm crazy. "Yeah, Dad. A blog. It's

similar to a journal, but it's online."

I nearly choke on my drink. "What's a fourteen-year-old got to write about?"

"A lot, Dad. Think about it."

"I'm sorry, Em. I didn't put two and two together."

"Dad, relax. I'm not using my real name. My account's private. If anybody wants to read it, they have to be approved by me first. I haven't said where I live or anything."

"Why can't you just write in a notebook like everybody else?"

She rolls her eyes, she does this far too much. "Are we going to Herb's or what?"

It's the first week of the summer holidays. I have it all planned out. Mondays and Tuesdays, Em's volunteering at the book shop. Wednesdays and Thursdays, she's at sailing school. Fridays and the weekends, she can be a lady of leisure and do what she likes. As long as it's within my approval.

The great thing about living in Drake Cove is everything's within a reasonable distance. I know certain people don't favour the thought of living in a small seaside town. Some don't like the familiarity; others have a bizarre idea we have no privacy. Well, it's pure bollocks. I don't know everyone in Drake Cove or their personal business and they certainly don't know mine. I grew up here, knowing I wanted to stay. If others didn't, they left, so be it.

I hate it when village or country folk are labelled as isolated or narrow-minded, or in some perverse manner, that we're inbred. That's the type of crap Drake Covians receive on a daily basis.

Derek greets us when we enter the shop. He's Herb's partner in work and in life. They've been together for years.

"Hi Uncle Derek," Em says.

They aren't real uncles but they've been in her life since day one, they might as well be family.

"Everything alright?" I ask.

"You haven't heard?" Derek utters in shock, looking paler than normal. "Herb's been at the police station all morning. He found a body washed up on the beach."

"Holy fuck," I say.

"Language, Dad." Em clocks me. "Is Uncle Herb going to be okay?"

Derek smiles pleasantly as his glasses fall down his nose. "He'll be fine, sweetheart. He's giving them a statement. He'll be back later." He ushers her behind the counter, sweeping a curtain of salt and pepper hair out of his face. "I need you to help me price the new stock." He glances at me momentarily. "She'll be fine, Jules. You can head off."

"Well, I've been called in even though we're not going out on the water, again. I'll be back when I can." I look directly at Em. "If I'm not here by closing time, I pray you can let yourself in?"

She rolls her eyes again. "I'll be fine, Dad. Home's only five minutes away."

I arrive at the office within ten minutes. Beforehand, I took a detour and Derek was right, the police have cornered off the beach with their iconic blue and white tape. The area's not just a political hotspot anymore, it's an official crime scene.

Great, the Fucking-Arsehole-Cunts-Against-the-Hard-Working Man, excuse me, the Fighters Against Animal Cruelty will be all over this. A handful of police officers shoo off the placard cretins to picket somewhere else. Summertime's their breeding ground. Except, this year they've been extra vicious and doubled in numbers. I swear some of them are only a couple years older than Em. They wear balaclavas, as if they're part of some secret army. I've had a couple of run-ins with them; it's mainly heckling, that I should piss off and fuck my mother. Did I mention that's the type of crap Drake Covians receive on a daily basis?

Our office is by the quay where all the boats are kept safe. There's a macabre atmosphere when I walk into the staff room. I don't like it at all.

I sit at the same table as my boss. "What's going on?" I ask.

"Police are interviewing in the meeting room," Mike replies.

"Why? What's happened?"

"Herb found Ian dead this morning."

I didn't know it was Ian and clearly neither did Derek. "What? How?"

"I don't know. Police haven't said yet. They found Serenity smashed up by Becks Hill."

Shit. My stomach's not feeling up to this. Swallowing half a bottle of whiskey the night before hasn't helped either but lately, it's been the only way to get to sleep. "What was he doing out on the water?"

Mike shrugs, stuffing his large hands into his jacket pockets. "Not too sure. Probably pissed cause our day got cut short because of those bastards."

"Why did he go out on his own?"

He sighs. "You know Ian, he's not afraid of them."

In my line of work, not being out at sea is nerve wracking. Ian must have felt the same way, so having a late night with the waves was a remedy to cure it.

"Do you reckon it's the FAAC?" I ask.

Mike nods. "The police are acting like it's an accident."

This makes me hate the group even more than I already do. "Do you think they're right?"

"Absolutely not. Ian was too careful for his own good." Mike looks me straight in the eye, his lips twitching under his greying red beard. "He's been fishing since he was a kid. He wouldn't drive his boat into the rocks. He was an experienced sailor. It's ridiculous. Something happened to him, I know it. With the picket, the culling, the fucking press and our new contract... I don't need this shitstorm right now."

As my boss rakes his meaty scarred hands down his face, the meeting room door swings open.

Daniel Cripps stands in the doorway along with two police officers perched either side of him. I hate Dan's pleasurable smile, it's unnerving and bluntly disrespectful to Ian. This guy's my deputy manager, he's been friends with Mike for years. I find it handy to stay out of his way. A former co-worker mentioned to Dan that his surname sounded like crisps, the salty potato snack. Dan didn't see the joke and he had a stare so threatening it'd startle even the most trained fighters to stop in their tracks. None of us brought up the association with his name ever again. Dan's always too upbeat when bad stuff happens, he loves a fight and the FAAC are his perfect opponents.

"Everything alright?" Mike asks.

"Of course," Dan laughs, scratching his shaved head.

"I'm heading out for a ciggie."

"Thanks for your time, Mr Cripps," the officer says, then she turns to me. "Are you Julian Finch?"

"Yes, I am." I try to show I'm not nursing a hangover.

"Best of luck," Mike says, tapping my arm. The action reminds me of when my dad gave me a reassuring hug before my sailing exam.

2

"Take a seat, Mr Finch," the officer says.

I do exactly that.

The officer doesn't look intimidating like the others guarding the beach. She's short, only coming up to my shoulder. She's not wearing a uniform either and appears to be the oldest one on patrol. She has short cropped grey hair and serious eyes with wrinkles arching around her mouth. I can't pinpoint her age; she could be in her late forties or early fifties.

"I'm Chief Inspector Lynda Drew. I assume Mr Blocksidge has already informed you about the unfortunate news concerning Mr Copton?"

"Yes, he did," I reply. "What happened?"

"Ian was found on the beach this morning. It appears he died from a wound to his chest. Please tell me what you know about Ian."

I want to be sick. This wasn't a fucking accident.

"Well, I've known Ian for most of my life. He wasn't originally from here; he came from up north, Liverpool way. We used to make fun of his Scouse accent. He never managed to shake it off. I worked alongside him, he's... shit, sorry."

"It's okay," she whispers. "Take your time."

"Thank you. He was a normal, friendly, hard-working guy."

"Did he have any family?"

"No, no wife, partner or kids. He used to tell me about

a woman he was seeing years ago but things didn't end on good terms."

"I understand," Drew says, taking notes on her pad. I notice a gleaming speckle of a gold wedding ring on her left hand. "Can you tell me if anyone would want to hurt Ian?"

I snigger and instantly regret it. Forget what I said about her height, the look Drew gives me sends an icy shiver down my spine.

"This isn't an amusing matter, Mr Finch," she says sharply.

In my panic, I can see Em staring behind a glass window with metal bars cased around me. "I'm, I'm sorry, I'm in shock. We've always had a running joke that if anyone was going to bump us off, it'd be the FAAC."

"Oh yes, the notorious Fighters Against Animal Cruelty group. Mr Cripps mentioned them in his interview. Can you tell me more about them?"

"Where do I start?" I say. "They call themselves animal rights activists but to be honest, they're anarchists. They come to Drake Cove every year to make trouble, shouting, threatening, hiding under balaclavas."

Drew nods, acknowledging my words and jots on her notepad. "Please continue. What's happened with this group?"

"Well, they started off small. People taking pictures on the hillside, at a glance, they were just tourists. Then someone took a photo of us at the culling and leaked it online. It was hideous."

"The Yearling Echo covered that story, didn't they?"

"Yeah, it was front page news and soon after that, all hell broke loose. Things here haven't been the same. Some of the protests got so severe, a couple of my former colleagues changed to different careers, some even moved out of Drake Cove completely. Since the leak, the number of working fishermen here has dwindled."

Drew nods again, keeping the mask she's wearing neutral. "My grandparents used to participate in the culling. But my mother and father didn't agree with it."

This doesn't surprise me. I've heard it before. I don't care if people disagree with my line of work, as long as they're not screaming and pouring their propaganda down my throat. It'd have to take a magic spell to change my opinion.

Drew taps her pen on the table. "Do you think someone in the FAAC could've killed Ian?"

"Honestly, I have no idea. I tend to avoid them if I can. They've been violent in the past, they still are. We're just trying to feed our families and get by every day. I know what we do leaves a rancid mess, but I have a daughter to look after and a bungalow to pay for."

Drew suddenly smiles with sincerity. "I understand, Mr Finch. Thank you for talking to me. I'm sorry for your loss. Take it easy."

"Thank you," I say, getting to my feet.

If I don't get out, I'm gonna throw up.

She opens the door, thanking me again and calls Damien into the meeting room.

Mike watches me with concern. "Everything okay, mate?"

"Yeah, it's fine."

He blanches. "You don't look it."

My stomach reacts and I race for the exit.

Cornflakes spew out over the bars, sinking into the quay. Mike's by my side as I retch. Sweat's dripping off my forehead.

13

"Sorry Jules," he says. "I know this isn't a good time."

"Drinking last night didn't help," I reply.

"You need to pack it in."

"I can't."

"Of course, you can. Don't say stupid things like that."

My stomach muscles contract painfully. "Mike, you know why."

"Jules, do it for Em." He pats me on the shoulder. "I've gotta get back. Stay out here and get some air. Work on your boat."

I do what Mike instructs and work on Henna, a small boat I built for my wife. The engine's bust so I have to replace it and there's something wrong with the pull chord, as if it's been snagged. It wouldn't surprise me if one of the FAAC's behind it. They've tried to ruin our boats before. Serenity's not tied up with the rest of the family. She should be here.

~

By lunchtime, Drew finishes her interviews. Working on Henna in the fresh air's distracted me from my stomach and the embarrassing vomiting. Mike and I head to the Crest Café, it's our favourite place to eat lunch.

Frank Blothio sits at the table in the front window, tapping madly at the keys of his laptop. I couldn't miss his bulky frame.

He has large hands like Mike, they're aged and scarred from fishing. His once golden hair's greying and thinning at the back, dark red reading glasses slip down his nose, the frown lines on his forehead are easier to see as his pale green eyes scan the screen.

Mike and Frank don't have the best history. They used to be best friends, colleagues and co-founders of the fisherie, Blothio and Blocksidge. Then their friendship broke down. What it was over, I have no idea. What I do know is that Frank decided to hang up the fishing net. He sold half of the business to Dan and is now a writer and, get this, an animal rights activist. If I'm being honest, from the echoes of past workers, things were better when Frank was co-managing our team.

When it comes to the activism part of his life, he isn't involved with the FAAC, they hate him just as much as they hate us. I've seen him argue with them relentlessly about their practices to know he isn't on their side. Frank has class, he protests with dignity and he uses his brains, something the FAAC lack. He's published books, been on the news and used to teach at the local sailing school. That was how he knew me, my wife and our daughter. I learned everything about living on the water from him.

There's a frosty atmosphere as we enter the café. Frank glares at Mike when we walk in, but then he nods at me. It's a silent greeting.

I don't like the tension between Mike and Frank. You can sense it in the room, dark anger and conflict festering under the surface. I've tried to pry the lid on their jilted relationship, but Mike keeps it firmly shut. I even enquired with Dan one time, which took encouragement but he just laughed, providing a sarcastic one liner, which made me think it was deeply serious. I mean, for a fisherman to turn his back on his livelihood and best friend, *something* bad must have happened.

After lunch, I text Derek, Herb's back at the shop. I'll pop by later. Mike and I return to the office and I continue to work on Henna. We have a meeting about the upcoming culling and I leave work, feeling deflated. No wonder Mike's so stressed.

15

The shop's closed by the time I arrive.

Derek smiles at me as he opens the door. "Em went home, Jules. Are you okay?"

"I've had better days," I reply. "Is Herb here?"

"Hi Julian," Herb answers from the back room.

An old pair of glasses with thick wedge lenses hang from a piece of string around his neck. His white shirt's untucked, normally when he's on the shop floor, it's strapped in. He has dark purple rings under his eyes and the light from above's shining on his bald head.

Derek's eyebrows rise. "I'm going upstairs, don't be too long, okay?"

Herb smiles tiredly. "Don't worry, I won't be." He turns to me. "Fancy some tea?"

"Yes, please." I sit at the chair next to his desk, glancing around the office as he makes the drinks. "I've heard you've been through the mill."

"If that's what you wanna call it," he replies. "I'm sorry about Ian. He was a nice man, one of our regulars too. He loved reading, especially the classics."

Ian's death still hasn't fully hit me yet. "I didn't know he liked those books."

"He probably kept it to himself because you'd all take the piss."

"I agree," I say. "Dan would've ripped him to pieces."

Herb smiles cuttingly, passing me the steaming mug of jasmine tea. "Dan's an idiot. He hasn't got any sense of style or culture."

"Again, I couldn't agree more. The police said Ian had a wound in his chest."

Herb takes a sip with wide eyes. "Half of his fishing rod was lodged in his chest."

I want to be sick all over again.

"This is so messed up..." I say.

"You're telling me," Herb utters. "I don't understand why anyone would want to hurt him."

"Well, the FAAC said they'd do something."

"They're just words, Jules. It's like a peacock preening its feathers, it's a method of intimidation, they don't actually mean it. They aren't the smartest bunch to pull off a murder."

"They've trashed our boats before."

Herb leans his chin on his hand. "Ah, I didn't know that. Well, I can see what you mean, but I still don't think it's them. If they wanted to kill someone, they would've gone for Mike or Dan. To dismantle your company from the top by taking out the leaders."

"Or maybe they've started with Ian to bump us off one by one..."

"Don't be ridiculous."

"I don't know, Herb. We've had some physical altercations in the past. Of course, they've got the balls to do it!"

Herb repositions the glasses around his neck, wiping the lenses with the cuff of his shirt. "Okay, let's say it was them. Why would they do it in the first place?"

I laugh. "Because they hate us and they want to destroy our way of life. I just wish my brain would stop thinking of conspiracies. I've got enough on my plate as it is."

"I reckon the culling should be postponed this year," Herb says. "It doesn't seem like the right thing to do. It might make this whole thing worse."

"Herb, listen to yourself. We can't call it off."

"Have a word with Mike. Talk to him."

"Mike won't be able to do anything. He's not the Mayor, plus he hasn't participated in years. I haven't seen him at a gathering since I was in school. What can he do?"

"You all admire him in some way. Except Dan."

"Be as it may, cancelling the culling would be like calling off Christmas," I say. "It's a Drake Cove tradition. It's been going on since Ragnar Lothbrok. Ian wouldn't want that, he took part every year too. If we call it off, then the fucking FAAC wins."

~

After our catch-up, I leave the shop half lying that I'd chat to Mike but I know he'd be just as helpless as me. Em's watching TV when I get home.

"How was your day?" I ask as I start to make dinner.

"It was nothing special," she replies. "I helped with pricing and tidying. They won't let me go on the till."

"Because you're not eighteen yet."

"I know that. But, it's not like I'm going to steal anything."

"Well, why don't you ask about shadowing them? Under supervision?"

Her eyes turn into slits. "I'll think about it."

I don't understand teenagers. They ask for advice and when they get it, they don't like the outcome.

~

We sit and watch a movie together. Afterwards, Em goes to bed with Keira following at her heel. I should probably do the same but I decide to do some investigating on my laptop, searching for her blog but I can't find anything. I type in her favourite songs, movies, characters, her birth year and get nothing. My stomach tightens when I think of a possibility. I add it in the search bar:

Hanna Finch blog

After I hit enter, it's there in black and white.

Hanna the finch, the writings of a teenage mind, tread

carefully.

Shit, Em was telling the truth.

She's set the blog to private as the profile's locked. The display picture is of a blue and grey zebra finch bird. Should I make an account under an anonymous name? Am I invading my daughter's privacy?

I can't look at it anymore and I turn off my laptop. I head to bed, making sure I take the rest of the whiskey with me.

3

As the investigation trundles on, the heartbeat of Drake Cove has changed significantly. I hear whispers when I drop Em off at sailing school or when I'm ordering at the Crest Café.

Ian's funeral is just as morbid. All of us fishermen turn up, Herb, Derek, even Frank shows his face, keeping a safe distance from Mike. I hate watching Ian's coffin being lowered into the mucky ground. There's anxiety in the air, we glance at each other with worry. Was it a mere, fatal accident?

Em and the rest of her sailing classmates are allowed out at sea. I feel a twinge of jealousy towards my daughter but I'd rather her be out in the fresh air learning, than sitting at home watching YouTube all day.

I'm working on Henna when I receive a text. My hangover isn't as severe so I can read her words in one great swoop:

I saw a lady dive off Drake's Tooth this morning! 😵

Drake's Tooth is our highest cliff, at the bottom is a lovely mound of sharp, jagged rocks. It's a suicide mission or an adrenaline junkie's ideal stunt. You wouldn't jump off there unless you had a death wish.

It was probably just a seagull.

It wasn't a seagull Dad! It was a woman. I drew her! Look!

I laugh when I see the picture. Her drawing skills wouldn't win any awards. *What's with the green hair?*

Because she had green hair!

Why are her ears lopsided and why does she have three chins? 😄

I'm not Picasso, Dad. Ur not funny!

Picasso didn't draw in biro. Anyway, how's class?

Learned about the port + starboard. She's being sarcastic. **Having lunch w/Jordan before we go out again.**

Say hello to your boyfriend for me!

Hilarious… 😕

She doesn't respond and that's when I hear a commotion. I chain Henna up and race to find my colleagues huddled together as if they're in a rugby scrum.

A man I recognise all too well and for the wrong reasons is Geoffrey Ward, the leader of the FAAC. He's standing in front of Mike, eyeballing him like crazy. His flock are gathered behind him wearing balaclavas, clicking away on their phones. It's pathetic and cowardly. Did any of us wear face coverings?

No, of course not. We're not weak. We reckon they wear them because of the risk. If their disguises fall, they could lose their jobs, be arrested and anybody they attack could seek them out for revenge.

"What are you gonna do, murderer?" Geoff jeers.

Mike smiles, his stance is solid. "I think you need to move along, mate. We're not fishing today and you're blocking the doorway to my workplace, that's illegal. You need to stop going to the beach, it's a crime scene remember."

Dan's itching for a fight, he's standing behind Mike, grinning wildly.

"Every day is a crime for you sadists," Geoff replies. "I guess you'll be sharpening your knives for the blood bath tomorrow."

I spoke to Mike about Herb's request at breakfast. It was a waste of time as I knew it would be. He replied that he wasn't the Pope and Herb clearly didn't have his head screwed on, probably from discovering Ian's body.

Mike holds his hands up in a peaceful gesture, some of Geoff's followers aren't enjoying his smooth composure. "Look, we aren't cancelling the culling, folks. I know you're angry but we need to make a living. It's a Drake Cove tradition, been going for centuries. You need to respect that."

Geoff hates Mike because he doesn't rise to the bait. FAAC use the Internet, their followers and fear tactics to project their views.

At last year's culling, one of them hit Dan in the side of the head. He was livid. The attacker wasn't jailed but they made two major mistakes. They chose Dan to target and didn't change their clothes throughout the chaos. So, what did Dan do?

He tracked the attacker down and waited till they were alone to pounce. Under the mask, the attacker turned out to be an eighteen-year-old joining in on the fun over the summer before heading off to university. Well, Dan sent him home in tears with a broken wrist. I reckon the lad told his parents he fell off his skateboard or something.

This worries me about the FAAC, some of the participants are young and impressionable, just starting out in life. Geoff Ward, their arsehole leader, is a grown man, an adult with life experience who can take advantage of their vulnerability. I mean, I understand the FAAC's fury, from an emotional position. I get why they think my work's barbaric and bloody but it's necessary for protecting the food stock. Someone has to do it. I'm a single father trying to earn money who's trained his whole life to fish. I live and breathe to be out at sea. We do the work nobody else wants to do.

"I had the police at my door the other day," Geoff says. "They think I killed your friend."

Mike shrugs. "They interviewed us too. You can protest and say whatever you want but we have a right to earn a living. Again, you need to respect that."

"Get another job, you prick!" someone yells behind Geoff.

I grab Dan as he shoots forward. "Don't do anything stupid," I whisper. "This is what they want."

From over the phones and balaclavas, Frank's talking to the police. He's pointing in our direction. Then, the officers edge towards us.

"Mr Ward, you can't be here," one of them says to Geoff. "We've warned you about this before, you need to leave the area."

The police weave themselves between the FAAC.

Geoff turns to Frank. "Fuck off, you traitor!"

"Coward!" another of the sheep shouts.

Geoff doesn't want to leave but he hasn't got a choice. They don't want to get arrested ahead of tomorrow. With one stern command, Geoff's followers turn off their phones and retreat like robots.

Dan shoves me off. "I can handle myself, Jules. We're mourning the death of a friend and he's fucking disrespecting us. Don't touch me again!"

"I was stopping you from doing something stupid. He's been messing with us long enough. You should know this!" I hiss. "We could've gotten into some deep, serious shit there!"

"He's right, Dan," Mike says. "We should thank Frank."

I'm truly stumped. Mike never talks about him.

~

The evening's normal and boring. Em and I have dinner, then we watch telly. I'm trying to be incognito on my phone as some young adult dystopian film plays out.

Spoke to Mike. Culling is still on. Sorry Herb.

He responds immediately. **Don't worry, I thought it was a long shot. Thanks anyway Jules. Hope you're doing okay.** 😊

I feel guilty because I didn't actually talk to Mike, I just made a comment about it. I watch my daughter sip her can of fizzy pop; her eyes are transfixed on the television.

Has Em spoken to you about her blog?

No, didn't know she had one. She's never mentioned it. Why???

Nothing. Only father worry. Have a good night.

My head aches. I don't want to think about the next day, but it has to be done. We do it every year.

When I wake up, the television's off and the blanket my wife knitted for Emily is draped across me. I must've dozed off from the exhaustion.

I stare out at the beautiful sight of the dawn looming over the sea line from the lounge window. One thing I love about my home is the spectacular view. It's utterly breathtaking but actually being on a boat in the early morning dawn, tops it.

I look over to find the bottle of whiskey on the coffee table. I'd bought more from the off licence after the FAAC's hostile preview. I was never to drink in front of my daughter. Now, I hate myself. I have to get away from the seductive view of the sun and the six cans of summer fruits cider sitting in the fridge.

4

Today's meant to signify a celebration, a Drake Cove tradition, yet partying is the last thing I want to do right now. I wake with the cold churn of dread in the pit of my stomach. I change my clothes, make a steaming mug of dirt coffee and chomp on two slices of toast lathered in peanut butter. I need my energy.

After I'm finished, I knock on Em's door. "Sweetheart? Are you coming?"

There's no response but I can see the shadows of her feet on the other side. She's pacing back and forth. When I knock a second time, her shadow freezes as if someone has hit pause on the television. She feels very differently about the culling. My wife and I have taken part since we were infants brought up on the ancient iron rules of Drake Cove. We took Em with us when she was old enough and she burst into tears within the first ten minutes, it was torture. A bad decision on both of us.

"Em? Are you okay?"

A piece of paper is pushed under the door.

Just go. I'll be fine. Please be careful.

"Okay my lovely," I say. "There's pizza in the freezer if you want it. I love you."

There's still no response.

I pick up my tools and leave the bungalow, locking the most precious thing to me inside.

5

The morning birds of the FAAC are fashioning their figurative knives by the time I arrive at the office. There's a film crew from the local news. The female presenter's doing a dry-run in front of the cameras, the make-up girl's standing out of shot, waiting patiently.

Mike allocates us into groups. I'm taking Henna out which is a great relief, but I'm going with Dan which puts a huge dampener on things. We relay instructions about what to do if we're caught in a bad patch, if the FAAC get on the wrong side of us. Mike makes a strict "no punches" rule, pointing at Dan in particular. The FAAC will say and do anything to rile us up. We are *not* to fall into any of their traps.

"Remember there's press out there, cameras and people who want to bring out the worst in us," Mike says, looking around. "Don't give it to them."

I can't help but imagine we're an army troupe storming out to battle.

We wait until some of the Drake Covians have showed up, they'll be helping us later on. Mike passes me a walkie-talkie.

"You do know the FAAC can hack the signal, right?" I enquire.

He shrugs. "I know, but you don't have any other choice unless you want to shout at each other."

I take it reluctantly. There isn't any point in arguing. We have to get on with it. Mike wishes us luck and disappears into the office to *drown in paperwork*, his words, not mine.

Damien and Earl leave first, followed by myself and Dan and lastly Lance, who's in a boat by himself. The sun's still asleep behind the clouds. I don't dare cast my eyes to the beach, hearing the slanderous words of the FAAC is enough right now.

We get into our boats and escape, letting the sea take us away. Damien and Earl have already scoped the waters, using a drone which belonged to Earl's granddaughter. They've discovered a pod of pilot whales nearby. We've had bigger catches but it's enough for Drake Cove.

Dan unveils his tools like a surgeon, a mischievous smirk sticking to his face.

Damien's crackled voice spits out from the speaker of the walkie-talkie.

"*Dan, Jules, make your way to Drake's Tooth. Earl's spotted the pod. Start circling them.*"

"Will do," I reply, pushing down on the handle of the engine.

Henna's made a miraculous recovery after my hands have done their magic. Her engine isn't making a metallic choke anymore, it's a smooth hum and her belly's gliding healthily on the water.

"Who's she?" Dan asks, glancing up.

"Probably a spy," I say.

"I don't think so. I've never seen this one before."

I turn and my heart does a jig in my chest. Standing on the edge of Drake's Tooth is a woman with a fiery stare and long… *green* wavy hair…

Shit.

It's the diver.

She isn't looking at Dan, she's staring and *glaring…* at me.

What did I do?

"That's the woman Em saw yesterday," I say to Dan. "She was diving off the cliff."

"*Utter bollocks*," he sneers. "No one's dived off Drake's Tooth and lived."

"This one has. Em said so."

"I think your kid's full of shit."

Now, I'm pissed off. "I believe her. You don't have to."

I keep my hand firmly on the steer, making sure Henna stays on course with the team.

The diver is dressed in a black and red striped scuba diving outfit. She's got to be a part of the FAAC. She's probably got a secret camera hidden somewhere.

I must admit, Em's drawing doesn't do her justice. My daughter made her appear like a timid pubescent teenager; the real-life result is far from it. She's grown up, perhaps in her late twenties or early thirties. She's tall, nearly my height. I'm over six foot. She has the physique of an athlete with strong shoulders and long muscly legs that go on forever.

I move my attention back to the pod of pilot whales; the tips of their tails rise and slap the water as they dive under the surface. I pull Henna around, circling them. Dan pulls out a kitchen pan and a ladle and begins to clang them together. My colleagues copy him and so do the other locals out on their boats. The actions send a chorus of noise to disorientate the pod.

The whales click their tongues and groan; the hammering sounds are confusing their communications. The largest whales in the pod; probably the mother and father drift, slow their pace, analysing the situation. The others wait behind obediently. That's when Damien and Earl move in, sailing right over the pod. The mummy and daddy whales watch our boats in fascination or fear.

Dan and the others continue to bang on the pots and pans, the parent whales dive and the others follow. We move with the pod; each boat's positioned around them so they can't escape.

Some of the Drake Covians wait by the shore, knives or hooks in hand. A line of the FAAC are gathered near the beach, the police are holding them off. I push down on the throttle, driving the pod into the beach. The whales call out to one another, they know something isn't right.

A handful of the locals charge into the water, clutching a long piece of rope. That's when the flapping and high pitch squeals start, from the whales and the FAAC.

The daddy whale is the first one to be caught, then the rest of the locals spear off taking down the rest of the pod. Damien and Earl hop out of their boat, pulling it across the pebbles as the daddy whale is hauled onto the shore, the rope is lashed around its head. Blood's already staining the sand.

"For fuck's sake, Dan!" I shout as he leaps out of Henna, grabbing his knife, hacking at the head of one of the smaller whales. He's meant to help me bring the boat in. The stupid selfish prick.

While he's slicing, I pull Henna onto the shore by myself. Thank God I've done this before. After I get Henna to safety, I grab my tools. Static's all around me, the atmosphere's full of electricity. I've done this so many times my ears block out the noise, finding silence amongst the chaos. The water's already transforming from a murky dark blue to a gory red. From the corner of my eye, I see her again.

The diver.

Now, she's standing on the edge of Becks Hill. It's opposite Drake's Tooth, parted by two and a half miles of ocean. How did she get over there so quickly?

I notice she isn't alone.

She's crying and talking frantically... *at Frank*.

His hands are up in surrender, a camera hangs around his neck. The diver's shaking her head, pointing aggressively to the pandemonium on the beach. Frank's trying to calm her down but it isn't working. She's hysterically furious. He's never told me about this woman. Who is she? His daughter? A young girlfriend?

The diver breaks away from Frank's embrace and runs in full speed to the edge of Becks Hill. She jumps off, her arms and legs forming into a perfect, balletic dive.

Frank races to the edge, watching the waters, he seems defeated and exhausted. Then he catches me staring. We watch each other for a while before he walks off. I don't know what just happened, but I can't ponder on it now. So, I take out my knife and get to work.

After it's over, the whales are hacked up and that's when the second war begins – distributing the meat. There are several colourful disagreements between the locals, debating who gets what and why they should get a certain amount over everyone else. I don't need a lot and I'm too tired to argue with anyone. I take my portion, I'm happy with whatever's leftover as there's only me at home who eats it. The others are off to get pissed at our local pub, The Sea Horse. A cold beer is tempting right now but I need to check on Emily.

I head home, put the meat in the freezer and have a shower. Sand, sweat and whale blood isn't a pleasant stench but after I get out, I feel refreshed. I grab a cider from the fridge before collapsing on the sofa. That's when the exhaustion sets in.

Em emerges from her room, her phone screen lights up on her skin.

"What's the matter?" I ask. "You look upset."

Her eyes are watering. "I told you to be careful."

"Aren't I always?"

"This isn't funny, Dad!"

She pushes the phone under my nose. On the screen, I watch myself working at the culling. My face is splattered with blood. I'm carving an unborn whale calf from the mother's stomach.

6

The next morning welcomes me with a head cracker of a hangover. I shouldn't have turned to the whiskey after the epic fight with Em, but my mind was bursting with dark thoughts. A place I didn't want to be swimming in. Alcohol seems to be the only way to extinguish them until I fall into a heavy sleep where no guilt trips or nightmares dwell.

I guess I deserved it, in Em's eyes.

She said the video has gone *viral*. I don't have any social media accounts, never seen the point of having them. The video's been *shared* and *retweeted* over a thousand times in the past twelve hours. People have gotten famous from viral videos and others have gone to prison or been sacked from their jobs.

"People are saying you should die," Em said, tears were streaming down her cheeks.

"Who the fuck said that?!"

"*Everyone!*"

"Well, they should say it to my face."

"It's the internet, Dad. It's anonymous. Nobody's on your side!"

Seeing her upset was truly hurtful and it was all my fault. I tried hugging her but she told me to leave her alone and returned to her room. She pretty much stayed in there all day so I grabbed the whiskey and can't remember the rest of the evening.

‸

Em's already left the house by the time I wake up. She's out with Jordan, her non-boyfriend from school. I have a shower and try to eat some breakfast. I can't taste the peanut butter on my toast.

My phone buzzes next to me. It's from Mike.

Call me. Right now.

I groan, phoning him. I'm gonna get it from both ends. I don't give him time to breathe when he answers. "Look Mike, I know what you're gonna say. But I didn't know I was being filmed. I was working. I'm really sorry."

"*What?!*" he exclaims.

"The viral video. The FAAC filmed me and put it online."

"*I don't give a shit about that!*"

"You don't?"

"*No, not right now.*"

I can hear an ache in his voice.

"Mike…" I say. "What's happened?"

"*It's Earl,*" he replies. "*He's dead.*"

~

My hangover evaporates after the call. Shock and anger must've snapped my body back to normal. I arrive at the office. The police are staked out by the beach, closing it off again with their tape. My stomach churns when a body bag, Earl's body is heaved into the ambulance.

Mike looks like his eyes could roll out of his head. I don't blame him, the stress he's under must be immense.

"I'm sorry mate," I whisper.

"Thanks Jules," he says. I can tell from the redness in his face he's been crying. Earl was the oldest one in our team. "Well, today just can't get any fucking worse, can it? The police want to talk to us again. Dan and I have got a meeting with our new contractors this afternoon."

Bugger. "Are you worried they'll pull out?"

"I have no idea. If they do, it's their decision," he says.

If they terminate our contract, we're royally fucked. I'll have to find another way to support myself over the winter period.

"Can we have a chat about the video?" I ask. "Em's really upset about it."

"Yeah, I'm gonna be busy most of the day. Catch me later on. Sorry to hear about Em."

He disappears into the office and the police arrive after sorting out the crime scene.

Chief Inspector Drew calls me into the meeting room and the memory of my last interrogation returns with a sickness. "Good morning Mr Finch, I hope you are well," she announces.

"I've had better days."

"I assume you've heard about Earl?"

"Yes, what happened to him? Same as Ian?"

"He was found lying face down on the beach, it appears he drowned."

Well, that's rubbish.

"Was he attacked?" I ask.

"We can't assume that at this time." Drew clicks her pen. "What can you tell me about Earl Harriet?"

"He was a good guy. Married with kids. He was a grandparent. Always came in on time and was rarely off sick. He was one of the older ones so he knew a lot about the business."

"Any enemies?" she asks.

I shake my head. "Not that I know of but we had a mutual dislike of the FAAC."

"You've mentioned this group several times. Why's that?"

"Because they hate us and what we stand for."

"And you seem pretty adamant they'd be the ones behind this…"

Because it would make fucking sense if it's them, that's why.

Drew pulls a phone from her pocket and taps on the screen. "I want to show you something, Mr Finch." She tips the screen towards me; I hear the clicks of the whales screaming and the sharp cutting of flesh and blubber. "What do you make of this?"

"I was at the culling," I sigh.

"Were you aware of the camera?"

"No of course not," I say. "I mean, I knew the FAAC were there making trouble as they always do but I didn't know they were filming me. They always record on their phones, we just ignore it and get on with our work."

Drew nods thoughtfully, her expression is calm and uncreased. She jots something on her notepad. I glance to the paper, her handwriting's just as bad as mine. I can't see what she's scribbled.

"Why did you show me the video anyway?" I ask, feeling my heartrate rise. "Do you think it's associated with Ian and Earl's cases? Do you think the person filming me's behind it?"

She slots the phone back in her pocket, making brief eye contact with the officer who's standing at the door. "We're not sure. Since chatting to you and your colleagues, the FAAC have been mentioned in *every* interview. Do you have any questions for me at this time?"

I shake my head. I'm too freaked out to enquire.

Drew reads through her notes and her attention is back on me. "That's all I need for now, Mr Finch. Thank you for coming in."

I leave the meeting room feeling uncomfortable and miserable. Dan is called in after me. I don't want to stay in the office. It's a Saturday, I've got fuck all to do. I want to make up with Emily but I don't want another verbal fistfight. I want her to relax and enjoy her weekend. So, I stuff my hands in my pockets and visit an old friend.

Frank's house is up near Becks Hill, by the old lighthouse. It's a hike but I need the walk. When I reach the top, I look out at the view of my hometown. It's lush in colour, a mixture of green, brown and blue. I know Frank's in because his old van's parked in the driveway. He smiles warmly when he answers the door and welcomes me inside.

I step over the threshold and walk down the hallway when I see the diver sitting in his garden.

"When did this happen?" Frank asks, taking off his reading glasses after I announce the dreadful news.

"They found his body this morning," I say.

"Shit. Sorry. I'll make you a drink."

"Thanks."

The diver's staring at the plants and flowers, muttering to herself. Her long wavy green hair's tied up in a loose bun. She's wearing green commando trousers and a long black sleeved top.

"Who's the lady?" I ask.

Frank sees me staring at her. "Shy Blothio, my niece."

Shy. Bizarre first name.

"Niece?" I say, this is getting interesting. "I swear you've never mentioned her before…"

"My step brother and his wife asked me to take care of her if anything happened to them."

I have to backtrack and sift through my memory. I

can't remember anything about Frank's family. "What happened?"

"Car accident," Frank replies. "A van cut across them coming out of a junction going too fast. There was no time to react. The van driver didn't make it either. Shy was in the back, she survived thankfully."

I'm either an ignorant friend not taking notice of the details or, he never told me. "Oh, I'm sorry pal." I choose not to delve further even though I really want to and we move to the kitchen.

"How's your book going?"

Frank smirks sarcastically, pouring tea into two mugs. "Draft after redraft, edit after bleeding edit. I've gotta get the final manuscript completed by the end of this month so it's crunch time."

"What's your book about?" I ask.

He passes me the boiling mug of breakfast tea. "My views on environmental issues and ideas about how we can reduce the number of animals we kill to eat. I've been doing a lot of research. Have you heard of mukbang videos?"

I shake my head. "I'm very unaware of what's *trending* nowadays."

"Are you familiar with the term social media influencer?"

I draw a blank. "Um, are they a politician...?"

"No."

"But it's in the title, they influence society?"

Frank grins. "Ah, Jules, you're so innocent. They review stuff on the internet and get paid for it, or they receive freebies."

"How is that a job?"

"Don't ask. Anyway, mukbang's linked to the social

media frenzy. The craze began in South Korea where people eat a large amount of food in front of a camera. Some of them don't even speak, they just eat."

"And people actually find that interesting to watch?" I ask.

"It's very profitable in the online world if you have a big enough audience. I'm not a fan. Certain mukbangers buy large quantities of meat, increasing the numbers of animals that are killed just for people to *watch them*. Would they be buying the meat if they weren't making money?" He shakes his head. "Plus, they're ruining their health. How some of them don't have gallbladder problems is beyond me. One guy on YouTube ate *seven* double cheese burgers and it generated over twenty *million* views. He probably earned a year or two's worth of wages for that."

"Wow," I say. "I didn't know about this. Should mukbang be banned?"

"Absolutely. It sends an unhealthy message about our relationship with food. And these people who do it are wasting resources. There was a controversial video swimming around the internet of a woman eating a live octopus. She didn't have the decency to kill the poor creature and she was biting its tentacles off. You can see it *wriggling*. She started crying when the octopus jumped on her face and bit her with its beak." Frank shakes his head with disdain. "It was being devoured while it was defending itself, trying to fucking survive."

The flaming passion flares in Frank's eyes.

"Sorry, got carried away didn't I?" he chuckles abruptly.

"Kind of."

"Look, I'm really sorry about Earl," he says. "He was a good man. Great to work with."

I gulp my tea. "I don't know who'd want to hurt him or Ian."

Frank blinks several times; he does this when he's thinking. "I don't know either."

"I reckon it's someone in the FAAC. Herb disagrees."

"It's a possibility. Animal activists have killed people before."

A laugh escapes me. "Oh, wonderful."

"A few years back, a dairy farmer committed suicide because an animal rights group were stalking and bullying him. They sent hate mail, made up horrible shuddering stories and then the village he lived in eventually turned on him. He lost his livelihood soon after. Pressure and animosity can kill just as much as a knife."

That's fucking morbid and infuriating. "It's just nice to hear someone agreeing with me for a change. Whoever this person is, they targeted Ian and Earl who were relatively quiet workers. If any of us were gonna be taken out, I thought it'd be Dan."

Frank sniggers. "Me too."

"I don't suppose you've seen the video..." I say.

"I write about animal activism on a daily basis, Jules. Of course, I've seen it."

"Em hates me."

"She'll come around, she wants to protect you. You know that deep down."

He's right. "She said people were saying I should die."

"It's the internet, people are vicious online because they're anonymous. Typing a threat's easier than saying it to the person's face. After I published my first book, I received a letter from a fisherman. According to him, he was going to drive to my house and shove his fishing hook down my throat and use me as bait. Course, he's never turned up."

"It's sinister stuff, Frank. I wouldn't ignore it."

He nods, glancing out of the window, his eyes falling on his niece for a moment. "I don't, Jules. You don't need to worry about me. I'm just saying it's all bravado. I got loads of weird phone calls from another animal rights group because I criticised their way of protesting. They walked into restaurants chanting, disturbing people having dinner, carrying lurid pictures of dead cows. Several of the female members would run around topless, covered in fake blood and on another operation, they tied their necks to a machine at a duck slaughtering house with bicycle locks. One of them was almost decapitated. It's not activism really, it's performance art. It had nothing to do with the animals."

"Their behaviour just confuses me, Frank. What makes someone wanna join a group like that in the first place?"

"Loneliness," he utters, swaying slightly in his chair, itching the early bristles of his grey beard. "Groups like the FAAC attract vulnerable people who have an empty hole in their life. Attacking a fisherman, holding up a banner, screaming at the top of their lungs, they feel like they're doing good for the world." He shrugs to his words. "It's like those stupid eco warriors who blocked the motorway as a form of protest. They thought they were doing something useful." Frank shakes his head in disappointment, there's a pinch of pain on his face as he speaks. "But they were actually causing more harm than good. One poor woman suffered a stroke because the ambulance was stuck in the congestion they'd caused. She didn't get to the hospital in time and lost her mobility and speech."

I remember when that was on the news, made me so

angry. They'd ruined a woman's life and took zero responsibility for the fallout of the catastrophe.

"You see, Jules. I receive agro from both sides of the argument. No matter what I do or how I do it, someone's going to be upset."

"Really?" I ask.

"Oh yeah, I receive threats all the time. Some of the Drake Covians have said I don't belong here anymore, but this place is my home. I'm not going anywhere. They're just words, Jules. It's actions you need to worry about." The phone rattles off in the hall. "I better answer that."

"Go ahead."

Frank vanishes into the hallway. Shy's still in the garden. I convince myself it's a good idea to speak to the infamous diver. Maybe it will cheer Em up, surely, well hopefully.

Shy must have heard me walking across the grass as her back stiffens and her muttering stops. She rises to her feet and turns to face me, that angry look from the day before reappearing.

"Woah steady on," I say, holding up my hands in surrender. "Hi, I'm Julian. I'm a friend of Frank's." I offer my hand. "It's nice to meet you."

She stares at my palm and frowns. I feel awkward and stupid. Perhaps she's not a hand-shaker, some people don't like it. I start to retract when Frank interrupts.

"Be polite, Julian's being a gentleman," he says. "Say hello."

I glance over my shoulder.

Frank's leaning against the backdoor with the phone in the crook between his ear and shoulder. "Yes, I'll hold. Go on, Shy. Say hi. Jules won't bite."

I turn back, Shy's closer to me. She has a Nordic

appearance, flawless pale skin with high cheek bones and pink kissable lips. Some strands of her green hair become loose, falling into her line of sight. Her gaze never breaks mine. Her left eye's a watery blue and the right, a deep dark brown. I've never seen anyone with different colour eyes before. Underneath her quirks, she's gorgeous.

She takes my hand, pressing her palm down on mine. She smells like freshly cut grass. What happens next, I can't really explain in the best details. A throb, like an electric current shoots through me and the image of a whale calf flashes in my mind. When I open my eyes, Shy's staring at me, watching carefully. What the hell was that?

She suddenly turns and marches over to Frank.

"Drake's Tooth?" His eyebrows rise. "Please be careful and remember to take your swimming costume."

She doesn't wave goodbye or even smile when she disappears into the house. Was that a good introduction? Or, was I a complete tit?

"Is she okay?" I ask Frank. "I thought she was gonna hit me."

"She can be like that, sometimes. But, she's just shy around new people. Like her name." He laughs momentarily. "She's had a hard life. Imagine being the only family member to survive a car crash."

"What's up with her eyes?"

Frank frowns at me. "Nothing's up with them, Jules. She's got heterochromia iridium. Her eyes are just different colours, she can see perfectly fine. My step brother had it."

"Oh, okay. I wasn't saying it as a criticism. What does she do for a living?"

"She's an artist, an out-of-work-one. She's been studying away and came back to Drake Cove to figure out her next steps. I can tell she has no ideas. Kids these days."

"How old is she?"

"Twenty-nine."

Then she's not a kid, she's an adult. She certainly has a peculiar personality for an artist, they normally do - like that Dali moustache fella and the ginger geezer who chopped off his ear.

"Em saw her diving off Drake's Tooth," I say.

"Oh yeah, she's a fantastic swimmer. She's been freediving for a long time."

"She must have no nerves."

"Heights don't frighten Shy."

"I saw her at the culling yesterday. She seemed really upset."

Frank sighs. "That was my fault. It was her first time witnessing it. To cut a long story short, she won't be going again. She gave me Hell for taking her there."

No fucking shit, it was obvious. "Is she involved with the FAAC?"

"No, she's not a fan. By the way, how's Mike doing?"

Why would he wanna know?

I thought he hated him.

"Um, he's fine," I say. "He's stressed out with what's going on. What's made you ask?"

"Nothing in particular."

7

Police officers protect the beach. I head back to the office. Mike's the only one in when I arrive, busy tapping at the keyboard, reading and responding to emails. His blue eyes are still red and puffy when I sit down.

"Are you okay, mate?" I ask.

"I'm exhausted and working on my weekend off. That's how bloody okay I am." He turns away from the monitor. "What's up, Jules?"

I let out a huge sigh. "Have you seen the video?"

"Yep, the police showed it to me. Don't let it bother you. Em won't like people attacking her dad. Ripping out fish guts isn't glamorous but someone's gotta do it."

"But it was a whale, Mike," I reply. "They have an emotional effect on the general public rather than your bog-standard cod or tuna."

"True but it's no different in the fishing process. We do it for food and money. Look, there's plenty of seedy videos out there. You should watch the Japanese whaling ships. They shoot them with gigantic harpoons and drag them out of the water while they're still alive."

"How is what we do at the culling any different?"

Mike shrugs. "People need to eat."

"Are you angry with me?"

He frowns. "Why would I be angry?"

"I was worried I was gonna get the sack."

"I wouldn't let you go. I need you here."

"What did our potential employers say?"

He mimes wiping his forehead. "We're still on. They said our current situation is tragic but it's not our fault. I could tell the director was finding the conversation over Ian and Earl difficult."

"When are we heading off?"

"September, back at the end of October," he replies.

I'll be away from Em for two months. Herb and Derek have agreed to look after her while I'm gone. I have no spouse, or parents or in-laws to watch over her so I have to rely on the kindness of friends. This is gonna be hard. I hate leaving Em. I have to make the most of this summer.

"I saw Frank earlier, he was asking after you," I say.

There's a nervous twitch in the corner of Mike's mouth. "He was asking after *me*?"

"Yeah, he wanted to know how you were."

Mike frowns. "That's bizarre. What did you say?"

"I said you were fine, just stressed with everything going on. He was shocked when I told him about Earl." The curious cat in me wants to enquire about their falling out. "I met his niece too."

"Niece?" Mike frowns even deeper this time. "Frank doesn't have a niece…"

"He does, he's been looking after her since his step brother and sister-in-law died in a car accident."

Mike shakes his head. "I've never ever heard of a step-brother in Frank's life, or a car accident. I've known him for a long time and he's never talked about it. He lived with a woman years ago, then I stopped seeing her around Drake Cove. I guess they broke up and she moved away."

"Why don't I remember this?" I ask.

"You wouldn't. You would've been five or six years old at the time."

"This is getting a little weird," I say.

"A little?" Mike laughs. "*A lot* more like."

A revolting thought scuttles into my head. What if Shy isn't family at all? What if she's actually Frank's lover?

"What else do you know about this niece?" Mike asks.

"She's an artist, just got back from university. Oh and she's a great swimmer. Em saw her diving off Drake's Tooth the other day and I saw her jump off Becks Hill yesterday. It was like a swan dive, really elegant. She should qualify for the Olympics."

Something in Mike's expression changes.

"Mike?" I ask. "You okay, mate?"

He blinks then he smiles tiredly. "Sorry, Jules. I was miles away. You better head home. This niece of Frank's sounds like an intriguing mystery."

"She sure is."

"And a beauty."

"What makes you say that?"

"Your skin flushed when you talked about her."

"Nah, only women flush."

"You're living proof that's not true," he replies jokingly.

A text arrives on my phone. It's from Em.

Dad, where r u?

At the office chatting to Mike. Everything okay?

Yeah, back home now. She doesn't seem pissed off anymore, that's good. **Can u get sum ice cream?**

There's some mint choc chip in the freezer.

47

Nope. U ate it last night. ☺

I don't remember stuffing my face with ice cream.

"I better go," I say to Mike. "Madam's home."

He stretches in his chair. "Alright, have a good evening. Try and put that video on the back burner, okay?"

"I *can't* stop thinking about it, Mike. That's the problem. It's driving me crazy."

"Remember, it's just the luck of the drawer it was you they filmed. It could've been any of us, fisherman or Drake Covian. We were all doing the same as you."

"None of you were carving dead babies out of stomachs."

"We've all done it, Jules."

⁓

I pick up some ice cream on the way home. The bungalow is engulfed in agonising silence when I get in and it makes me wonder where Em is. I hang up my jacket and put the ice cream in the freezer. I switch on the lights, calling for her.

She runs out of her bedroom in a speed stampede.

"What's wrong?" I gasp, my head's spinning, immediately running to the worst scenario.

I'm engulfed by her arms. "I'm so sorry Dad," Em says, giving me a tight bear hug.

"Why are you apologising?"

"I didn't mean to shout at you."

I stroke her hair tentatively. "It's okay, hun. You had every right to."

She peers up at me. "But I was horrible."

"We all have our days. Oh by the way, I met your mystery diver. She's Frank's niece, well step-niece really."

"Oh, I didn't know."

"Me neither."

We bury the hatchet and spend the evening watching *another* dystopian disaster film. Em heads to bed, along with Keira, her shadow in cat form. I lie across the sofa and my thoughts rush to Shy: her eyes, her figure, the way she watched me and the whale calf flashing across my mind when she touched me. It was such a random moment. Am I overthinking this?

But there is… *something* about her. I can't put my finger on it. I haven't touched a sliver of alcohol this evening. I should be drinking till my eyes roll back but I don't want to. Why's that?

I'm dropping off when I hear the window smash.

Em's screaming my name.

I shoot off the sofa and run to her room. *"Emily! Emily!"*

Keira shrieks, zooming out the door like lightning. My daughter's curled up on her bed.

"Are you hurt, hunnie?" I ask.

"No! I don't think so!"

"Did you see anything?"

"I saw a man outside wearing a balaclava!" she whimpers.

Em's window is now a giant gaping, jagged hole. There's a rock wrapped in white paper lying on the carpet.

I edge forwards, trying to avoid the shards of glass. Em begins to uncurl, watching me. "*Dad, be careful!*"

"I am. Stay where you are. Don't move."

I pick up the rock and unwrap the paper, clearing the specks of glass. There's a message inside. I feel a twinge of violent anger hit me right in the gut.

"What does it say?" Em squeals. "*Dad?!*"

"I'm calling the police."

"*What is it?!*" Em asks fearfully.

I stuff the note into my pyjama pocket and move over to Em. I heave her over my shoulder, carrying her out into the living room so she doesn't cut herself. I grab the house phone, hugging Em to my chest as I bellow what's happened to the operator. I've made the poor woman deaf I'm shouting so much. They tell me someone's arriving in ten minutes.

"It's okay. It's okay," I whisper to Em. "Someone's on the way."

"What did the note say?"

"It doesn't matter."

She snatches it from my pocket. I've memorised the message already. It's a slow agony as her face morphs with realisation, exploding into raw hysteria. She's had enough sadness to deal with this year. I've failed as a man and a father.

Two down. You're next, baby killer.

One thing's for sure, whoever did this has crossed the line. Heads will fucking roll.

I'll make sure of it.

8

It doesn't take long for the police to arrive. I'm flabbergasted when Drew climbs out of the car. I guess she must work all hours. A tall male officer accompanies her. I stand in the doorway with Emily holding onto my arm. If she pulls any tighter, she'll snap it off.

"Mr Finch?" the police officer asks.

"Yes, that's me," I reply.

"And the little lady?"

Little lady? She's a teenager. "This is my daughter. Emily."

"Where's the crime scene?" he asks.

"In the bedroom, just through here." I point to Em's room and the officer trudges off, putting on some gloves.

"I'm sorry we keep meeting in these circumstances, Mr Finch," Drew says thinly as she steps over the threshold.

"It's okay. Actually, it's *not* okay. Whoever did this could have killed my daughter!"

"I completely understand why you feel the way you do," she replies.

We move into the lounge and sit on the sofa. Em's still holding onto me.

"Do you think this attack is related to the video?" Drew asks.

"Of course, it is." I pass the note to her. "This was wrapped around the rock."

Drew reads it and doesn't react to the words. She pulls out a plastic bag from her pocket and dumps the paper inside. "Cooper, get in here."

The police officer returns to the lounge. "Yes, gov?"

"Make sure you're taking notes," she says, handing him the plastic bag.

Cooper puts it in his rucksack and pulls out his phone. I guess the police have upgraded their systems.

Drew positions the foot rest by the coffee table, in front of Em before sitting down. "What's your name, darling?" she asks.

Em looks at me nervously.

"Go ahead hun," I encourage. "They want to help."

"Emily Finch," she replies.

"Can you tell me what happened here?"

"I...I was sleeping. There was a loud smash. It woke me up. Someone had thrown a rock through my window."

"Can you tell me what they looked like?" Drew asks.

I glance at Cooper who's studying Em and texting as my daughter recounts her story.

Em turns her body into mine. "I couldn't see their face. They had a balaclava on. I think it was a man."

"Not to worry." Drew nods. "What was he wearing?"

"A hoodie, maybe tracksuit bottoms. It was too dark to see what was on his feet."

"Did he do anything else?"

"He watched me, then he ran off."

"You've been very brave, Emily. I'm sorry you've had to go through this." Drew's facing me. "Do you think it could be someone you know, Mr Finch?"

"It's gotta be the FAAC," I say. "They posted that video. It has their fingerprints all over it."

"Have you two got anywhere you can stay for the next couple of days?" Drew asks.

My mind draws a blank. "I'm not sure. Do we have to leave?"

Drew stares at me seriously. "This is dangerous."

"We could stay at Herb and Derek's," Em says.

"No hun. Their place isn't big enough."

"Mike's?" she asks.

"His flat's too small. Plus, he has enough on his plate. We'll just have to stay in a bed and breakfast somewhere."

"We can reimburse you for the costs if this helps," Drew says.

Em scowls at me. "I don't want to stay at a B and B. Call Frank."

"I don't think it's appropriate, Em."

"Dad, please try," Em pines.

I notice my daughter's behaviour makes Drew smile. I excuse myself and head to my bedroom. My heart's beating rapidly as I hear the dial tone. It sounds like a funeral dirge.

Within five rings, his groggy voice answers. "*Hello.*"

"Frank, it's me."

"*Julian?*"

"Yes."

"*Why are you calling me so early?*"

"Someone threw a rock at Em's window with a horrible message attached to it."

"*Oh my god.*" I can hear him moving in the bed. "*Is she alright?*"

"She's fine, a little shaken up but she's coping. I'm fucking furious."

"*I bet you are.*"

"The note was intended for me. Apparently, I'm a baby killer and I'm next to be picked off."

"*Jesus Christ, Jules...*"

"I know. Well, you did mention actions being worse than words." I hear him laugh uncomfortably. "Look, Frank. The police have told us to find somewhere to stay for the next couple of days while they investigate. I really didn't wanna call but I couldn't think of anyone else. Em doesn't wanna stay in a B and B..." I let my words trail off, holding my breath as there's a beat of silence before he speaks.

"*You can stay for as long as you need to...*"

"Are you sure?"

"*Jules, your family have been through enough,*" he says softly. "*I have a spare room but it's a single bed.*"

"That's fine. Em can have the spare bedroom. I'll take the sofa. Are you alright with Keira coming with us?"

"*Of course, she's family.*"

The relief washes over me. "I really appreciate this, Frank. Thank you so much. I hope I haven't ruined your Sunday."

"*Don't worry. My alarm was about to go off anyway. I'll tell Shy she has to be pleasant for our guests. When are you getting here?*"

"Not too sure. The police are still here."

"*Okay, text me when you're on your way. I'll get the tea brewing.*"

"Maybe something stronger. Thanks mate," I say, hanging up.

Drew's on the phone when I walk into the lounge. Em wraps her arms around my waist.

"Hey, Frank says we can stay at his. Looks like you'll get to spend time with your mystery diver."

"I'll be here." Drew clicks off her call, turning to me. "I've got some help arriving. They'll need to replace the lock of the front door."

I hate the idea of leaving my home.

~

Em and I get ready. I gather as many clothes as I can carry, my laptop and bathroom essentials. Em's taking longer, she's carrying four massive bags. I grab two of them, swinging them over my shoulder. We wait outside while the police officers lock up the bungalow. Some of the lights in the houses opposite glare on, a handful of the Drake Covians watch from their windows.

"Do you want a lift, Mr Finch?" Drew asks.

"No, my friend only lives up the hill. We need the walk anyway. Thanks for the offer."

"Make sure you both get some sleep," she says. "I'll be in touch."

~

Frank's true to his word.

When we arrive, he's standing by the front door and helps us carry our belongings inside. Emily has Keira squashed to her chest. Getting my cat out of the bungalow was a challenge. She was so frightened, she was trembling, hiding under my bed. When I grabbed her, she nearly took a chunk out of my arm with her Freddy Kruger claws.

Frank's made tea and hot chocolate, it's brewing on the coffee table in the lounge along with a plate of biscuits. He's added a drop of whiskey in mine. Em downs her drink and falls asleep. Keira lies along the arm of the sofa, staring at Frank as we chat.

"Do you reckon it's the FAAC?" he asks.

"It's gotta be," I say. "I think I've convinced the police to take me seriously."

"It wouldn't surprise me if Geoff *the bastard* is behind it. Trouble follows wherever that moron goes."

"Well, the police better find out who it is because I'm not putting up with this shit anymore. The FAAC can hate me all they want but they *don't* target my kid."

"You need to get some sleep, mate." Frank smiles cautiously. "Have my room. I'm going to work in my study."

"Thanks, Frank."

I carry Em upstairs to the spare room, Keira's right on my heel and curls up at her feet when I tuck her under the covers. I head into Frank's room, collapsing onto the bed. I haven't felt this tired since Em was a new-born. I didn't know what true stress and exhaustion was back then. The shame overwhelms me, rushing over my mind like a tidal wave.

I couldn't protect my daughter.

Someone dwelling in the shadows is trying to ruin my life.

9

I awake hearing the bells of Em's laughter. My phone screen's blown up with missed calls and texts from Derek, Mike and Herb. I head downstairs to find my daughter playing in the garden with Shy performing cartwheels. It's nice seeing Em smile after what happened, and it's good to see Shy in a better mood too. She stands on her hands, pointing her feet beautifully like a ballerina. Then she pushes off the ground, curling her body backwards, flipping her feet onto the grass, uncoiling from the knot she's wrapped herself in. She did it so swiftly, without breaking a sweat, as if her bones are made from elastic.

"Wow, that's amazing," Em says.

Shy nods and points to the ground. Em giggles, hurling herself into a handstand. Shy grabs her waist and holds her legs up. Em starts to giggle as Shy pushes her forwards, my daughter breaks concentration, falling in a heap on the grass.

"Damn, I lost it! I'll do it again." Em hops to her feet, curling her caramel hair behind her ear. "Okay, here we go. Don't drop me!"

I can't help but grin to myself. Frank's in his study, typing on his keyboard. Music seeps from the radio in the corner. Lines of shelves are filled to the brim with books. His work station's positioned by the French doors, looking out at his garden. Above his head is an old fishing net, the rope's frayed. Next to it is a fishing rod, the metal on the handle's a rusting dirty orange. Why are they pinned up in his office?

"Did you have a good sleep?" he asks, sensing my presence.

"Yeah," I say, half way through a jaw cracking yawn. "Your bed's really comfy. Looks like Em and Shy are having fun."

Frank spins around in his chair, he's wearing his dark red reading glasses again. "We've got a match made in heaven. I've told Shy to be on her best behaviour, she's not used to having guests over."

"Not a problem." The scent of cooked food wafts under my nose. "Is that lunch?"

"It'll be done soon, but there's no meat options. As you know, we're vegetarians. If you want meat, you'll have to get some from the shops. Sorry, I didn't think to stock up."

"I don't mind vegetarian food."

Frank's eyebrows rise sarcastically. "Really? You'd eat soy mince?"

"That's what you're cooking? Oh bleh, then no. I'll get some grub then. You veggies enjoy chocolate, don't you?"

"Love it," he says grinning.

I grab my trainers and head out to the shops. I ring Herb and Mike as I chuck crisps, biscuits, eggs, cat food and sausages into my basket at the supermarket, informing them of the latest fuck up in my lousy life. Mike's silence intrigues me when I mention that we're staying at Frank's. It's the first time I've heard him stammer in a while.

~

I stuff Frank's cupboards and fridge with my shopping. Frank comments on the amount of sugary, heart clogging food I've bought. Em and Frank are sitting around the table in the kitchen when I chuck sausages in the saucepan.

"Is Shy not joining us?" I ask.

"She will be, she's in the shower," Frank answers, heaping carrots and broccoli onto his plate.

"But she had one earlier," Em frowns.

I stir the sausages, watching the meat bubble and squeak. Maybe Shy's got OCD. It'd make sense if she's a germaphobe. I finish cooking the sausages. I put them on a plate in front of Em and I sit opposite her. My stomach gurgles as the meat hits my tongue, there's nothing better than a greasy cooked meal.

"Your niece is funny," Em says to Frank, stuffing broccoli into her mouth. "I like her, she's nice. She doesn't say much though."

Frank nods pensively. "She talks when she wants to. She's not a chatterbox like you, Em."

"Dad, can I dye my hair?" she asks.

"*Nnnnope*," I reply.

"Why not?" Em protests. "Shy has!"

"She's a grown up, you're still a kid."

"*Fourteen* is not a kid. I'm a teenager."

"Fine, you're a teenager and you're not dying your hair," I reply. "School won't allow it."

"I can buy the non-permanent stuff. I'll wash it out before term starts. It's just for the summer."

"*No*," I reply.

"Well, I can wear eye contacts like Shy does," Em chats. "There's a goth shop in Yearling and they sell these yellow cat lenses."

Frank coughs, wiping his mouth with a napkin. "She's not wearing contacts, Em. Her eyes are naturally different colours. She's got heterochromia iridium."

Em winces with embarrassment. "Oops, sorry. I didn't know."

Frank grins. "Don't worry about it, sweetie."

I smile at Em, she reminds me of the little girl she once was, adorable and happy.

We eat lunch in silence. I'm bloody starving. Upstairs, I see the bathroom door swing open and Shy emerges, a cloud of steam following behind her. She rakes the towel through her hair. I expect to see patches of green hair dye on the fabric but I can't see any. Hair dye normally drains out after a couple of rinses, doesn't it?

Shy comes downstairs barefoot, dressed in a dark red t-shirt and blue jeans. Her damp hair's lashed back from her face in messy horsetails. She seems hesitant to join us but Frank points to the empty space between me and Emily.

I pull the chair out beside me, nodding encouragingly. "It's okay, I don't bite."

Then she smiles. I like it, it's cute.

Shy sits and reaches for the vegetables, helping herself to the soy mince placed in the middle of the table. We eat in silence again; Keira sits by the table legs, sniffing the air for food.

A question I've been wanting to ask bubbles up from my core. I can't help it, I'm a curious bastard. "How have you been, Shy?"

She stops eating and turns to me, her unusual eyes staring back. "I'm okay thank you," she whispers.

I notice a pink streak on her right arm, it's peaking under the sleeve of her t-shirt. "Yeesh, that looks like a nasty cut. What happened there?"

Shy's eyes widen and she glances down at her arm. "Oh, I misjudged the distance when I was diving. Landed close to the rocks. It's healing now."

That must've hurt, a lot.

"Have you been working on any art lately?" I ask.

She looks at Frank with concern, did I say something out of line?

"She hasn't been working on anything since she got back from university," Frank interjects. "I think I mentioned before, she's got artist's block."

"Oh yeah, I remember now." I glance at Shy. "Well, I'm sure you'll find some inspiration. They nearly filmed that Doctor Marvin show at Drake Cove."

"Nobody watches that sitcom Dad," Em scoffs. "It's for old people. You're not old."

Frank laughs, showing his teeth. "That's a pretty bold statement, Emily. I watch Doctor Marvin."

It's funny watching my kid squirm between a rock and a hard place as her brain races to conjure up some kind of response.

"I'm only pulling your leg," Frank adds.

I clear my throat. "Shy, Em drew a picture of you when she saw you diving off Drake's Tooth. Do you wanna see it?"

"*Shut up, Dad.*" Irritation spreads across my daughter's face. "Ignore him. He's being a knobhead."

"Knobhead?!" Frank laughs, leaning back in his chair.

My fingertips dance across my phone screen. "Hang on. I've got it here somewhere, let me find it."

Em yanks my phone from my grasp. "Stop it, Dad. It's not funny."

It's really fucking hard to suppress a grin.

"Shy, have you seen The Apocalypse Tribulations?" Em asks.

Shy shakes her head, heaping mince into her mouth.

"You haven't?!" Em blurts, her eyes almost bursting out of her head. "Have you read the books?"

Shy shakes her head again.

"Do you wanna watch it?"

"Okay," Shy whispers.

"You got Netflix, Frank?" Em asks.

"No but you can install it on my telly if you want," he answers.

Em leaves the table excitedly. I roll my eyes, stabbing my fork into her sausages and finish her food. She loads Netflix onto Frank's television, inputting my email address and password. Nothing's sacred anymore, my kid knows all the crooks and crannies of technology better than I do. She's growing up too fast.

I clear the table. Frank doesn't stay to watch the film and returns to his study. Shy sits cross legged on the carpet, she has fantastic posture, I wonder if she does yoga. My eyes trace the curves of her slim muscular arms, and I wonder if she lifts weights too.

We watch the first Apocalypse Tribulations film again. Emily pauses it occasionally, explaining the plot and characters to Shy. She did this with me too. I had to tell her to stop or we wouldn't've finished the film till midnight. Shy doesn't say anything through the entire thing, but she watches and listens to Em. She seems interested in what my daughter has to say. Keira seems to like Shy too, she sits beside her, docking her head, letting Shy's fingers swirl around her fur.

I feel the rush of embarrassment when the young heroine pulls the hero into a kiss when he's injured. We watched this medieval show a while ago and I turned it off the second a pair of pert breasts flashed on the screen. I always get like this when a sex scene springs up on the telly.

I peek through my fingers as the kiss scene continues. I

notice Shy's watching it, leaning forward, caressing the back of her hand against her lips. My phone rattles beside me, and I mouth thank you to some invisible force and excuse myself to the garden.

It's Drew.

"Hello," I say.

"*Good evening, Mr Finch. How are you doing?*"

"I'm coping. It's late."

"*How's your daughter?*"

"She's fine, better after a good sleep."

"*I'm glad to hear that. I have an update on the investigation. We interviewed your neighbours.*"

She's talking about Gary and Felicity, an older couple who keep to themselves. I don't talk to them much.

"*They heard the window break but sadly didn't see anyone. I've checked the CCTV cameras around the area. There was a figure running away from the scene.*"

"Did you get a look at their face?" I ask.

"*They were wearing a balaclava, Mr Finch.*"

"Emily reckons it was a male."

"*It might be, we need to keep our options open. Bodies come in different shapes and sizes regardless if they are male or female.*"

"Did you see where the perpetrator ran off to? Maybe he had an accomplice waiting in a car nearby?"

"*We couldn't find anything I'm afraid,*" she replies. "*The attack seemed premeditated. They may have known about the positioning of the cameras.*"

My fingers tighten around my phone. "What's happening next?"

"*I'll be interviewing Geoff Ward again.*"

I laugh sarcastically, I don't mean to but I'm pissed off. "He won't admit to anything. I think he's linked somehow, especially to whoever uploaded that video."

"*That's exactly what I was thinking,*" she utters.

"Okay, great. Do you know when we can go home?"

"*Not yet Mr Finch,*" she replies. "*Not until I find more answers.*"

Fucking wonderful. "Alright."

"*I know it's not the best situation but we're working really hard. Enjoy the rest of the evening.*"

"Thanks for your help."

I hang up, anger shuddering through me. I stare at the flower bed and walk the circuit of the garden.

Frank leans against the back door, his reading glasses resting on the top of his head. "Anything?"

"They can't identify the guy who smashed Em's window," I say. "It's like he vanished into thin air. Drew said she's going to interview Geoff Ward."

"It's definitely linked, they want to frighten you. It's disgusting, Jules. This is how they operate. Geoff won't tell her the truth. It'll be one of his henchmen."

"I know. Em and I can't go back home yet, so you've got us for a little while longer. Sorry."

"You can stay here as long as you want. Don't let it bother you."

I chuckle at him.

"I know it's harder than it sounds," Frank says.

No shit.

~

After I return to the house, Shy goes out for a walk. I should've gone with her. We eat dinner. Shy still hasn't returned. I'm dropping off on the sofa when she finally comes through the front door. She doesn't acknowledge us. Her jeans are wet.

Em's head is lolling on my arm, tired from the day.

Frank's falling asleep in his comfy chair. Keira snoozes next to me.

Shy heads up the stairs. Her back stiffens as if a cold breeze just blew past. She looks over her shoulder at me. I give her a gentle smile, hoping I don't scare her. She smiles back faintly and disappears into the bathroom. She's in the shower for a long time, she's had three of them today and emerges wrapped in towels. She doesn't say anything or even look at me when she vanishes into her bedroom.

"I'm going to bed," Em says, stumbling off like a zombie. Keira wakes up on cue and pads after her.

"Alright hunnie, sweet dreams," I reply.

"I better head up too." Frank heaves himself out of his chair. "Are you sure the sofa's comfortable enough, Jules?"

"Yeah, it'll be fine. I've slept on the floor of an old boat before; this is like a five-star hotel compared to that."

"Oh yeah, long nights on the water," he says, smiling momentarily off in the distance as if a memory just caught him. "It's been a while since I thought about it."

Why did you stop fishing Frank?

What happened between you and Mike?

The questions want to burst out, but I can't ask him. Not now. He's taken me and Emily in, I can't pry. Yet.

Frank says goodnight and leaves the lounge. I switch off the television and cosy up on the sofa. Frank's house is high up on the hill, I can hear the waves and the cranking wheel from the lighthouse. My bungalow's only a small walk away but I miss it.

My mind begins to wander. I want to know who's behind attacking my home. I imagine confronting them, slamming their face into the ground. Was I supposed to be the third victim? Did the same person upload that ugly video?

I drift off as I ponder. My imagination plummets into the unconscious depths and I visualise floating through the ocean, letting the power of the current pull me away.

My body jolts awake when I see Shy in the reflection of the television. She's standing behind me, watching...

Our eyes find each other in the mirror of the screen. I sit up, twisting my body as my heart shudders.

She's not here.

The only things keeping me company is the lingering darkness and the pulse of nature.

10

When my life can't get any worse, I receive a text from Mike. He wants all of us in the office first thing this morning. We're having a visit from our new employer today *and* we're to be on our best behaviour.

Everyone's in a non-cheery mood as we sit around the large oval table waiting for this director to arrive. There's an uneasiness floating around us. Ian and Earl should be here too.

Dan's looking bored as if he'd rather be someplace else. He owns half of the company; he should be out with Mike doing the meet and greet. I bet when Frank was working here, he wouldn't've left Mike out to dry.

Damien, Lance and I chat as we wait. I slurp my coffee, trying to answer their questions about the window attack. Dan's attention switches when I talk about staying at Frank's, then the topic of Shy suddenly springs out of nowhere. I dunno how they know, maybe Mike told them. Lance and Damien tease me, asking when I plan to jump in bed with her. I wave them off. They've been working alongside me for years. They should bloody know better.

We hear Mike laugh in the background. Our new guest has arrived.

Matthew Waldemar isn't the type of person I expect to walk through the door. He's slim, well dressed in a dark blue tailored suit. He has a golden crown of thick wiry hair. He doesn't have dark bags under his light brown eyes from long shifts like the rest of us. He doesn't have a broad chest and wide toned shoulders either. His hands aren't scarred from fish hooks or rope burn, his fingernails aren't stained from dirt and blood. He's clean. *Too* clean in fact. I'm willing to bet he's never held a fishing rod in his life.

We click on our smiles and introduce ourselves, routinely shaking hands with Waldemar. We all sit down and he starts to go through the housekeeping. Mike's taking minutes on a notepad. Dan's doing nothing, he's slumped back in his seat like a moody teenager. He needs to pull his fucking weight and do more to help Mike.

"My name is Matthew Waldemar and I'm the director of Waldemar & Sons," our potential new employer says. "Do you know anything about our business?"

We shake our heads, except for Mike and Dan.

Waldemar continues. "My company distributes fish and mammals around the world for meat produce and pharmaceutical purposes."

"Sorry Matthew," I say, adding a smile. "By mammals for pharmaceutical purposes, what do you mean?"

He beams gently. "I'll answer that once we complete the initial paperwork."

Alright then, I was only bloody asking.

Mike hands out a sheet of paper to everyone.

"What's this?" Lance asks.

"Confidentiality statements," Waldemar replies. "I need you to read and sign them before we talk any further."

Mike points to the paper. "Please proceed, gentleman."

Lance laughs. "I feel like I'm in the Special Air Service."

The document's full of the typical legal jargon about not revealing procedures, items discussed at meetings, how we fish, conversations and actions heard or witnessed. This is odd: fishing's fishing. It's a universal practice. Toddlers can fucking fish.

Damien glances at me, he's uncertain too as he twiddles his biro between his fingers. I look at Mike. He smiles back tiredly, giving a reassuring nod: *It's fine, Jules. I've checked it out.*

Reservations aside, I sign, pushing it towards Waldemar who smiles as he sweeps the rest of the papers into his case.

"Anyway, going back to Julian's question," he replies. "If you're not aware, there's a popular demand for the distribution of whale meat. The oils, blubber and cartilage have been used to create wonderful health products and supplements. Have any of you purchased candles?"

We all nod in unison.

"There's a pretty high percentage some of the candles you've used in the past contain whale oil. Even certain perfumes consist of a substance called ambergris, to make the scent last longer. This comes from the faecal matter of sperm whales. Of course, not all companies use this, some ambergris is made synthetically but you can't beat the organic version."

I didn't know this and I bought my wife tons of perfume. I wonder if it's been made with whale shit.

"What about other mammals?" Damien asks.

"Machine lubricants and fertilizer have been made from dolphins," Waldemar replies, taking a sweeping glance around the room. "I can see from your perplexed expressions that you're unaware of these investments."

I really wasn't.

"So you want us to hunt for whales out at sea?" Damien asks.

"That's correct," Waldemar responds.

"But we only fish for *fish*," Lance utters. "You know cod, mackerel, the normal stuff to be eaten, not to be made into face cream."

"I'm aware of this," Waldemar says. "I know it's a big step in a different direction. However, I was watching the culling the other day and I felt your skilled expertise of handling the whales was beneficial for the work."

Waldemar was at the culling, why didn't he say something?

Did Mike and Dan know he was there?

Mike scratches his head, as if he's been holding his breath. "How would the project work, Matthew?"

Our future employer smiles. "Well, I own a large ship where we do most of our catching. You'll have room and board, work in twelve-hour shifts and be paid handsomely." He pushes more papers around the table. "This is what you'll receive at the end of your six-week assignment. We plan to start in mid-September and finish at the end of October before the winter weather fully sets in."

I nearly choke on my drink when I see the amount. I wouldn't have to worry about the winter period, it'd tide me over. The fishing industry's a hit and miss market, sometimes I make enough where I can work on my boats, and other times it's a short drown. I've nabbed some temporary factory work in the past to pay my bills when sailing the waves dried up.

"Do you have any questions?" Waldemar asks.

"I do," I say.

He smiles. "Yes, Julian. Go ahead."

"I've never hunted whales from a ship before. We've only done it at the culling. I assume the method of killing will be different?"

"Brilliant question," Waldemar says. "I have a colleague called Craig who coordinates the live catches and conducts the health and safety regulations. It'll be very safe when you're working."

He's not answering my question. "What do you use to hunt?"

Waldemar smiles again. "A harpoon. It's the same size as a military device."

"We've never used them before," Lance utters.

"You'll be trained beforehand," Waldemar replies.

"Bloody hell, it's like being in a spy film," Damien utters.

There's polite laughter around the table. I think about the whaling videos Mike mentioned and my stomach churns. My working tools are nets, rods and carving knives. Deep sea divers carry a harpoon gun in case they run into trouble, but fishermen don't.

During our break, I hang by the quay drinking in the fresh sea air. I notice there's a text from Herb.

Frank's niece is quite unusual isn't she. She's very pretty. ☺ ☺

What's with the wink emoji? What are people insinuating? And, why do they keep telling me how attractive she is?

I send him a reply. *I thought you didn't swing that way? Is she at the shop?*

A response lights up my phone screen. **Just because I'm gay doesn't mean I can't appreciate a woman's beauty. Emily brought her. Shy's been helping with the book stacking.**

What do you think of her green hair?

I like it, an unusual sight in Drake Cove. She looks ethereal, as if someone moulded her from a fairy tale. How come you're asking?

I frown at his text. Why am I asking?

Another text blinks on. **Do you think she's pretty?**

I reply instantly. *Yes. You'd have to be blind not to see that.*

☺ **Are you sure you don't have a crush, Jules?**

Nope, I'm admiring her beauty... just like you. ☺

I don't get a response and I'm thankful for it. What was starting off as a joke, is now getting on my nerves. First Mike comments on me blushing, then Damien and Lance insinuate about us shagging and now Herb's doing it. Okay Frank's niece is an attractive woman. I admit it. She's strong and athletic, but she's also really weird, and she hardly speaks, and she *stares*. She stares *a lot* as if she's x-raying my brain. *And* I swear she was watching me sleep last night.

I go back to the meeting and we discuss the scheduling. I opt for the day shifts but I'm not bothered either way if I can't work them. As long as I'm not paired with Dan, I'm happy. We all agree to do three weeks of day shifts and three of the nights. Thankfully Lance is grouped with Dan, I can tell by his face he's not happy about it. We sign the contracts and Waldemar pulls a self-indulgent smile as he gathers up the paperwork.

A pool of nerves form in my gut when I picture the monstrous harpoon gun.

"I'm delighted to be working with all of you," Waldemar says, then his smile melts away swapped with a mask of sympathy. "I'm sorry to hear about your colleagues. Ian and Earl sounded like great men - it's such a pity I never got to meet them."

Mike crosses his arms over his chest. "The past couple of weeks have been rough on all of us."

"It's been fucking awful," Lance sneers. "Our friends murdered, the FAAC blowing smoke up our arses and then

Jules gets his window broken in."

"And that bleedin' video too," Damien adds.

Waldemar clocks me.

Thanks guys, I really didn't want the boss of our boss to know.

"I heard about the incident, Julian," Waldemar utters. "I'm very sorry."

I wave off his apology. "Thanks, Matthew. The most important thing is my daughter didn't get hurt. The police are on the case, I'm sure they'll catch the culprit."

11

The meeting's adjourned, Waldemar says his goodbyes and leaves the office. He drives off in his shiny BMW and a cloud of uncertainty floats over me. Lance and Damien go to work on their boats. Mike and Dan sit behind their desks, typing away. I pop my head around the door. "I'm heading to The Crest to grab some grub, wanna come?"

Mike rakes his hands down his face, he does this far too much. "I better not."

"Oh come on, give yourself some head space for once."

My boss smiles tiredly. "Yeah, you're right. I need a break or I'll crack."

We don't walk in a hurry, we take our time. I notice some of the Drake Covians stare at us as they stroll past. Rumours travel fast in a small town.

"How do you think it went?" Mike asks.

"Better than I expected," I reply.

Mike smirks. "It was, by the way I never told Matthew about the video. He already knew about it."

"It's fine. Don't worry. It wouldn't surprise me if Dan let it out. With Ian and Earl, I'm sure he did some background research on all of us."

"How do you feel about the project?" he asks.

"The money's great," I say. "But I'm nervous about leaving Emily for six weeks. This is the first time... Hanna's not around."

"I know, Jules. It's been tough for you. But you've coped better than you think."

"Herb and Derek have agreed to look after her."

"That's very kind of them," he sighs, breathing out slowly. "I saw your expression when Matthew mentioned the harpoon gun."

"It freaks me out, Mike. If the FAAC find out what we're doing, they'll make things ten times worse for us than they already are."

"They can't find out about it. We signed confidentiality statements. Matthew and his crew can't talk about it either. The FAAC won't come out to sea, unless they have a boat or a sponsored ship floating about."

"It's still violent. We hunt whales for their meat to eat."

"True but we're not making their bones into chandeliers." Mike laughs. "It sounds like Frank's views are rubbing off on you."

I stare at him briefly, the questions lingering in my mind. *What happened between you two? Why don't you talk anymore?*

But, I don't say anything.

~

We arrive at the Crest Café and I order my usual. Mike chomps through his BLT sarnie and slurps his tea. I miss the days when Drake Cove was completely oblivious to social media and the internet, even Dylan (the café owner) is staring at me more than normal. Everyone's intrusive eyes make me think of Chief Inspector Drew. Is she questioning Geoff Ward and the rest of his zombies?

They have every reason to benefit from my misery. They paint what we do in a mean, sadistic streak as if we get off on gutting whales. It's a job, that's all it is. Do you see farmers crying every five minutes after they've killed some cattle?

No. It's hard, exhausting work and its everyday life. We've numbed ourselves from the "violence" of it.

Then it hits me as I gaze around the café in silence. The distressing video and the attack on my home, it makes us villain fishermen look like we've received some kind of karmic justice from our "bloody, barbaric" work. This whole thing is a mind puzzle and it's tipping towards them, in their favour.

~

We eat leftovers for dinner. Emily's talking in tongues about her day. I give her the news when I'll be away, she isn't pleased but she knows it's got to be done. Shy isn't with us again; she's gone out for another walk. I haven't received an update from Drew, which must mean there's nothing to report, or she's still investigating.

After dinner, Frank and Em watch telly. I beam up my laptop, making sure to keep the screen tipped so they can't see. I load YouTube and type in the search bar:

Whaling ships

I plug in my headphones and click on the first video. The screen explodes with several images of dead whales. Before I watch, I read the description. The video consists of B-roll footage from the whaling ship, the Mission Ark during a fishing tour in 1993.

I hold my breath momentarily, pressing play.

Two fishermen dressed in yellow and brown uniforms load a harpoon. Waldemar's right. It reminds me of a huge machine gun. The camera angle changes to a shot of the open ocean where a blue whale rises to the surface exposing its pale belly.

The gun shoots loudly and the harpoon skewers the creature. The camera cuts and the blood oozes around the whale. The fishermen yank the rope attached to the harpoon; heaving the whale onto the ship. It flaps its tail, trying to escape.

Another harpoon from the other side of the ship fires, water spray jets out from the high pressure when another whale rises to the surface. A group of fishermen pull on two sets of rope. The whales are heaved out of the water. Pink pulsing tubes of the intestines bulge from the gaping wounds of their bellies. The sharpness of the harpoon has ripped several deep holes into their flesh. Being pulled onboard is causing more flesh to rip when they try to flee. They're being heaved up the ramp, their fins and tails wiggling still. They're still alive, even when their intestines are sprawled out all over the deck.

I skip through the video until I come to a section where one of the whales (now dead) is lifted up on a winch, then its tail is sliced off. It falls to the wet ground in a huge splodge and the skin's peeled off in chunks. The video cuts to a conveyer belt, shifting whale meat and blubber. The fishermen brandish cleavers, dicing the meat into cubes, then a line of others package it in boxes, ready for distribution.

I press stop on the video. Mike's right, it's not a glamorous business, but people need to eat. No wonder Waldemar's hiring us for the work.

I look up when Shy walks through the front door, again her jeans are damp. That's the second time. She doesn't say anything and disappears upstairs into the bathroom. I pull the lip of my laptop down, closing the YouTube video.

"Your niece loves the shower," I say to Frank.

He glances at me, nodding and goes back to watching the television.

"Should I make her something to eat?" I ask.

"Don't bother," Frank replies. "She'll eat when she wants to."

"But she didn't eat last night either. It can't be good for her to run on two meals a day."

"We went to the coffee shop this afternoon," Em says, her chin bobbing on the arm of the sofa. "She ate loads."

"See?" Frank says. "Shy's fine."

"I'll make her something anyway." I put my laptop on the coffee table and march to the kitchen. "Does she like cheese?"

"Yeah, she does. What are you gonna make?"

"A sandwich."

"That's sweet of you, but you really don't need to. Shy can look after herself."

"Well, she's been great company for Emily and I want to say thank you, in my own special way." I slap some bread together and smear the cheese on. I nuke it in the microwave for a short burst and heap Kettle crisps on the plate.

Em says goodnight, cuddling Keira to her chest.

I wait in the lounge with Shy's dinner. "Frank, what do you know about whaling ships?"

He turns to me, folding the newspaper on his lap. "Why are you asking?"

"I'm just curious..."

"Well, whaling's been going on for centuries, since the dawn of time. The blubber and meat's been a resource in commercial industries. Back in the olden times, whales were just eaten for their meat. The Vikings used to hunt them, it's where our culling came from. An adult whale could feed an entire village twice over. According to Drake Cove history, the celts fished normally and when the Vikings invaded, they brought their ways with them. Then as the industrial revolution began, humans realised whales weren't just meals in the sea."

"They could be used as machine lubricants?" I ask.

"Yes precisely," Frank replies, smiling with scepticism. "Have you been reading my books?"

"Nope, been telly hopping. When did whaling start being controversial?"

"Pretty much when television began broadcasting. Ordinary people discovered how whaling ships worked and they witnessed the devastation it can cause. This includes farms and slaughter houses. A whistle blower leaked footage of how pigs were killed at this farm. They were doused in water, electrocuted and slit open while they were still alive and... they bled to death. The worker brings in the next pig and the animal *knew* it was gonna die, you could see the fear on its face, it was backing up trying to get out of the room. It was distressing to watch. But, it's a business. They need to get the pigs through the line, hacked up and shipped off. That's why you have places that pile animals in together. There's no conscious thought, it's a factory process, still… it doesn't make it right."

I think about the YouTube video of the Mission Ark, it must have been a shock for people if they aren't in the profession like me. The whales were still alive, just like they are at the culling.

Frank continues talking. "I was invited by a farmer to visit his business when I was working on my second book. It was an enlightening experience. His cattle had plenty of space, they were healthy, they had water, food, they were cared for and had a huge field for grazing. He even showed me how they were killed. A single nail gun bolt to the head, fast like a silent bullet. There was no blood, the cow didn't feel any pain. Farms protect animals from predators and the elements. Some activists forget animals *die* in the wild, hunted by others, starvation, infections and so forth. This farmer said that the breeding and killing of his cattle helped mankind. Their lives *and* their deaths served a purpose. He wasn't uneducated or old fashioned. He cared for the welfare of his animals and he attended more animal agriculture seminars than me!"

I want to grab Frank and give him a big kiss on the forehead. It's such a relief to hear that he's explored both sides of the argument. Not like the FAAC who just focus on one sword of an opinion - their own.

"It's not just the killing fields under fire," Frank explains. "On the other side of the coin, you have aquariums who capture killer whales from the open ocean, breed them, separate them from their young and train them to perform tricks for an audience, and what for? So, they can accomplish a couple of flips through a hoop to get bums on seats? It's the same with those bloody dog shows."

"You really hate them, don't you?" I ask, my head's exploding with all of this new information.

Frank wipes his face. "Don't get me riled up, Jules. It benefits nobody but the owner. Anyway, back to the whaling shows, some of the orcas have attacked, even eaten their trainers." The passionate flare blooms in Frank's eyes as he speaks. "They keep them in tanks, work them hard, until their old, still performing flips when they have chronic arthritis. Whales, orcas, dolphins, they're much like us. Put a man in a cage and tell him to dance for his food, he'll do it. But one day, he will snap, violently. If a human's treated like an elephant at a circus, the owners would be imprisoned, labelled monsters, criminals, and rightly so. Why are animals treated so differently? Is it because we're the kings and queens of the planet?"

I stare at him, shrugging. I really don't know.

"I guess it's always been that way," I say. "Humans are at the top of the pecking order. Whales didn't discover morphine. Tigers didn't invent trains. *People* did."

"You're absolutely right, Jules. Homosapiens are wonderful creatures, but then, look at the atrocities we've caused, the wars and the soaring number of deaths, not just with animals but our own kind. We're monsters too, and we need to take accountability for our actions. Did you know scientists discovered that whale meat contains a high concentration of heavy metals?"

"Really?" I ask.

"Yes, people have died from mercury poisoning. Didn't you know that?"

"No, never."

"When I started writing my first book, I volunteered for any signs of mercury poisoning. The research group took some hair and blood samples and the results came back positive. The poisoning can cause headaches, sleeping difficulties, neurological and behavioural disorders. It can also harm the kidneys and thyroid. I've consumed large amounts of whale meat and blubber in my time, so sadly I can't be saved from it." He watches me, his gaze searching for a reaction. "When this town participates in the culling, the blood from the whales pours into the sea. The mercury will be in the water, other fishes swim in it and then the humans consume the fish. It's a depressing, toxic cycle."

"How come I've never heard of this before?" I ask.

"Drake Covians don't like the truth, especially if it hurts their long-standing traditions. I've said it before, it's why some of them don't want me living here. They'll be plenty of Drake Covians with positive mercury readings and don't know it. It's the same with smoking, if you keep doing it, you *will* have health problems. Despite all the anti-smoking adverts, people still choose to do it because we have freedom of choice."

My mind's shaken. My parents didn't talk about mercury poisoning, neither did Mike, or Herb and Derek and they're against whaling. I'm amazed by Frank's attitude, he's respectful and he listens to my argument. We stand on opposite sides of the fishing debate and we're friends. He's not punching me or wishing my life to end. Not like the FAAC.

"What made you change your view about fishing?" I ask.

"I went on holiday. I'd never tried octopus before, so I was curious and ate some. The tentacle was squidgy and tasted of moss. I remember sitting there, thinking, octopuses are incredibly intelligent and the poor thing died so I could have lunch. And I didn't enjoy eating it."

"Maybe you just had a bad chef. Is that why you chose to leave the industry?"

Frank nods.

He had an epiphany. Over an octopus. Really?

I don't believe it.

"Is that why you and Mike don't talk anymore?"

There's an uncomfortable silence.

Frank watches me before smiling. "That's private, Jules." He gets up from his chair. "It's late. I'm heading to bed."

"Shit, sorry, Frank. Have I upset you?"

"No, not at all. I know our history must baffle you but it was a long time ago and I've moved on. Mike has too, I can tell. It's best that I leave that box bolted. Do you understand what I mean?"

I nod slowly, feeling like a kid again.

"Anyway, if you want to know more about whaling and so forth…" Frank turns to the bookcase and chucks a book in my lap. "Have a read, you might find it interesting. It changed my life, quite literally too." He laughs politely, I must've pissed him off. "Have a good night."

"Goodnight Frank," I reply, watching him disappear upstairs.

Shit, shit, *shit.*

He's told me to back off after I leached his brain for information. Well done, Julian. Well fucking done.

I glance at the book in my hands.

Underneath the Fisherman's Net, a memoir by Frank Blothio.

The front cover is of a man (I assume is Frank) glancing out at the shoreline. The lighthouse of Drake Cove is off in the corner. I read the blurb:

Frank Blothio is a fisherman turned animal rights activist. In this deep, raw account, he tells his story about why he left his long-standing profession and the darkness of the fishing business, revealing secrets the media refuse to publish.

I open the book, flipping through the dull pages about copyright. Then my heart freezes when I see the dedication.

To my Shae.

I'm sorry for everything I've done. Just know the work I do from now on, is because of you. It's all for you.

I sit back and think.

Shae?

Who's Shae?

I've never heard of her. Frank's never mentioned anyone by this name. His dedication sounds sorrowful, as if things didn't end on the best terms. Was this the woman Mike mentioned, the one Frank lived with when I was a child?

More mysteries seem to be blooming every which way in this man's life.

I flick through the book and skim the pages. Frank talks about how he got into fishing (like all of us, it was learnt through family) and then he goes on about some of the dealings when he co-managed the company. He names and shames the businesses. No wonder he's hated by so many people. One of them we've worked with and according to Frank, they sold fish that had expired to customers!

How could that happen?

If fish is kept in the freezer, it can last for nearly a year.

The bathroom door opens as I swear in confused whispers and Shy emerges wrapped in a comfy night gown.

"Oh, Shy," I say, grabbing her plate, heading upstairs. "I made you some dinner."

The nape of her neck shines with moisture from the shower vapour. Her eyes travel from the plate to my face. She takes it from me and walks into her room.

Oh-kay…

I stand, feeling a tad stupid that she's brushed me off. What do I do now?

I knock on her door which has been left open. Shy's sitting on her bed, munching through her sandwich hungrily. Well, at least she's enjoying it.

"Can I come in?" I ask.

Shy nods. I step over the threshold. She's watching me closely, there's flecks of crisps by the side of her mouth, strands of green hair peak through the towel wrapped around her head.

"I wanted to say thank you for spending time with Emily, she seems happier being around you."

Shy smiles sweetly. "I like her."

"She likes you too. Frank says you've been going for walks," I say, hoping I don't sound like a snooping idiot. "Why do you go out for so long?"

"I enjoy being outside," she replies. "The sea air's good for you."

That doesn't explain why her jeans have been wet and why she's in the shower for so long, unless she *is* a germaphobe with OCD.

"Can Em and I accompany you on one of your walks?" I ask. "It'd be great to do some exercise rather than binge watching TV all night."

Her eyes widen and her lips purse as she thinks. "If Frank's okay with it."

Why would Frank not be okay with it?

As he said himself, she's a grown woman.

I indicate to the pictures. "Did you paint these?"

"Yes."

There's a portrait of a crowd of people with war paint smeared across their faces. Then I notice a landscape of Becks Hill in a wash of blue and green, the light pours out onto the sealine. I hear the delicate crunch as the crisps disintegrate between Shy's teeth. I'm growing nervous, as if her eyes are burning into the back of my skull.

There's posters on the walls of David Bowie in his Ziggy Stardust persona.

"Oh, you're an admirer, are you?" I smile.

Shy places the plate on the floor and stands next to me. I wonder if her mum or dad had the tall gene. She taps her finger on David Bowie's face and then points at her eyes.

I look closely, staring into her face. "Oh of course, you both have different colour eyes."

My attention switches nervously to her paintings and drawings. A mixture of colours spark from the wall. "I like your work, you're really talented. They're so realistic."

"I paint from memory," she replies.

"That's impressive. I wish I could draw like you. These should be in an art gallery."

Shy picks up a canvas from the carpet, tipping it towards me. "I'm working on this right now."

My heart lurches in my chest, where there are natural shades in her other paintings, this picture's devoid of it. The image is of a gloomy sea swarming with blood, whales are screeching in pain, grey faceless figures hack at their heads with gutting knives. The lighthouse of Becks Hill stands, one ray of its eye shining down on the monstrosity.

"It's the culling." I look into her eyes. "You don't agree with it, do you?"

"No," she utters. "It's not right."

She stares at me, something in her face is drawing me in. There's an intensity in her expression as if someone's lit a blaze. My palms grow clammy as I try to formulate some sort of response. "I... know it looks awful from the outside, Shy but..." I lick my lips as my throat goes dry and I cough. "You see... people have to eat."

"Then why does it bother you so much?" she asks.

"What?"

Shy touches my cheek and images flash through my thoughts. A lonely whale calf. Shadows loom at the surface. Blood engulfs the sea along with a piercing scream and the calf escapes into the depths.

My heart palpitates painfully in my chest and I sit up in a shudder. I'm drenched in a cold sweat, lying across the sofa. Frank's book is on the floor next to me. I must have been dreaming. I wipe my head, pulling the blanket off me.

Shit.

I can see Shy's reflection in the television screen.

12

I receive a call from Drew with news I don't want to hear. She interviewed Geoff *the bastard*, he has a solid steel alibi proving he wasn't in Drake Cove at the time of the attack. Apparently, he was visiting a family friend. Drew followed it up and it was confirmed with this "family friend" so she couldn't arrest him. I protest that Geoff's probably lying and so is the contact, the guy does it for a living. He may not have been present at the attack but he still could've orchestrated it. Drew agrees with me and says when she asked Geoff if she could have access to his phone, he refused, spouting crap about his human rights and that she'd have to take it up with his solicitor unless she charged him with a crime. Emily and I can't return home as she delves into their barracks. I wish her all the best, but I'm worried there's no hope for an outcome. They hide their cynical existences for a reason, to get away with shit like this.

On the lighter side, we've been given the green light to be back out at sea and the first shift was wonderful and euphoric. I find being out on the ocean, away from Drake Cove a bizarre release. I don't have anyone whispering about me, judging me for my profession. I wonder what it'd be like to pack a ton of supplies, take Henna out and let the sea drift me off into the glorious sunshine. I wouldn't have to answer to anyone, or anything. No wonder so many become lost with the waves.

~

As lunch ticks by, I head to the Crest Café for my usual and decide to visit Em at the bookshop. When I walk to the town square, I immediately regret my decision.

The fucktards of the FAAC are here.

There's about eight of them, all wearing masks. One of them is shouting rubbish into a megaphone and a black Labrador's barking loudly. They're holding a long banner with pictures of deceased whales and other marine mammals.

The words on the sign make my blood run cold:

EXPOSING THE DARK HEART OF DRAKE COVE

My hometown's always been busy with tourists during the summer, but the volume this season has spiked significantly. I wonder if the deaths of my friends and the viral video has anything to do with it. People stand and watch eagerly filming on their phones, others are talking calmly to the masked twativists.

I pull my hood over my head and catch a family walking by. I huddle in, matching my footsteps to theirs. They're the appropriate camouflage.

Em looks up from the till. "Dad?!"

I smile at her as I close the shop door. "Hello hunnie."

"What are you doing here?"

"Just on my lunch break, thought I'd drop by and say hi."

"I'm working, it's not that interesting."

I correct her. "You're volunteering."

Em shrugs sluggishly. "Volunteering, working, it's the same thing."

"Well, it's not." I pull my hood down. "The FAAC are outside, I didn't want them to see me."

"They've been getting on my nerves all day. They've

made such a racket. I'd love to shove that loudspeaker where the sun doesn't shine."

"Emily…" I press.

"I mean it. We haven't had any customers because of them!"

Out from the back of the shop, Shy carries a massive heavy box of books.

"Hi Shy," I say, trying to hide my embarrassment from the night before.

She smiles briefly. "Hello."

"Where's Derek?" I ask Emily.

"He's out back making drinks. I'm watching the till for him after I did some shadowing."

As she talks about her day, Shy steps up the ladder, still holding the box.

"Dad?"

I hope she doesn't fall off and break her neck.

"Dad?"

She's pulling a book out with one hand, while the other steadily holds the box.

"Dad?"

Shy has great balance; she's not teetering on her feet or making the ladder sway. It must be the gymnastics and all the swimming.

"*Dad?!*"

"*What?*" I blurt.

"So, can I go to Jordan's birthday party on Friday?"

"What party?"

"You weren't listening to a word I was saying, were you?"

"Yes…I was…" I mutter uncomfortably.

"Okay, where's Jordan's party taking place then?"

I squirm. I was too busy staring at Shy. "A burger bar?"

"That was when he was eight." She rolls her eyes. "Fine, as you clearly weren't paying attention. It's Jordan's fifteenth this Friday. We're going to Yearling for the day, gonna do some bowling, have pizza then go to the cinema. Is it okay if I go?"

"Do you want to?"

"Um, *yeah*. I need to escape this place now and again."

"Of course, you can, as long as you're safe," I reply. "Have you got him a present?"

"No, not yet."

"You could give him one of Shy's paintings, they're really good," I say, noticing Shy's head turn. "Is it okay if Em buys one of your pictures?"

"Sure," she answers, smiling faintly.

"Dad, Jordan won't want a painting!" Em hisses. "He'll want the new Foo Fighters album."

"Oh, okay, sorry. I just thought it'd be a nice present."

"No, Dad."

I feel stupid and embarrassed, but what are fathers for?

I hear the creaks as Shy climbs down the ladder, the box in her hands is empty. Her attention's been robbed from us, something is going on outside, her eyes are still and serious.

"Shy, are you okay?"

She places the box on the ground, ignoring me and leaves the shop, her shoulder brushing mine. My heart drops when I clock what's going on.

Frank's standing in the town square, talking to the FAAC. Some of the activists are congregating around him. This can't be going anywhere respectable. The one with the megaphone has stopped spouting and he's leering at Frank who's standing calmly, wearing a casual smile. Some of the others are filming Frank, while the rest are still holding the crude banner.

"Stay here," I say to Em and head out after Shy, hoping to avoid a scuffle.

I shouldn't be doing this, especially with everything going on. But I can't stand by and watch Frank be heckled and pestered. He's done so much for me.

"I'm not scared to show my face when it comes to expressing my views, sunshine," Frank quips to the leader. "I don't hide behind my phone, or a mask, or a morphed voice."

I find the relationship between Frank and the FAAC fascinating. They share the same opinion but dislike each other's execution of their views.

"Is everything cool here?" I ask.

The FAAC turn to me, phones clicking in my personal space. Shit, just what I don't need right now.

"It's alright, Jules," Frank says. "I can handle this."

Shy's standing next to Frank, watching with caution. Her fingers hooking around the cuff of his jacket.

"You were at the culling. You had your window broken in," the leader says, swinging his megaphone by his hip. His dog peers up with worry.

"Yes, I did," I reply.

The FAAC laugh at me, some utter that I deserve it. I can feel myself getting angry, their words validate my suspicions. They *are* the culprits.

"Whoever threw the stone got the wrong room," I say. "They've could've killed my daughter."

I don't see a flicker of interest or empathy that a child was targeted and nearly bludgeoned to death.

"Well, it wasn't me," Megaphone replies snobbishly.

"Do you know who did it?" I ask.

"*Piss off!*"

Megaphone, the leader of the group is in his mid to late twenties. He has copper, golden hair sprouting from the crooks in his coal balaclava. It's not Geoff the bastard. I wonder where he's scarpered off to. Maybe he's told them to do this because of Drew's interview. I won't tell them the police are investigating their organisation.

"Who are you?" Megaphone asks, green eyes beaming at Shy with delirium.

"Take off your mask and I'll tell you." She grins flirtatiously, stepping in front of Frank.

"Nah, I'm not taking it off, love."

Her gaze shines. "What have you got to hide?"

A glimmer of irritation glows in Megaphone's eyes. "Do you support the fishermen?"

"No," she replies.

"Were you there at the culling?"

"Yes, and I hated it. It made me sad."

Megaphone points in my face. "Then why aren't you angry at him? We're spreading awareness. We're the good guys. Look at what he did to that whale and her unborn baby!"

Shy glances at Megaphone's dog who's waiting obediently by his master's feet. "He doesn't like the speaker. The volume's hurting his ears. You should take him to the vet, he has a bad paw, it's sore when he walks. Have you not noticed he's limping?"

"Shut up lady," one of the activist jeers.

Shy smiles with gratification, her eyes burning into Megaphone's. "If you keep ignoring his injuries, he'll bite your hand off one day."

The dog cries hysterically, tapping its paws on the ground.

"He wants to go home. He hates being here. You

should listen to him," Shy utters. "For once."

She turns around and walks away. I grab Frank's wrist, pulling him from the bubbling chaos. They taunt us, calling us cowards for fleeing. Nobody says anything to each other until the shouts of the FAAC fade off in the distance.

"For fuck's sake, you two!" Frank hisses. "I don't need a security team. I was fine back there!"

I laugh from shock. "Are you serious? Did you not see what they were doing?"

"Yeah, the old scare tactic, huddling in. I've seen it before. It doesn't scare me."

"I don't want you getting beaten up," I say.

"I won't. They're words, Jules. They don't mean anything."

"Yeah and a threat smothered stone thrown through my window late at night by a masked tosser doesn't signify anything remotely threatening or sinister." I change the subject, pissed off and irritated. "Anyway, where are you off to?"

"I'm on my way to visit my publisher," Frank says. "Got the final draft finished! Hurrah!"

"Good for you," I say.

"I'll be back tomorrow," Frank replies.

"Tomorrow?" I ask. "Where are you staying?"

"A hotel."

"Why don't you just drive?"

"Have you ever driven to the big posh metropolitan cities, Julian?" he asks.

"No…"

"The parking's really expensive plus, it's a nightmare to drive round there anyway."

A red and blue bus swans into the bus stop.

Frank looks at Shy and caresses her arm with reassurance. "Be nice to our guests. I'll only be gone for one night."

By the evening, Em and I are chomping our dinner in front of the telly. Shy isn't here, again. When I came back from work, she pulled on her jacket and legged it. I get pulling a decent hour in the gym, or a run, or even cycling but she's been gone all evening. How is she not tired?

We're watching a documentary Frank recommended about killer whales in captivity. There's a moment in the film where a trainer's yanked to the bottom of the tank by his foot, and the orca won't let him go. It twirls the guy around underwater for several minutes. How the guy doesn't drown, I don't know. The trainer manages to wriggle free, and then the orca charges after him as he tries to get out of the pool. He shakes with fear, he knows the orca has the power card. It's menacing viewing, according to the film, the trainer has a broken ankle.

"They shouldn't have whales perform in these shows," Em replies, staring at the screen. "It's cruel."

As the documentary continues, I research about the FAAC on my laptop and find their Facebook page.

A new video has been uploaded. The video's entitled:

Who is this woman?

I mute the volume and play the video. The camera shakes, it's been filmed behind Megaphone. It focuses on Shy's face; she's smiling at him as he demands to know her name. Whoever's edited the video has provided subtitles too. I feel sick when I catch my face peeping over her shoulder. I must admit, I don't look nervous or scared, just exhausted.

As the argument continues, they film us leaving and

the camera pans to Megaphone:

"*You see, this is the type of people we have to deal with,*" he says with defiance and pride. "*People who say they don't support the fishermen who commit cold-blooded murder, but on the flip side, they can't provide a decent argument to back up their views.*"

The video ends and I read the comments below:

She really likes Frank. Ugh, what a pity, she's pretty cute too. *Retch* ⌧

I've tried to do a photo reversal on her face, but nothing's coming up on google, she's got no social media accounts or email address. If she did, I'd be spamming her arse!

She was deflecting. Did you notice how she kept talking about the dog?

The comments are odd and creepy. Why do they care so much about Shy's identity? Are they intimidated by her in some way?

Their actions reek of sadness and desperation. I understand them hating me because of what I do for a living, but not Shy.

My mind rushes to Emily's blog when I remember their lack of empathy about her life in danger. I type it in the search bar. Her blog's still private, thankfully. I don't know whether to make an account or if I'm interfering in her personal business.

Okay, I'm not proud of it…but I sign up for an account. I choose a random nickname and click the friend request on her blog. I have to know my fourteen-year-old's okay and she's using the internet securely.

~

After we go to bed, I have a sandwich ready for Shy when she comes back. She spends a lot of time in the shower, as she always does. I lie on the sofa, pretending to be asleep. Shy walks into the kitchen wearing her pyjamas. She crunches through her food. I open my eyes in a squint. She's not saying anything. She's standing, eating, and staring… at me.

My heart races as I realise, she must've been watching, the whole fucking time.

It gets worse when her soft footsteps approach the sofa. Shit, Julian. Snore, let one off, stink the house out. Em says my farts can empty a room in seconds.

Do something. Anything to make her stop.

Slender fingers prod at my chest.

"*Shy?*" I murmur. "Are you okay?"

She's kneeling next to the sofa. "Thanks for looking out for Frank."

"It's fine, you don't need to thank me. You did a far better job, standing up to that guy with the megaphone."

"He wanted to hurt him," she says.

"I know, that's why I couldn't ignore it. I wish Frank was more careful."

"He's stubborn."

I smile. "I agree."

An instinct within me wants to place a strand of hair behind her ear. Her gaze doesn't break from mine and I start to feel awkward. I blurt out a question. Shy ignores it and leans forward. Shadows move across my eyes; the air grows thin and her lips find mine.

I'm overwhelmed by her warm skin. Her fingers curl through my hair. Her kiss is passionate and powerful, as if she's sucking the life out of me. She clambers on top of my legs, our tongues dance and I picture Emily walking down the stairs, having the fright of her life.

I pry Shy from my chest, panting from her intimacy.

"Wow. T-That was a...really, *really* nice kiss." My words shake with shock. "But, I...I can't do this, Shy."

"Why not?" she asks, unclipping her pyjama shirt, revealing her bare breast.

My heart pumps into over drive. My throat's dry. Shy takes my hand and leads it to her bosom, watching me the entire time. It's been such a while since I've done this.

"I...I can't," I whisper, raising my other hand so she can see the golden wedding band. "I'm sorry."

Shy glances away, hastily clipping her bed shirt together. She's embarrassed and I feel for her. I *never* take off my ring. Ever. She would've seen it surely.

Shy looks at me and leans forward. I push back on the sofa thinking she's going to kiss me again. She presses her hand against my face with a curious expression in her eyes. Images rush over my vision. They come thick and fast. I can't flee.

Hanna's watching me on our first date, her caramel hair floating in the breeze. Our first kiss, the first time we made love, our romantic dance as husband and wife. The piercing screams of baby Emily squiggling in her mother's arms. Hanna at the hospital, hearing the diagnosis, holding her when her motor skills start to fail. Her body hooked up to a monitor because she can't breathe for herself.

My body jolts painfully and I stare back at Shy. "*What was that?*"

She doesn't say anything but I know from the seriousness in her face - she knows what happened to my family.

"This was a mistake," Shy whispers. "I... shouldn't've done it."

She rises to her feet and I grab her wrist, pulling her back down to me. I stroke the blade of my finger against her cheek. My gaze doesn't budge. A hunger's rising within me. I press my mouth against hers and we begin our dance once more. I love the way she feels in my arms. I've missed this.

So much.

13

The smoky aroma of coffee teases my nostrils. The fog melts from my sight. Frank's eyes burn into mine. His mouth's thin as if he's sipped the juices from the skin of a lemon. Then I hear the chime of a groan roll from my chest.

Shy rises, scrubbing the back of her hand against her face, massaging the tiredness from her eyes. She smiles at me, until she notices I'm not looking at her. The second she sees Frank, she jumps to her feet in a sprightly manner, adjusting her shirt. She approaches him, twiddling her fingers. Frank turns his back, chucking the spoon into the sink. It hits the basin with a loud clang.

"Just go to your room," he says bluntly.

Shy storms off, heading upstairs, slamming her bedroom door.

"Do you want some coffee?" Frank asks.

I clamber off the sofa, passing a hand through my hair. *Fuck.*

Here goes.

"Frank," I sigh, hoping he's not concealing a knife; he may not fish anymore, but he still knows how to disembowel. "Look, I know how it must appear. Nothing happened between us, she just wanted a cuddle. We were exhausted last night and we fell asleep. She was upset because the FAAC were hassling you."

He doesn't say anything, instead he leans on the counter, breathing heavily. "I'm not stupid, Jules."

My pulse hypes up in pace. "What do you mean?"

"I've seen the way you look at her."

"Shy looks at me too, Frank. We didn't have sex, I promise. I wouldn't do that. Emily could've woken up and seen us."

"I could've woken up and seen what?" a voice asks.

Shit.

I turn around to find my little girl squinting with messy hair, pulling on her dressing gown.

"You need to get ready for sailing school," I say.

"I will, after I eat my breakfast," she replies, shuffling past me, reaching for the cereal.

The silence is agonising.

I've made a massive cock-up.

Em clocks the situation, crunching through her cocoa pops, frowning at Frank. "What's up with you?"

"Nothing," he mutters. "I'm just tired." He's avoiding my gaze and walks out of the room.

"Is he okay?" Em asks.

"I think he's just stressed about his upcoming book launch." And that I was making out with his niece most of the night, and I've lied to him about it when he probably knows what we were up to.

~

I head to work after the awkward shitstorm. Mike, Damien and Lance are out fishing, Dan's in the office doing clerical duties and I'm working on the maintenance of the boats.

During my break, I receive a notification. Em's accepted my request to view her blog. She's done it very quickly considering, there's nothing on my profile. Hasn't she checked it out? Doesn't it feel suspicious to her?

I sip my tea as I flick through her page. The display and tagline remain the same as before. The left-hand side of the blog is now dotted with dates and titles. I tap on the first tab and words fill my phone screen:

Vanishing Acts

It doesn't hurt as much as it did. If you'd believed in me, you wouldn't have driven that train so fast. You didn't have to get out of the wreckage alone when I was standing there offering my hand. You'll be the one leaving with scars. It won't be me, not this time.

The smoke spills across the broken tracks. The tension falls like the rain minute by minute. The wounds you dug in deep are closing - I can see the sun climb and kiss my skin again.

I always thought you were the one who would heal my scars. I thought I was the vulnerable one. I had no idea you were the demon. Your crash has made them melt through the mist. I'm thankful I can see them now.

As you have vanished to board another train, covered in ash from the wreckage. You have walked without looking back, not even to wipe the debris from my skin.

I stroll the other way. I may be alone and you know, I'm okay with that.

I taste the horizon and the beauty before me.

Thanks for setting me free.

I sit back, letting her words sink. I'm not sure what I've just read. Is it a letter or a poem?

It doesn't rhyme. It's not in stanzas. Her words are angry and depressing. She's only a child. Who's she writing to? Has she based this off anyone from school?

It's been awarded with three love hearts and there's a comment from someone called, **vividphotos29**:

Really well written, Hanna. I could feel the angst. Hope this isn't based on any real-life situations! They'll need to talk to me first.

Mate, you're talking to a fourteen-year-old who's using her dead mother's name as a pseudonym!

I click on his profile, it's also set to private. Under his photo are the words:

A portrait is worth a thousand whispers.

The display picture is of a man holding a camera, the lens's covering his face, tuffs of yellowish-brown hair peak out from the top of his head. I can't see his eyes, nose or mouth and the picture goes blurry when I zoom in.

I see the response.

Hannathefinch:

Thanks, V. Nah, don't worry, it's not based on anyone.

I return to the menu on her blog and hunt through the entries. I'm not liking this. At all. There's about fifty more poems written in the same style and in every entry... **vividphotos29** has commented. Am I overreacting? Is this V person a simple lovie admiring my daughter's writing ability?

I scan through it again, there's no pictures of her. I'm relieved but I haven't seen every entry. She hasn't mentioned where she lives, she hasn't used her legal name. There will be other people called Hanna Finch on the internet who may be teenagers themselves but... it's gotta be Emily. It's too much of a coincidence.

Right, put your phone away, Jules.

Get back to fucking work.

~

Mike, Damien and Lance return to the office and we stack the catches into boxes outside. Mike's pulling a face, it drifts between worry and a smile - as if he's talking out loud in his head.

"What's up with you?" I ask.

His smirk disappears when he looks at me. "Oh, nothing, just glad to be sailing again. I saw your diver today. She's very...beautiful."

"Not sure if the green hair suits her," Damien utters, carrying a box. "She looks like one of those hippies from the seventies."

"That's Shy, Frank's niece," I reply. "What was she doing?"

"She was walking across the rocks to Drake's Mouth," Mike says.

Drake's Mouth is composed of a bed of sharp rocks, the opening of the cave inherited the name. A brown grey entrance with serrated teeth looming on the ceiling. The cave's a dark dank hole, there's nothing inside. Why's she going in there?

"Did she have her diving suit on?" I ask.

They begin to chuckle.

"*What?*" I say, noticing a sting of irritation in my voice.

Lance mutters with an edge of sarcasm. "Sounds like somebody's got a crush."

"Well, I am sharing a house with her." And playing tonsil tennis with her the night before.

"She had regular clothes on if you must know," Mike replies, closing up the company van.

"Wanna go to the Crest?" I ask.

"Nah, need to get this supply out." Mike hops inside. "Maybe we can get a drink when I get back?"

~

I walk to the Crest Café and eat my lunch alone, swarmed with buzzing thoughts. There's so much going on right now; my job in jeopardy, my daughter's secret blog, the threat to my home by a masked criminal and the murder of my friends.

And now, Shy Blothio…

I think about the images from the night before. They weren't just thoughts. I *saw* them, the second her fingertips touched my face. Every memory, every detail was precise to how I remembered it. Shy knew what had happened to me without asking, she knew why Emily was motherless. I didn't tell her; she *saw* it - in my mind.

My God, look at me, thinking of such ridiculous things. I wish Hanna was here, she'd know what to do. She always made the right decisions, she made lists, weighed the pros and cons and…she had a profound romantic spirit.

I think of a plan for later on, there's nothing wrong with conducting my own detective work. Shy has returned to Frank's several times with wet jeans and now she's been seen clambering into Drake's Mouth.

What is she up to?

I need to know.

14

I haven't been to The Sea Horse for a while, not since Hanna was alive. Despite the bittersweet association, it's nice to spend time with Mike now the contract has been signed. We chat over a couple of pints at the bar, noting the atmosphere. It's busy this evening. There's the Drake Covians and the non-Drake Covians. Patrons are standing and sitting in groups, words spill over one another. A young woman sits in the corner filming herself on her phone. A plastic smile's plastered all over her heavily made-up face. What's going on with the youth nowadays?

They seem more obsessed by the hidden world humming in their phones than a human soul sitting opposite them. I turn back to the bar, trying to ignore it but I can't help but eavesdrop. The young woman in skin suffocating make-up mentions something called a *livestream*, whatever that is. Then she mentions the FAAC and *two murdered fishermen* in the same sentence. Then she goes on about a *sponsor...*

Her voice sounds mechanical and rehearsed as she gushes about this *wonderful life changing face cream.* Apparently, *it will turn back the clock and obliterate any wrinkles.*

Ugh... and this is entertainment?

These modern townie people make my head spin. I hope Emily doesn't corrupt her brain with this crap.

"You better not have anymore," Mike says, patting me on the shoulder before ordering another round.

I chug the dregs of my beer, sensing the slow dreaminess creeping up on me. "Why not? You're having one!"

"I can handle more than you *and* you need to be on your best behaviour around Frank, especially with this niece of his."

"Nothing's going on between us, Mike."

He laughs. "Yeah, I've seen denial like that before."

"How would you know?" I scoff. "When have you ever been in love?"

"I have, it was years ago. When you were a kid," Mike mutters. "You would've been too young to remember."

"What happened?"

"It didn't go the way I wanted. She left me."

Ouch. "I'm sorry, Mike."

He shrugs. "It's okay, it was a long time ago."

"How come you haven't been with anyone else?"

He smirks slightly. "Who says I haven't?"

"Okay, but was there anything long lasting?"

He sips the white frosty froth of his beer. Then he takes a big gulp, remnants of the drink sparkle in his beard. "No, nothing since. Haven't met anyone worthwhile."

"Do you know a woman called Shae?" I ask. "Frank dedicated his first book to her."

Mike's eyes widen in alarm. "How do you know that name?"

"I just said, it was in one of Frank's books. Is that the woman he was living with?"

"Jules, go home. Em will be waiting for you."

What? What the hell was that?

Fucking hell. I've plucked another nerve. I'm doing this a lot lately.

~

I stumble back to Frank's. Mike's wrong. I'm not drunk, just tipsy. Frank doesn't greet me. I apologise for being late and come up with the excuse we overworked. I have a shower. The warm water hits my skin, trickling the tension out of my arms and legs, it's so relaxing I could fall asleep. I change my clothes and head to the kitchen. Frank and Em are watching television, my daughter's tapping on her iPad. Is she writing another poem? Is she interacting with that V guy?

She better not be. I'll make a mental note to check her profile later.

Frank doesn't acknowledge me. I sit next to Em, crunching through my food. She's completely engrossed in her iPad; white wires are hanging from her ears. She smiles now and then. I glance at her screen; she's chatting to someone. I wonder if it's that guy, the old man with the camera hiding his ugly mug of a face.

Some will think meddling in my daughter's privacy is wrong but what if something bad happens, I'll be in the firing line for being unaware and not protecting her.

Shy emerges from her bedroom, she's fully clothed and stomps past us.

"Where are you going?" Frank asks sternly.

I recognise the parental intention in his voice.

"*Out*," she replies.

"Drake's Tooth?"

Shy nods innocently.

"Okay, but only for *one* hour and you come straight back. Understand?"

Shy glares at Frank, turns on her heel and disappears outside.

The violent slam from the door makes Em jump.

"Is she okay?" she asks, plucking out her earphones. "She hasn't said anything all day."

Frank's looking at me and a jolt erupts in my chest.

Shit.

He's gonna throw me under the bus. Please, Frank. Don't do this to me. There's enough nails rummaging around my kid's head, she doesn't need more to trifle through. I plead with my eyes. I'm on my knees, Frank. Please don't.

He presses his lips together; his gaze moves to Em. "She's fine, she's not had the best week."

My daughter frowns. "That's odd, she seemed to enjoy herself at the shop."

"She's someone who can't sit on her backside all day," Frank utters. "She has to keep herself occupied. She'll be better when she finds a job or sells a painting."

"She can come to Jordan's party if she wants. It might cheer her up," Em says. "Jordan likes her."

"Has he met her?" I ask.

"Yeah, he came by the shop the other day and they started chatting."

"But won't it feel weird?" I say. "You know, a group of teenagers hanging around with a grown woman?"

Em shrugs. "No idea, I'll ask Jordan and see what he says."

"It's probably for the best. I don't think he'd appreciate it if you invited people without his say."

"Of course I'm gonna ask him, Dad!" Em exclaims. "*Jesus!*"

Frank's eyes gleam with a quiet annoyance.

Thank you, I say silently.

He watches me. *Don't mention it*, he mouths back, switching his attention to the television. A couple of minutes trickle by and I tap my phone screen. I flick to the settings and turn up the volume, pretending I'm texting. The notification bell chimes loudly.

Em and Frank's heads snap to me when they hear it.

"Crap. I better go," I say, getting to my feet.

"But it's late?" Em takes out her earphones again. "Where are you off to?"

"Mike's at the office, he's got a clerical emergency with the deliveries." I deliberately choose a work-related issue because I know it bores Em stiff and she'll switch off. "He's in a bit of a tizz, I better head down and check on him." I pull on my jacket. "Don't worry, I'll be back soon."

"Okay, be careful," she says.

"I will be."

I look at Frank, his scornful face shoots right through me. I wonder if he knows my plan.

~

I walk hastily to Becks Hill. The sun peeps behind the clouds, the sealine's radiant against the backdrop of Drake

Cove. I'm five minutes behind Shy, she's faster than I thought. She's not at Drake's Tooth, but when I cast my gaze to the rocks; her green hair bounces as she performs a hop scotch. She lied to Frank; she's heading to Drake's Mouth. What the fuck is she up to?!

I race to the beach, praying Shy doesn't see me. She's balletic in her movements and leaps into the cave, disappearing inside. I step onto the first rock, slipping. The water and fresh seaweed coat the rock to keep it moist. I hop to the next rock, again its slimy when my foot touches it. I jump again and again, navigating myself across the map of rocks.

The tide comes rushing in, smacking against the cliff, splashing my legs. The water bleeds into my jeans, seeping into my trainers. Drake's Mouth lingers before me. I grab onto the large rocks; they're like razor-sharp teeth. I climb into the cave. The smell of dampness and sea salt hits my senses. I get to my feet, wiping the dirt from my knees. I can't see Shy anywhere. The glare on my phone screen lights up the inside of the cave. The ceiling of Drake's Mouth looms down on me, and soon enough, I'm back on my knees feeling like I'm in the mouth of a monster. My heart's beating rapidly against my ribcage. Why has Shy come here? What's so special about it?

When a place can't get any more menacing, the cave mouth morphs into a throat and cranes to the left. I shimmy on my knees and stop when I see Shy, how deep does this place go?

I dim the light on my phone and hide, staying in the shadows. The cave must open somehow because she's standing up. Shy's removing her clothes and throwing them to the gritty ground. There's a bright blue sleeping bag, a stack of books and a pile of clothes sitting by her feet. How on earth can she read in this place?

She pulls off her tank top and climbs out of her jeans. I grow warm at the neck as my anxiety shoots up. I can't see her red and black swimming suit anywhere. She's standing in her bra and underwear. I cover my mouth when she removes them.

Oh my goodness…

You've got to be fucking kidding me…

I bite into my hand, sinking my teeth into my knuckles as Shy stands in all her naked glory. Her waist goes in and out and her hips curve like a ripe succulent fruit. My lower lip trembles when I think about the night before and our passionate kissing. My imagination splints off in tangents, picturing myself beneath her on the sofa, she's on top of me, squeezing me between her tight thighs…

Shy stretches her arms. The muscles flex under her snow-white skin, her blue veins pump and pulse underneath. Her hair falls around her shoulders, then she clicks her neck and I hear the bones crunch. She crouches and leaps into the darkness. I hear a splash and the whistle of the wind passing through the cave.

Blood rushes through my ears, dancing with the rhythm of my pulse. I scoot forwards, rising to my feet, my phone screen filling the cave with light. A hole filled with water rests quietly next to her belongings. She must've dived in, but there's no bubbles rippling to the surface.

I wait a couple of minutes, peering over the hole holding my phone. I can't see below the surface, it's so dark as if she's jumped into nothing. I turn to the pile and search through it. T-shirts, bone dry jeans, towels, underwear, bras, multicoloured socks and books. There's a back pack, inside is a heap of old newspapers and a lighter.

This place is devoid of any warmth or comfort.

Has she been sleeping here?

Some adventurers stay in the radiating heat of the Amazon, surrounded by wild gorillas, but they have a food supply, minders and guns to protect themselves. Maybe Shy's just a different version, she twirls off Drake's Tooth without a care in the world. She makes the concept of diving seem so effortless.

A river of cold sweat runs down my spine when the air changes behind me. I turn around to find a drenched Shy glaring. Water's dripping from her hair and chin, her eyes are burning into mine. "What are you doing here?" she demands angrily.

"I...uh, just wanted to see where you disappeared to every night," I reply, my throat's burning. "You're gone for a really long time."

"Why do you care?"

"Because..." I'm lost in her, absolutely terrified. "You intrigue me, I... thought, maybe, perhaps you liked me."

She doesn't say anything and the silence grows around us.

"Did you kiss me just for fun?"

Shy blinks at my words. "I didn't do it for fun." Her lower lip trembles abruptly. "I do...like you. I'm just not very good at romance."

I find that hard to believe after how she kissed me.

I'm distracted by a movement in the darkness. A pair of large black eyes stare out from the small hole.

"*What the fuck is that?!*" I gasp, my back hits the rock wall.

"An orphan." Shy kneels by the little pool, clicking her tongue.

The little face in the water turns to her, snapping and ticking erupts from the depths. Whatever or whoever, is talking back.

"What is it?!"

"Come and see for yourself," Shy replies.

"Are you crazy?"

"Fine. I'll show you." She reaches into the water. The clicks grow louder and louder and the front of the pilot whale calf flaps in her arms. Shy clicks her tongue, cradling its head. "She doesn't like you very much…"

"What?"

Shy looks at me. "Don't you recognise her?"

"No, not at all."

"*You killed her family!*"

I've never heard Shy shout before.

"She was at the culling," I say. "*Shit.*"

Shy strokes the calf's skin. "I found her hiding in here after it was over. She was so frightened. I've been looking after her ever since."

"Let it go."

"*She's not an it!*" Shy hisses. "Where will she go? Tell me that! She has no family, you wiped them out! Whales learn from their pod! Just like humans, they have to be together. She's got nobody else."

"You can ring the local aquarium. I'm sure they'll take her in."

Shy cringes at me as if what I've said is stupid. She kisses the whale on the head, pushing and sliding her back into the hole. "She doesn't belong in a glass cage. She deserves to be free, like we are."

I glance away, shame filling my heart. "Can you put some clothes on please?"

"But I thought you adored seeing me like this," she utters. "You enjoyed it last night."

"*Please.*"

Shy sighs with irritation. I hear the fumble of the towel as she rubs it up and down her body. After a minute, she's fully dressed in her jeans and hoodie, watching me. "Are you going to tell Frank about the calf?"

"Um, I was planning to yes."

"You can't."

"Why? What's the problem?" I frown. "I'm sure he'll wanna help. He'll be proud of you."

"He won't be proud." Shy kneels in front of me, gazing into my eyes. "I want to show you a secret." She leans in, so much I can smell the sea salt on her skin. Her damp hair gently hits my cheek like a bunch of cold green wires. Her fingers cradle my face, her brown and blue eyes burn into mine once more. "I think you should know the truth…"

I don't understand her words. "What truth?"

She pulls me into a deep kiss, a thread of adrenaline soars through me as she parts my lips, rolling her tongue into my mouth. A flash zips across my vision, flooding my polluted mind with white mist.

15

The fog surges around my skull. My fingers plunge into warm sand. I'm back on the beach. Did I faint again?

I shout for Shy but I can't see or hear her. I rise to my feet, gazing up at the hills. There isn't a single house in sight, there's no shops either. I turn to Beck's Hill, there's no lighthouse, no roads, no sheep munching on the grass. A cluster of tall, giant trees stand where there should be a farmhouse.

This is Drake Cove. I know from the shape of the shore line and the muddy texture of the cliffs. This is my hometown but it's not the same. The heartbeat's different.

From the corner of my eye, a line of men and women stand by the edge of the shore, they weren't here a minute ago. They're dressed in leather and furs, plaits and rags dangle in their hair. Each one is clutching a sword or an axe, some have nets. I don't recognise any of them but I realise how they are dressed. I've seen it in documentaries and my old school textbooks. These people…are Vikings.

I sense electricity in the air, a moment of calm before chaos ensues. They're preparing for something. I know this feeling. A man in the middle of the line steps out and bashes the necks of his weapons together. The others copy him. A chorus of noise is sent across the sea, tips of tails flick up among the waves. Oh fuck, I know what's coming.

I stagger towards the group, the pilot whales are drawing closer, disturbed by the clatter of noise. I tell them to stop, the line of men and women ignore me and they keep bashing. One of the whales swims forward, the rest of the pod trails behind. The people holding nets race onwards, casting the rope so it lashes and tightens around their fins. One of the armed men hacks at the whale's head and the creature begins to screech, swishing its tail. The others swarm the rest of the pod, repeating the fierce sequence. Above the squeals from the whales, I hear a ruckus and then a raw, human scream.

A dark-haired woman springs out of the water, clutching a stone dagger and plunges it into one of the men who's slashing at the head of another whale. She's covered in a blanket of seaweed; it shapes her physique like a body suit. Her weapon's lodged between his ribs, he's screaming, twisting in pain. She rips her weapon away, blood spills from his wound and he collapses into the water, drowned by the raging sea.

The dark-haired woman shrieks, her call punctures my soul. Several others, men and women dressed in the same attire emerge from the water like an army platoon. The Vikings halt their hunt, swapping to defending themselves against the strange water people.

I walk through the violence, arms and blades slice through me. I don't feel a thing. I'm a witness to the mayhem, unable to stop it. Metal clashes against stone, weapons break, people fall with fatal injuries.

The Viking leader from the shore stops and stands still, watching something with confusion and fascination. I follow his line of sight and the face of a woman peers out from the water.

She's wearing a crown of shells. She's broken the nets. The whales are escaping.

A white flash punches across me. The beach seeps back into view. The battle from before has disappeared. The Viking leader sits by the shore, playing a wooden whistle. It has a beautiful choral sound and it echoes over the hills.

A figure swims to the shore, it's the shell crowned woman.

The leader jumps to his feet, dropping his whistle in surprise. She crawls along the sand on her hands and knees, slowly rising so they're facing one another. Who is she?

She smiles gently, her deep green eyes are warm and welcoming. She looks at his scarred hands and covers his fingers. They stare at each other for the longest time. There's a connection growing between them. He smiles in return, the anguish from before melts as her hand cups his face.

Then the surroundings spin as if I've had too many drinks. Everything solidifies and hardens when I realise I'm in Drake's Mouth. The crowned woman's waiting and worried, biting her fingernails. The Viking leader clambers through the entrance. She smiles with relief and he pulls her into a deep, feverish kiss. Woah, I didn't see this coming.

They undress each other and within minutes, they're making love on the dirty ground. I watch their muscles contract with intensity, embarrassment creeping up my skin. I'm actually grateful when everything drunkenly spins again.

Now I'm back on the beach. The Viking leader stands with his axe and sword. He's glaring at his people, some I recognise from the fight, some I don't. A wail of pain booms from inside Drake's Mouth. The Vikings argue with the leader, I don't understand what they're saying but they're not happy. His people protest, shouting and cursing, some spit at his feet, a rock is thrown and it bounces off his eyebrow.

Yeesh.

A deep red cut oozes from his skin and he wipes off the blood. The scream jets out from Drake's Mouth again. It's high pitched, filling my mind with memories. A baby's cry spills out from the mouth of the cave. The leader's people fall into stunned silence, staring at one another helplessly.

The crowned woman emerges from Drake's Mouth, shaken and tired, she's paler than usual. Blood stains her inner thighs. A baby howls against her breast, squirming in her arms. The Viking leader cradles the baby, smiling sweetly at the little darling. I know the feeling, it's the most amazing emotional rollercoaster ever. When I held Emily for the first time, I was so happy she arrived intact with no missing limbs or anything. I was excited and terrified for the new unknown chapter of my life.

The leader looks back at his people, he's pleading with them to see what beauty has just taken place. Some of them feel defeated, others are merciful, and the rest are confused. But one of them glares with insolence, snapping with cutting words.

Heads turn and a woman with dirty blonde hair steps out from the crowd. Her body's covered in leather armour, a sword hangs by her hip and she's wearing a bow like a backpack. She was at the culling battle, standing next to the Viking leader when they started bashing their weapons. Her face is streaked with white paint and she grins with malice.

The leader turns to the crowned woman, he pulls her into a hug, whispering in her ear. She shakes her head, talking back in the same language. He places a loving kiss on her forehead. The crowned woman cries, pulling the baby to her chest. She walks through the crowd of people – some of them watch her with pure disgust, others dodge back as if she's got some sort of horrible disease.

She whistles at the edge of the shore, several heads bob up from the surface. I notice another person from the culling battle, the sea warrior who killed first is there too. They circle the crowned woman, protecting her as she swims into the water, clutching the crying baby. The longing in the leader's face dies when they dive underneath, disappearing into the waves.

The tension between him and his people ripples. He throws his sword and shield to the sand. Defeat is etched all over him. No, come on, man. Don't give up.

The blonde woman pulls an arrow from her quiver, sliding it into the bow, counting slowly under her breath. The leader stands still, he's not moving. The final number rings out and the arrow speeds towards his chest.

White light flashes over my eyes again. I'm still on the beach. Thunder and lightning crackles in the sky. The clouds darken and the waves crash violently. Something's coming.

A naked woman is trapped inside a fishing net, stranded in the sand. She's beautiful with immense dark hair, heavy lidded brown eyes and a gaze as dark as the water at night. I recognise the rope and it's modern material, we use it at work. She's staring at me, panicking, she doesn't want to drown in the lake trickling around her. I try to prize her out but my hands glide through the net. I feel helpless. She's vanishing and I can't save her.

Footsteps erupt in front of me and the trapped woman is now free, standing before me. The net falls away from her body like she's whipped off a cloak. Now I can see her face up close, there's something, a niggle in the back of my mind. Maybe it's the slender angle of her cheekbones or the deep sultry ripple in her eyes.

I know you…

The woman smiles at me, blood leaks from her skin, pouring down her legs and arms, transforming into pools by her feet. I hear a high-pitched cry which collides with the storm brewing in the sky. A baby girl with tuffs of green hair curls into the naked woman's arms. One of the baby's eyes is blue and the other is dark brown, just like the woman cradling her.

I've only seen those features on one person…

16

I wake up on Frank's sofa with the scent of his coffee brewing. He stands watching me, stirring slowly. "Are you okay, Jules?"

"I don't know," I murmur.

"Don't know?"

"Yeah…"

"Shy said she found you asleep on the beach. She helped you into the house. Don't you remember?"

"*No.*" I try to get up but my stomach tightens, squirming unpleasantly.

"Are you feeling alright?" Frank places a mug on the coffee table. "You don't look very well."

My stomach twists and I groan. "I'm gonna throw up."

Frank presses his palm against my forehead. "You've got a temperature."

"I'll be better once I get on the boat."

"Really?"

My stomach contracts. "*Uh no.*"

"I'll make you some toast."

"Thanks, I think missing work's a good idea."

I manage to grab my phone and text Mike.

A message immediately pings on my screen.

I told you to steady on.

It's not a hangover. I've had plenty of those, this is definitely not that. It's something else. Think it's a stomach bug.

Okay, hope you feel better soon. Damien and Lance are going out on the boat with me while Dan manages the office. Rest up. Hopefully we'll see you tomorrow.

Fingers crossed. I'll keep you updated.

Frank returns with toast and places a bowl on the floor in case I vomit. I like my toast soaked in peanut butter but it's desert dry. I nibble on it, slurping my coffee tentatively as I ride out the nausea. I hate calling in sick but the idea of being out on Olivia feeling the way I do. I'll be more of a hindrance than a help.

"What were you doing on the beach?" Frank asks, sitting in his armchair.

"I seriously don't remember." I really can't. I was in Drake's Mouth, with Shy, and that scared, helpless calf. Shy's kiss and then the dream. "I…went to help Mike and that's it. Nothing more."

Frank watches me, taking a slow sip of his coffee. "You must have been really poorly."

"I passed out."

"You're lucky Shy found you. If any of the FAAC discovered you…"

"I would've got my head kicked in."

I wonder If I should tell Frank about last night, would he believe me? Who were those sea people?

"Maybe I had a funny turn," I say, adding a little cough to cover my anxiety. "Perhaps it's a sign I should slow down."

Frank sighs, staring into his mug. "Jules, how long has it been since Hanna passed away?"

My heart lurches in my chest and a surge wants to erupt behind my eyes. "It's been a year," I reply. "Why?"

"When I saw you cuddling with Shy the other day, I must admit I was angry, with the both of you."

Oh God, what's this gonna be about?

"I was angry because you're a widower and Shy, because I told her to be on her best behaviour. I can't begin to describe what you and Em are going through, dealing with a loss in the family then Ian and Earl, the FAAC and the window attack-"

I raise my hand, cutting him off. "Frank, what are you trying to say?"

"I know Hanna would've wanted you to move on." He swallows painfully as if he's fighting a war in his mind. "If things between you and Shy are genuine." He stumbles on his words, closing his eyes momentarily to compose himself. "Then, she can find no one better than you. I just don't want you to lead her on."

"Frank." I try to sit up but my upset stomach reminds me not to move. "I'm not trying to lead Shy on in any shape or form. The concept of dating anyone makes my brain feel scrambled. I'm not ready for anything that intense yet, plus who'd want to take on my baggage. Though I have to admit, your niece is beautiful." I notice a flicker of a smile on his face. "Everyone else thinks so."

He grins with admiration. "Really?"

"Yeah, Herb does and so do the guys at work. Even a couple of the FAAC think she's cute." A bout of nerves pull at my chest. I feel like I'm a teenager again, having 'the talk' with my dad. "It's weird to say this but, Shy intrigues me. She's *untamed*." And she's more than that, something I can't quite put my finger on. She bewitched me the moment I clapped eyes on her. "But I...don't know where it's going, Frank. I'm just as clueless about it as you."

He nods, taking a swig of his coffee. "Sorry, Jules. I didn't mean to make you uncomfortable."

"Don't worry," I say. "You're looking out for her, and you're keeping me in check. I appreciate it. Out of curiosity, has Shy been with anyone before?"

"Not that I know of. If she has, she's been keeping any past boyfriends a secret." Frank smiles, rising to his feet. "I'll leave you to rest. I've gotta prepare for a Zoom interview. PR for my book starts today."

"What's a Zoom interview?" I ask.

"A video call."

"What's that?"

"Seriously?!" Frank cackles. "Jules, you've got to move with the times! Stop living in the Viking age. Ask Em, she'll know more about it than me. Young people always do."

~

I manage to sleep for a couple of hours. I dream about the ocean and the Viking leader's whistle melody. When I wake up, I glance at my phone, noticing a text from Em:

Hi Dad. Saw u asleep on the sofa when I was on my way 2 school. Frank said u were sick so I didn't want 2 disturb u. I spoke 2 Jordan about Shy coming to his birthday party & he said she can come. I think he fancies her. Wow, wait till she finds out her dad was snogging her. **Do u want me 2 bring u anything on my way home?**

I look at my watch, it's lunch time so she'll be free. *Thanks Em. Feeling much better, I think the sleep's done it. Don't need anything. Did you ask Shy if she wanted to go?*

Yeah, I've asked her. She's coming along.

I don't hear from her after that. I feel well enough to shower and change. Frank's chatting in his study; he sounds more professional when he's being interviewed. I try to be quiet around the house as I don't want to disturb him.

I knock lightly on Shy's door, she doesn't stir. I peer through, she's asleep, comatose. Her green hair spills across her pillow. She looks beautiful when she's asleep. At peace, relaxed. I wish she was like this more.

Yesterday changed things. I need to talk to her but right now isn't the time. I don't want to wake her. I leave a note for Frank saying that I'm heading out for a walk and I'll be back. If he needs me, he can call me.

I head into town and go straight to the book shop. Herb's facial expression is a comedy sketch. "You want a book on mermaids?" he asks.

Derek peers out from the office. "Why'd you want that?"

Shit, what do I say?

They'll think I'm crackers. How do I squirm out of this?

"Um, well, Em's always been a fan of mermaids," I say nervously. "I was thinking about getting her a book for her birthday."

Derek frowns. "But her birthday's not for another six months…"

Shit. Well done, Jules. And damn you Derek for having a better memory than me.

"Yes…well the idea's fresh in my head and I'm off sick so I wanna take advantage of the free time."

Herb taps on the keyboard. "Other than fictional books, I do have one in stock about the folklore of mystical creatures, written by Alice Green. She's a supernatural fiction writer and a former English Lit Professor. There's info about vampires, werewolves, ghosts and mermaids. Is this okay for you?"

"Yeah, I'll buy it," I reply. "Em loves the supernatural."

Herb locks the till and retrieves the book. I completely underestimated its size. It's fucking heavy.

When I leave the shop, Derek's standing by the till chatting to Herb, they're both watching me. Whatever, no time to think about it now. It's probably because I've bought a book. Me, a working-class fisherman reading for pleasure. *Shock horror!*

By the time I return to the house, it's like I haven't left. Shy's still asleep and Frank's working. I heat up a bowl of tomato soup and sit at the dining table, sighing inwardly at the scale of the book. Thankfully, there's an index at the back. I chug tea and begin to read.

M.

Mage, no.

Medusa. Ha, definitely not. Well, I hope fucking not.

Mermaids.

Sixty pages?! Bloody hell!

Come on, Jules.

Power through.

I didn't realise there was so much about the legends of mermaids. Alice Green writes a pretty substantial foreword at the beginning stating that the historical details of her research cannot be viewed as entirely accurate because they change with time and social influences. Each country and culture has their own take on the mermaid. It's extraordinary. According to Alice Green, mermaids are related to, or commonly associated with water spirits, sea nymphs, sirens, merfolk and elemental creatures. In the index, they all have their own sub categories.

The Scottish phrase for mermaid is Ceasg, pronounced *see-ask*. They appear as half woman, half salmon and keep their souls in a shell. They're feared for luring men to their deaths. If a man or woman fall in love with a *ceasg*, they'll transform into a full human and grant luck. The Scots also call them Finfolk, they can shapeshift, appear as fish or fully formed humans. They're known to be very beautiful and can suck the life out of someone.

Yikes.

In the Chinese legends, known as Jiaoren, *gee-a-run*, a mermaid's tears can morph into pearls. If they're given a home, they'll reward the successor and they wear white cloth which never gets wet.

There's more!

A Dutch story about a woman discovered swimming in a river near a village, she had green hair. This part makes my stomach clench. When she's taken out of the water, her fish tail transforms into a pair of legs. She's a selective mute, the villagers announce her as deaf and dumb. They make her wear normal clothes and she has to go to church. She makes endless attempts to escape but the villagers always bring her back. Wow, this sounds depressing, but it's more realistic. Shy has green hair but she isn't a mute although, I thought she was at first.

I find a couple of legends which are nearer to what I'd been told as a kid. According to British folklore, mermaids are a sign of an imminent disaster, others say they wreck ships and kill sailors.

I think back to the sea people in my dream, they knew how to protect themselves. They were armed and well versed in combat like the Vikings. Shy possesses a strength; I saw it at the culling and when she was protecting Frank. The book's been informative but it doesn't provide me with any concrete lock and key information.

Damn it, Shy. Why did you have to walk into my life and bewitch me?

I have enough crap going on right now.

Who are you?

What are you?

I don't realise how engrossed I am until Emily's caramel hair dips into view.

"What's Davy Jones' Locker?" she asks.

I must've been reading for hours. I snap the book shut, missing the tip of her nose. "Oh, nothing. I'm just doing some light reading."

Em smirks. "It's been a long time since I've seen you read a book, Dad. Since when did aquatic mythology interest you?"

Frank turns his head slightly as he's cooking at the stove.

"Well, I'm a... fisherman, so there's some natural curiosity. Plus, I wanted a break from the telly." I get off the sofa, tucking the book under my arm. "How was school?"

Em shrugs. "Same old, same old. Nothing interesting to report. I'm nervous about the exam."

"It'll be happening before you know it," Frank says, taking a can out from the fridge. "You should revise. The sailing examinations are nerve wracking. It's like learning to drive a car."

"Frank's right," I say.

"Can I borrow Henna?" Em asks.

I stare at her. "Why?"

"To practice, for the exam," she replies. "Like Frank said?"

"Yes, you can but not on your own. We can do it together, and have some decent father and daughter time."

"Sounds good to me," she says.

"How about this weekend?"

"Sure."

Hearing her words perks me up and then I see Shy upstairs, emerging from her room. The second she notices me, she immediately retreats.

I race up to her, my heart's beating like the clappers. "What happened last night?"

Shy blanches. "You fainted and I helped you get back."

"You're lying," I press. "You kissed me and then I wake up here. I had this weird dream about..." I glance at the

131

jumble of paintings in the corner of the room. One of them is the blonde-haired woman with the white face paint. She's looking straight at me, as if I'm the Viking leader, pulling that smirk before releasing the arrow. I pick up the canvas, showing it to Shy. "This woman. *I saw her.*"

"That's Ursula the Usurper," Shy replies.

"Who?"

"A ghost from a long time ago."

There are more paintings.

"I saw these people too," I say, pointing at them. "Who are they?"

Shy takes me through the line. The crowned woman is Octavia, the head of her tribe, a Sea Queen. The dark-haired menace is her sister, River and then there's Erik, the Viking Leader.

"What did I see?" I ask.

Shy bites her lower lip, taking the canvas from my clutch. "Glimpses."

"Of what?"

"The past."

"*What past?*" The sides of my head pulse with pain. I'm so fucking confused. "How do you do it?"

"Do what?"

"The mind-fuck thing."

Shy shrugs. "When I touch someone, I can show them dreams and sometimes…I can extract memories."

"Is that how you found out about Hanna?"

She nods sadly. "I didn't mean to meddle. The images were bubbling. She's always in your head."

Because I'm still drowning from losing her.

132

I don't want to believe this. A couple of weeks ago, I would've gladly swam in blissful ignorance, except the same face, the same dream is sitting in the corner of her bedroom, staring at me.

Shy doesn't stop me when I hunt through her work, my stomach double flips when I realise it's the beautiful Sea Queen with her shell crown and Erik playing his whistle. It's as if she's pulled the dreams from my brain and sprayed the scenes across the canvas. But there's more, passages I haven't seen yet. Octavia's circled by a group of Ursula's people; she looks terrified. Erik's tied up, Ursula's leaning down, glaring into his face. River's dark eyes wide and angry, her teeth shiny and lethal, her face scrunched in a shriek of agony. I wouldn't want these on my wall.

"What happened after Ursula shot Erik?" I ask. "What happened to the baby?"

"I don't know. I paint what I remember. Sometimes they come out in sequence, sometimes they don't."

I'm trying to compose myself but she's not answering clearly and it's grating at my insides. "Shy, I've been thinking about what I saw. I've done some research." I fish out my phone, showing her the screen. "There are some local aquariums not very far from here. I'm sure they'll take the whale in." I glance at her; she's staring at the screen but her expression's blank. I can't read her. It's frustrating. "Look, see, there's a Sea Life Centre in Yearling. It's a short drive from Drake Cove. They offer medical care. She'll have a fresh tank and she'll be fed. I can take you there if you want."

"No, she deserves to be free," she replies.

"She's not free stuck in a cramped hole living off dead fish!" My phone screen flashes, the loud ring makes my ears rattle. "Shit, sorry. I need to answer this."

It's Drew.

Wonderful.

17

Emily

Jordan's messaged me, he's on his way. I can't wait to get to Yearling. Drake Cove's been a bore fest since, well, since everything's gone up the shitter. Shy and I are waiting in the lounge.

My phone jingles loudly.

Fuck. It's not Jordan.

On the bus heading into town. Can't wait to finally meet the finch in person. V ☺

Dad walks into the room. I hide my phone. He had a face of thunder when he got off the call with that Chief Inspector lady last night. According to Dad, she was extremely apologetic and said we can go home. She'd interviewed the FAAC and not a single one of them have any knowledge of who the masked bastard is. There's some shit bag out there who tried to hurt me, to bait my dad because of what he does for a living. And they've got off scott-free. It pisses me off.

Pushing all of that depressing stuff aside, Dad's recovered from his stomach bug. He doesn't get sick easily, he's tough in that field.

"You feeling better today?" I ask, walking into the kitchen.

He's busy pouring chocolate chip cereal into a bowl, humming to himself.

"Dad?"

Nothing. He's in a world of his own.

"*Dad?*"

He jumps at the sound of my voice. "Oh sorry, I didn't know you were there."

"Yeah, I figured."

"Hey, have you shown any pictures of your mum to Shy?"

"No, not a single one. Why are we whispering?"

"Are there any on social media?"

"I haven't uploaded any since she…it's not the right time for me yet."

"I agree, sweetheart. Sorry, just thought I'd ask."

Shy's never asked to see pictures of Mum.

Jordan's text pings and I grab my coat. "We're off."

"Have fun!" Dad says, waving his spoon.

~

Jordan seems obsessed with Shy. I'm not sure if it's her neon hair, her cool eyes or the fact she dove off Drake's Tooth and didn't break any limbs. I swear I've seen Dad sneak a couple of hard glances at her, and I think Frank's noticed too. He's more like a father to Shy than an uncle, he's always watching out for her, the way Dad does for me.

Dad makes this silly assumption there's something going on between me and Jordan. He's not bad looking but, he's like a brother more than anything else. The thought of kissing him unnerves me, I've known him since, well…*forever*. It'd be weird.

We're sitting upstairs on the bus. I'm next to Jordan. Shy's sat in a seat in front of us, complimenting Jordan's raven bushy bubbly hair, saying it's like a load of springs jumping out of his head. His mouth drops when she announces she doesn't own a mobile. How can you not have a phone?

We have a laugh playing around with some camera filters. Shy likes the cat and dog ears. As Jordan and Shy chat, my phone rests on my leg, perched on my knee.

I send *him* a text. **On the bus now. See u in about 10 mins.** ☺

I should've turned the volume down but they haven't noticed.

Phew.

Waiting in the square, sitting on the benches. Can't wait to see you. <3

We have some quiet time watching the houses zoom past. Jordan nudges my shoulder, stooping his head, lowering his voice. "Does Shy know *Thingy's* coming?"

"Oh no," I say. "She doesn't. V's already waiting for us."

"Why haven't you told her?"

"It didn't pass my mind."

"I don't like this, Em. It doesn't feel right."

"What do you mean?"

"You only know him as *V*. He hasn't given you a full name. It's fucking strange. Did you video call him?"

"No…we never got round to it. He was always busy when I brought it up. We did speak on the phone though, he sounded alright."

"*Alright?*" My best friend's eyes widen with horror. "*Em!* This is really dangerous. Text him back right now and say we're not coming!"

"No, shut up. It's fine, he sent me some pictures. You're overreacting." I go into my gallery, skimming through the ones he sent me. "See? He's well fit."

"He could've got them from anywhere. Don't you watch those catfishing shows?"

"No, I hate them," I say. "They're scripted!"

He sighs tiredly. "Fine then."

"What's wrong with you?"

"I just hope you know what you're doing, that's all," he says, shaking his head with disappointment.

I did but with my best friend's reaction, I'm not really sure anymore.

⁓

I'm feeling claustrophobic. Ten agonising minutes pass and we're unchained from the bus. We walk to Yearling's town square. The heat and sunshine have brought the city people in flocks. Kids waddle around carrying buckets and spades. They head for the beach, or cram into the arcades like battery chickens.

My heart's thumping when we approach the centre of the square. There's no tawny haired teen with flames painted on his skateboard and blue headphones hanging from his neck. I can't see V anywhere.

Where r u?

People swarm past. I'm glad we're meeting here.

Ping.

At the benches. I can see you!

My stomach performs an acrobatic dance. Someone's waving and staring at me, smiling from ear to ear. He doesn't have tawny hair or own a skateboard. He'd probably break a hip if he did. I bet he hadn't heard of My Chemical Romance. He must've googled them.

"There's *no fucking way* that dude is sixteen," Jordan utters. "He's gotta be in his forties. You've invited a psycho pervert to my birthday party!"

"Oh my God." I want to cry. I'm the biggest idiot alive. "I'm so sorry, Jord."

What have I done?

I can't ring Dad. He'll hit the roof, he'll never let me

out of his sight again. If I call the police, they'll tell him and he'll know I wasn't careful.

Fuck, shit, fuck.

What do I do?

"What's going on?" Shy asks. "Why do you look so scared?"

"I think I'm gonna faint," I say, my knees are wobbling.

Jordan curls an arm around my waist, propping me up. "Em forgot to tell you that she invited her internet boyfriend along." He nods over to V, well it's no longer V, it's an imposter. "And *clearly* he hasn't been honest about his age or what he looks like."

V's expression changes when Shy stares at him. There's a glimmer of fear in his gaze, then it turns to anger. His eyes snap back to mine, his face scrunches in confusion.

"I see what's going on," Shy says. "Don't worry. I'll deal with this."

"You will?" Jordan asks with shock.

"What are you gonna do?" my voice is shaking.

"Just don't be here," she replies. "I'll meet you somewhere else."

"Let's go eat," Jordan says. "I could use a fatty milkshake after this."

"Yes, good idea," Shy replies, looking over her shoulder, glaring at us. "*Go. Now.*"

The authoritative pound in her voice makes us jump.

~

We scurry into the burger bar. Jordan's hand is clasped around mine, his palm's clammy. "This friend of yours is a bit scary," he says. "Has she been in the army?"

"No, she was a student. She's not normally like this. She's usually quite gentle."

We bag a front window table. Jordan's clicking his fingers, he does this when he's anxious, it's really irritating. He leans over, gazing out of the window. "I can't see her or that creep. Do you reckon he's killed her?"

"Don't be silly!" I feel even worse when I notice the bench V was sitting on is now empty. And I can't see Shy, at all. Where the hell did they go?

Before I know it, Jordan's slurping on a large banana milkshake. His knee's jigging. This type of scary shit is why *everyone* should have a phone.

Jordan pushes a large cup towards me. "Drink, you'll start feeling better."

"What is it?" I ask.

"Strawberry, your favourite."

I drink and drink until my stomach hurts. "Jord, I'm sorry I've ruined your birthday."

"It's okay. I knew something didn't feel right. I've got great instincts!"

"I feel terrible. Let me pay you back for the milkshake."

"Nah, fuck it. Pay for the cinema and bowling instead."

I nearly vomit when I see Shy walking towards us. There's no V. She's not being followed, thank God.

A group of lads standing outside check her out as she opens the door. One of them ogles her bum, sticking his tongue out cheekily at the rest of his friends.

"He's gone," Shy replies merrily, scooting in beside me.

"Seriously?" Jordan laughs. "Well, what did you do? Did you pull some serious mafia shit on him?"

She frowns. "Mafia?"

My best friend's eyes light up with joy. "Whatever you

did, you're my fucking hero."

"It was nothing." She turns to me, touching my shoulder before pulling a reassuring smile. "Don't worry, he won't be bothering you anymore."

18

Julian

I promised Em some supervised practice for her upcoming exam. Other than the intense heat, the wind isn't rough which is a really good condition for sailing. It feels so much better being back at home in the tranquil house of Finch. I bet Frank's glad to be rid of me and my piling heap of problems. I've had distance from Shy and all of her enticements, even though she's living rent free in my mind. Ian and Earl's cases are still open, I asked more about it, but Drew wouldn't say.

Em's sleeping in my room. I'm occupying hers. If the FAAC have a problem, they can take it up with me instead of attacking a sleeping kid. When Em came back from Jordan's birthday bash, she was quieter than normal. I ordered pizza for dinner, she only ate two slices. She even dismissed a Netflix movie of her choice to go to bed early. It bothered me but then this debacle has been exhausting for everyone.

I sign into my account on her blog and dart through her pages, she hasn't posted anything since my previous visit. But one thing's different, it sticks out like a sore thumb. On nearly every single post, the account which once read as **vividphotos29** is now **Deleted User**. This keeps getting odder and odder.

Em's sitting in her lifejacket, scowling at me as she reels off the different components of Henna. She needs to know them off by heart.

"Okay, what's the hull?" I ask.

"It's the structural skeleton, the part which rests in the water," she replies.

"Very good. What's a cleat?"

"A metal fitting you tie to a rope; it normally sits on the gunnel."

"And what's a gunnel?"

"The top edge or half of the hull of a boat or ship."

"Brilliant. And how do you spell it?"

"*G-u-n-w-a-l-e.* Dad, there's no spelling in the exam."

"I'm just testing you, that's all."

"Can I just sail now?" Em asks tiredly.

"Sure, you can."

We swap places and gently leave the quay. We have a shaky start but Em takes control, correcting her errors. The main sail is up. Her hand's tight on the steer. She takes us out past Becks Hill, the boat bobs up and down on the gentle waves. If you're not like me, this is normally when people feel nauseous. The sensations are similar to the dips on a small roller-coaster.

"Is everything okay, Em?" I ask.

"Yeah, why wouldn't it be?" she utters, frowning in concentration as she steers.

"Are you sure? You've been quiet ever since you came back from Jordan's party. Did you enjoy yourself?"

Her face drains of all colour and I notice she's staring over my shoulder. "Why's Shy heading into Drake's Mouth?"

I turn. Em's not wrong. Shy hops across the bed of nails and disappears inside the cave. Henna's nose is sailing towards it.

"Em, what are you doing?" I ask.

"I wanna see what she's up to."

The boat sails towards the beach and my daughter springs out, racing towards the death rocks.

"*Em!*" I shout. "*Em! For fuck's sake!* Wait for me. I need to tie Henna up!"

I pull the main sails down to the decking, tying them shut and haul Henna onto the beach. Thank fuck I have the strength to do this. The boat can't be left unattended. It needs to be secure and locked up, like any vehicle.

Em leaps from one rock to another. My heart's pumping into overdrive as I imagine her skidding into the water, striking her head off one of the rocks.

"*Em!*"

My stubborn child ignores me and leaps into Drake's Mouth.

"*Shit, Jesus Christ! Why don't you bloody listen to me?!*"

I make my way across the rocks, glancing back at Henna.

"Aaawww she's so cute!" Em sings from inside the cave.

I really hope Shy's got clothes on or I'll go nuts.

I crawl through the crevice, snagging my jeans. The grit from the ground's rough against my belly when I heave myself to my feet. "Em, when I tell you not to run away from me. *I fucking mean it!*"

"Ssshhh, Dad be quiet!" Em glares, cradling the calf.

Shy watches me. Thank fuck, she's fully dressed. "I told her not to come in but she didn't listen."

"My kid has the tendency to do that," I sigh.

"*She's so cute,*" Em coos.

"Put her back," I order. "Don't put her on your lap, she's too heavy. She'll dislocate your knees."

The calf coughs. They can't live out of the water for

very long. I step forward, my hand inching towards the whale. It notes my presence and backs up, squishing its tail against Em's chest. Shy clicks her tongue, the baby clicks back in frantic negotiation.

"How are you doing that?" Em asks curiously, glancing up at Shy.

Shy coils her fingers around mine and the calf calms down. I hesitate for a moment and Shy nods, encouraging me. I stroke my palm across the smooth cold skin of the calf. She feels warm and not in a healthy way, she's feverish. If Em was this temperature, I'd be ringing the doctors.

"Shy, I think she's sick..." I state apprehensively.

"Dad's right," Em says. "We should tell Frank, he'll know what to do."

Shy shakes her head, her fingers still joined with mine. "No, I don't want him to know."

I step back, my hand falling away and I take out my phone. "Sorry Shy, I'm calling him."

~

As I thought, Frank knew *exactly* what to do and in no time at all, he's accompanied by a Sea Life Centre van full of people carrying a grey and red stretcher. From their conversations, Frank's work and knowledge has reached and touched many individuals. They seem so happy to see him, as if they've met the queen or something. Since staying with Frank, I've seen a completely different side to his life. I've learned so much about what he does, but there's a strand of curiosity still living in me. I don't know what *drives* him. You don't throw in the fishing nets and turn your back on everything... because you ate some octopus on holiday and felt bad about it. Something significant must have been the root cause, something deep and painful that burned him to the very core.

Shae…

Who is she?

Why was Mike so hostile when I mentioned her?

I watch the Sea Life people do their work. My hands rest on Em's shoulders as they bring the calf out from Drake's Mouth. Her tail dangles between the sheets. Shy stands absent from it all, she seems sad and disappointed, slumped in some sort of defeat. Frank smiles and pats her on the back, a loving gesture.

The presence of the Sea Life Centre has attracted the attention of the locals. They're standing outside the pub, holding their pints, watching as if they're kicked back in the lounge at home.

Frank asks if we want to go to the aquarium and accompany the calf. We agree. I tie Henna back in the quay and return to the beach. We stay close behind the Sea Life Centre van as Frank drives. Em's got her earphones in, nodding to the music but Shy's silent, staring out of the window, her mind in another world.

~

I feel like a VIP when we enter the Sea Life Centre, they don't charge us for an admission fee. The staff are yapping to Frank, decorating him with compliments. They take the calf to a large room and pop her in a water tank. We stand behind a glass window, Em's watching with captivation. Frank stands with the medical crew, he's dressed in blue scrubs and he's wearing a surgical mask. He watches eagerly, asking tons of questions. They seem happy to answer him.

After a while, the door clangs behind me, Shy has left. I wonder what's wrong with her. Being here is good news, the calf is getting the care she needs. I leave Em with Frank as she watches the experts work their magic.

The aquarium corridors snake off into different routes. Families sail past, kids run along the tunnels with sharks gliding over their heads. A little girl with pigtails twirls on her feet, besotted with the creatures swarming above her.

I walk past the shark area and head into the octopus enclosure. Shy's standing off to the side. Her hand rests on the glass, her eyes are closed and her peachy lips move silently, as if she's muttering a prayer. On the other side, sits a red and brown blotchy octopus with one of its long tentacles propped against the glass. I think about the time I saw her at Frank's house, she was sitting in the garden, in front of the flowers, she was muttering then too.

"Are... are you okay?" I ask, feeling like I'm treading on egg shells.

Shy's hand snaps from the glass at the sound of my voice.

I smile warmly when her eyes lock with mine.

"I didn't mean to make her sick," she utters.

"It's not your fault." I place a hand on her shoulder. "You did all you could, Shy. She's in the best care now. They'll look after her here."

She turns back to the octopus; the creature watches me cautiously. Then, it slithers across the pebbles and sand to another part of the tank.

"You can understand them," I say. "Can't you?"

Shy smiles at me, she isn't shocked or taken back. "What makes you say that?"

"I don't know. I guess, it's just a gut feeling I have. So... am I, right? You can speak to them?"

"It's an instinct," she replies, staring into the tank. The water ripples, bright lights cascade patterns against her skin. She sighs deeply, her jaw tightening. "None of them

147

belong here, Julian. It's not natural."

"Some of them might not survive in the wild," I whisper, my hand trickles down to her lower back, yearning to stroke her cheekbone.

We stand there for a while watching the octopuses and fish float around us.

"What happened to Hanna?" Shy asks, looking back at me.

My chest tightens at the sound of her name. "I thought you already knew."

"I wasn't prying."

A wave wants to explode from behind my eyes. "Are you sure you wanna know?"

Shy nods. "I do, I think it'll do you good to get it out."

"Fine then. She… had Huntington's disease."

"How did it start?"

"Hanna always had a shake; most people have a tremor but it doesn't hinder their life." My fists clench up as if my body doesn't want me to go on. "A couple of years after giving birth to Emily, Hanna's symptoms got steadily worse. She started forgetting stuff, dropping things. She'd stumble and be clumsy. Then there were the dark times where nothing I did made her happy. I thought it was stress, from postnatal depression or something. Then she lost her job because of her shakes. I wanted to have another baby but she didn't and for a while, I just told her to pull herself together."

Shy smiles briefly.

"I know it didn't help," I say. "But, I was frustrated. Then, Hanna had these involuntary movements, her legs and head would twitch. I took her to the hospital; they did countless tests and then… they gave us the diagnosis." A shiver shudders along my spine. "I remember feeling relieved that we had answers and… devastated because there was nothing we could do."

"Couldn't they save her?" Shy asks.

I press my lips together, shaking my head. "It's hereditary. Sadly, the illness existed in her family."

"Does this mean Emily has it?"

"Possibly, but she doesn't want to get tested. I don't blame her. She's fourteen. Who wants to be reminded of a potential death sentence?"

"I'm sorry, Julian," Shy utters softly.

"Thank you but… I'm sick and tired of hearing how sorry everyone is. Apologies are not what we need. My daughter… *needs* her mother back."

A sigh of frustration escapes my lips as Shy's fingers trickle up my arms and along my shoulders.

"Keira misses Hanna too," she says.

I laugh pathetically. "My cat told you?"

"She's not stupid, she's worried about her family. It's why she sleeps with Emily, to keep an eye on her. She used to sleep with you and Hanna before…"

I've never told her that. Oh my God. *She knows.* I was right this whole fucking time. I think about Frank's frightening yet complimentary words about her choosing me. He couldn't be more wrong. I'm a mess, a complete fuck-up but…

I'm drowning for Shy, especially when I stare into her face. I lean forward, wrapping my arms around her waist and kiss her. Shy's lips feel cold against mine for an instant. I cup the back of her head, pulling her closer. My mouth trickles down to the well of her neck, tasting her skin. I hear her trapped breaths as her heart begins to race. I rub my cheek against her skin when her body freezes under my fingertips.

"What's wrong?" I whisper.

Shy's pulling away, her head's stooped in submission as if she's ashamed. Then, I realise who's observing us…

I don't know how long she's been standing there or what she heard…

"I know you helped me out yesterday but…" Em glares at Shy with disgust. "You will *never* be my mother."

"Excuse me?" I walk towards her. "Repeat that. What happened yesterday?"

Em blinks several times. "N-Nothing."

I knew it. I'm better at reading my daughter than she thinks. I turn to Shy; she seems so small with her head and shoulders hunched. "What happened yesterday?"

"It's not for me to say," she utters.

"What does that mean?" I look at Em. "What does she mean? What happened?"

My daughter's eyes widen and shine, fermenting in fear.

I hate the silence. No one's saying anything. If they don't, I'll snap. Silence succeeds and I grab Em's wrist. "*What happened yesterday?*"

"Nothing!" Em squeaks. "It was my fault!"

"What are you talking about?"

"Ow, Dad! You're hurting me! Let go!" She pulls her hand from my tight grip, rubbing at her skin. "I…invited someone to Jordan's party, it was a big mistake. I should've been more careful."

"Who was it?"

Em's gaze races between me and Shy. "Someone I met online."

"*Who was it?*"

"He said he was sixteen," Em replies. "He was nice to me, he made me laugh."

"He was a grown man," Shy interrupts. "There was *nothing* youthful about him."

"Why didn't you video call him beforehand?" I ask. "That would've been a dead giveaway."

"He said he couldn't," Em utters. "I spoke to him on the phone, he had a deep voice. Most teenage boys do. I just assumed he was telling the truth."

"Oh God, Em." My head falls into my hands. I've been feeling so guilty about logging into Em's blog yet clearly my instincts were guiding me in the right direction. "What the fuck were you thinking?!"

My daughter begins to cry and it's attracting the attention from the other families. "You don't need to say it like that! I feel bad enough as it is!"

"But you know so much about the online world and there are *so* many horror stories out there!" I say. "You're not a dumb kid!"

Em looks at the floor with guilt. "I don't know why. He made me happy, and I missed Mum."

Her words are like a dagger in the chest. Em didn't need to run into the arms of some arsehole. "Did he touch you?" I ask.

"I wouldn't let him," Shy replies.

My imagination's conjuring all types of scenarios I don't want to be thinking about. "*What's that supposed to mean?*"

Shy looks at me with defiance. "He never spoke to Emily in person. When I realised what was going on, I told her and Jordan to leave the square. I took him to one side, had a word and he left."

"Just like that?!" I ask.

"He never laid a finger on Emily," Shy says. "I promise you. I was quite persuasive."

If I'd been there, I would've killed the bastard.

"Was this vividphotos92?" I ask Emily.

Her eyes light up in horror. "How do you know?"

"I've been reading your blog. His name came up frequently in the comment section." This made so much sense why the pervert deleted his account.

"It's not supposed to be for your eyes, Dad. It's personal. It's my escapism!"

"I wasn't planning on making you aware," I growl. "But after hearing this, when we get home, you're deleting that blog and you are *never* to use your mother's name for your scribblings ever again. Do you hear me?"

Shy attempts to comfort her.

"*Don't touch me!*" Em shrugs her off, leering right up in Shy's face. "I know you want my dad."

Em moves to wallop her but Shy grabs her arm, blocking her blow. Shy's grip is strong and there's a standoff. She glances over at me, the hostility returning, the same fury I saw at the culling. She shoves Em to the side before trudging out of the octopus area. I hear the angry loud clang of the doors.

"*Jesus Christ Em,*" I whisper, melting onto the nearby bench.

"You like Shy, don't you?" Em sobs, wiping her nose on the cuff of her hoodie.

"Yes, I do. I'm sorry."

"You're forgetting about Mum..."

Oh, God.

Em's crying hysterically now.

This is such a mess.

Fuck.

Hanna, what do I do?

19

It's been several days since everything poured out, leaving a searing pinch. Em's not talking to me, she's been going to the book shop and sailing school in silence. She utters the occasional hi or when she's done with the telly, she'll pass me the remote. The awkward atmosphere is like picking at a scab which refuses to heal. I want to reconcile with her but I don't want to upset her more than I already have.

My feelings for Shy are not replacing Hanna. I can see why she'd think it because she caught us kissing but it's not the case. I feel bad for making her delete her blog, but look what materialised from it!

When it comes to vividphotos92, yes I was angry with her because she wasn't careful. I want to destroy the piece of shit who thought he could deceive my daughter. I want to know who he is, where he lives, where he works, if he's married, if he has any children. What makes a grown man think he has the right to do such a thing? What makes him think he can get away with it?

Shy said she spoke to this loser. She seemed so confident. Well, what did she say?

Work's keeping me afloat for the time being. My thoughts are exhausting, like a whirling wind launching around my head in a relentless pendulum. I chomp through my egg and bacon sandwich at the Crest Café, barely tasting it. I sit opposite Mike who's reading the newspaper. My phone pings loudly. It's a text from Derek:

Is Em okay, Jules? She's been very quiet.

I roll my eyes. *We had a huge argument a couple of days ago. She's not speaking to me.*

Uh oh, not good. Sorry, am I snooping if I ask what it's about?

Not at all. She thinks I'm forgetting Hanna. It's been a year. I omit the part about the paedophile. I'm not telling him about kissing Shy either.

It's not easy. Can I do anything to help?

Nah, I'll let her sulk and then I'll try and sort it.

She's missing her mum, Jules. We all are.

I know.

Are you coming to the rally later?

What rally?

You don't know? Geoff Ward has organised a big protest. Frank's been asked to speak at it. They've been setting up all day.

I've noticed a buzz around the town like an electric current swimming in the air. There's been more visitors and news vans turning up. It makes so much sense.

I send my response. *No, never heard of it!*

Really? Em knew.

And she's cut me out of the information, thanks Em. I know you're pissed off with me but that's big fucking news, anything remotely to do with the FAAC bastards.

She never said anything.

Probably because of your disagreement. This is why I want us to join a neighbourhood WhatsApp group, so we can look out for one another.

People are private about that sort of thing.

NOTHING is private in Drake Cove Jules…

~

During the afternoon slog of a shift, I inform the others about the upcoming rally. It's starting in the town square at five thirty. Geoff Ward's speaking, and then Frank's presenting.

Lance stamps a distribution sticker on one of the boxes. "Why are you going? Do you want more stones chucked through your window?"

"Frank's helped me out. I owe him," I say. "Are you coming?"

Lance and Damien gawp at me like I'm mad. Dan will only go if there's a smell of a fight and I don't wanna be anywhere near his bad behaviour.

"I'll go with you," Mike replies.

I nearly drop the box. "Are you sure?"

He smirks, swiping it out of my hands. "Yeah, you need a bodyguard."

Mike and I arrive at the rally after work. The town centre's crazy and not in a cool rock concert way. The aggravation and unease is powerful. I can smell it looming over everything. A line of police officers wearing bright hi-vis jackets stand in the centre of the crowd, preventing everyone from devouring one another. The Drake Covians are positioned on the left, some of them hurl abuse at the FAAC who shout behind metal fences, their cowardly faces concealed under balaclavas.

A non-Drake Covian stands off to my right, her phone's propped up on a selfie stick, just like that girl at the pub. She's talking to the screen, repositions her hair and smiles brightly before swivelling the phone, pointing to the crowd.

"Shit," Mike utters. "We've had bad, but never *depraved* before."

"It's a mini revolution," I reply. "I wonder how much of our tax money is being spent to keep these shits at bay."

"If the FAAC wanna make a noise, they should pay for it."

I laugh at his words. "It's called freedom of speech, Mike."

"I thought so. Frank's influence *is* rubbing off on you."

The crowds descend into a chilled silence as Geoff Ward slogs across the stage. Megaphone stands beside Geoff wearing a balaclava, he has a bandage on his hand. There's no dog with him. Geoff pours tedious words into the microphone, spewing about the freedom of animals. He shouts gory questions, asking how we'd feel if we were hung by our feet, our throats sliced as we slowly bleed to death.

Yawn.

I disconnect from Geoff's rambles. Mike and I make our way to the left-hand side of the podium where the Drake Covians congregate. Frank waits offstage, he doesn't look nervous at all. He must have some built-in bullshit barricade. How does he do this?

Geoff finally finishes his bore of a speech and is politely clapped off stage. He doesn't go to the area where the FAAC are standing, instead he walks past Frank who doesn't clock his presence... but Shy does. There's some tension between her and Megaphone as he says something but I can't make it out.

Frank walks across the stage and stands behind the microphone. Shy watches on anxiously. He taps the mic, clearing his throat:

"I know a lot of you aren't happy I'm here to talk today. I know some of you dislike my opinions, or how I conduct myself. But I want to give you a scenario." Frank glances at his notes. "If we were separated from our young, it'd be labelled a travesty. If humans were ravaged for their resources, it'd be called a rape of human civilisation. But, we do it every day for the milk in our tea, the eggs in our breakfast and the meat in our cheese burgers. Humans don't see themselves as a part of nature …we're *apart*. We cannot continue living at the rate we're heading. Climate change continues. Rainforests disintegrate day by day and our fishing statuses are violently plummeting. I've done my research and it'll be our descendants who will suffer the consequences. Do you want this for them?"

There's a pause and strangely, nobody fills the space.

"I haven't come to shame you all with doom and gloom. I don't want this for anyone. Amazing work is being done as I speak. Conversations have grown seeds and given birth to strong plans of action. But it's not enough, we need your help and compassion. We can make baby steps to rewind the clock and rewild the earth." Frank glances at the crowd, a couple of the locals tell him to fuck off. "We can start by making this change on our very own doorstep. The culling is a long-standing tradition for Drake Cove, it once signified harmony for a little village. It's a practice that was necessary for our ancestors but in the modern world where food is available at the swipe of a button, it's simply not needed anymore."

There's a chorus of boos from the Drake Covians. I'm sweating under my jacket.

"He needs to shut his mouth," Mike whispers. "People are looking at him as if he's a four-course meal."

"He won't stop, Mike. It's what he believes in," I reply.

"It'll get him seriously hurt or killed if he's not careful."

Frank's no longer reading from his notes, he's addressing the charged crowd full on. "Every drop of whale blood spilled into our oceans is poisoning the course of our future, not just for us, but for our children and our grandchildren. I've seen the effects of mercury poisoning. I'm one of those people and I wish someone had told me about the heavy metals in whale meat when I was a fisherman. I have headaches and difficulty sleeping. A doctor said my hearing and my sight could deteriorate. Am I frightened? Of course I am. The consequences of my decisions are coming for me, and there's nothing I can do to stop it. I don't want that reality for your children or for you. Humans are the most powerful animals on this planet. We've made Earth ours and we dominate so much of it. I haven't come here as your enemy. We can find a resolution if we are united. We must reverse the damage before it's too late. And we must do it *together* as one. Thank you."

Frank nods diplomatically, stuffing the notes into his pocket and walks off stage. There's a smidgen of respectful clapping but it's being drowned out by the furious souls in the crowd, local and non-local alike. I don't understand the aggression, especially from the FAAC. He's on their side. And they still hate him? Because he doesn't believe in violence against us fishermen?

From speaking to Frank and flicking through his books, he wants us to eat *less* meat (beef, pork, chicken and so forth), not to cut it out completely whereas Geoff Ward wants all meat banned. *And* the sad wanker wants criminal charges against people who eat it. Well, it's not gonna fucking happen. The guy's a complete and total nutter.

Humans need meat to survive, it's vital for our health. We're carnivores, eating meat is in our heritage, it's in our blood. The FAAC wouldn't tell a lion to change their ways unless they had a death wish.

My heart lurches when Frank and Shy walk casually from the stage. Shy smiles sweetly, patting Frank on the shoulder. She's so proud of him. Then I notice something I wish I hadn't. Geoff clocks them as they walk off, he's grinning manically and follows them with Megaphone trailing behind.

"You see, this is the type of shit I was worried about," I say, looking at Mike.

"I told you, Jules. Nothing good comes from this," Mike replies. "Frank should've stayed at home."

We march over. Frank and Shy stop as Geoff and his man servant talk to them. We spring into a run as the second a dollop of spit escapes Geoff's lips and splats across Frank's cheek.

Megaphone leaps forward, shoving Frank in the chest. My friend stumbles back. Shy steps in front of her uncle, her eyes lighting up, her temper flaring. Before I shout, Shy slams her foot into Megaphone's gut and he doubles over, crashing to the ground. She squares up to Geoff who's grinning proudly. Megaphone's groaning in agony and Geoff's completely ignoring him.

"*Frank!*" I yell. "*Frank!*"

He acknowledges the sound of my voice. "Jules, what are you doing here?" His eyes die at the sight of Mike. "Why are you here?"

"Oh look it's the whale killers," Geoff coos.

"Fuck off Geoff," Mike grunts. "I saw what you and your friend did."

"*Shy no!*" Frank cries.

She slams her face into Geoff's nose, in the middle of his annoying chuckling. His head snaps back like a Pez dispenser. I wrap my arms around her midriff, pulling her to my chest. She glares at me, panting with rage, blood's seeping from her lower lip. A force pushes at my back and my arms break away. A police officer slams Shy on the ground, shouting at her to calm down.

"Please leave her alone!" Frank yells. "She doesn't know what she's doing!"

"She assaulted me!" Megaphone winces under his breath.

"They were aggravating them," Mike says. "They started it. Geoff spat in Frank's face and his friend pushed him. This woman was protecting him."

Shy growls as the officer yanks her hands behind her back, cuffing her wrists together. Some of the FAAC have clocked what's happening, they're clicking on their phones. Another group of officers shoo them off, telling them to keep a strict distance. Frank's almost in tears, pleading with the police to release Shy.

Geoff the wanker groans, clutching his bleeding nose. "She attacked me!"

"Oh shut up you big baby," Mike mutters. "You've caused this. It was gonna happen to you sooner or later."

Frank turns to Mike. "*Why are you here?*"

They stare each other out. I pray that a part two of this chaos doesn't unravel.

"I'm trying to help you, Frank!" Mike growls. "Jules was worried about you, so I thought I'd come along."

Frank smirks sarcastically. "Thanks Mike but… I don't need anything from you."

"Hey, hey, stop this." I stand in between them. "What the fuck is going on?"

"Nothing," Mike utters. "Coming here was a mistake. Sorry Jules. I'm going home."

"Mike-"

He ignores me and I watch him stalk off in a huff as

the police throw Shy into the back of their van. I look back at Frank; his eyes are tired and grey. I've never seen him frightened before.

20

I check on Emily, she's having dinner at Jordan's house. A slice of me feels sceptical if she's telling the truth. I expect a tirade of fire when I press her for more details, instead I receive a photo of Em and Jordan playing the Xbox, so I let it go.

After Shy's arrest, everything else kicked off, more police officers were called in. The FAAC and the Drake Covians clashed in a massive brawl. The local media were there to record every single second of the debauchery.

"I thought what you said up there was amazing," I say to Frank as we wait in the police station. "You're really brave to speak up when others have turned their back on you."

"Thanks, Jules. You don't have to stay with me."

"Of course I'm staying," I say. "How do you write a speech like that?"

The take-out mug shakes in his hand as he takes a delicate sip. "I paraphrased some of the crucial points from my new book." He sighs under his breath. "Shy shouldn't've come, she's really sensitive about environmental issues."

"I think there's another reason for her actions, Frank. She's really proud of you, and so am I." I hope my words offer some kind of comfort. "I didn't realise until I stayed with you, how hard your job is. You've got a lot on your shoulders. I couldn't do it."

This time Frank smiles but it only lasts for a short spark

until stress and sadness reappear. "I told her to be on her best behaviour but she doesn't listen to me."

"You got spat at and pushed around, Frank. It made me angry just watching it. If it wasn't Shy striking first, I would've done the same. Geoff the bastard deserves a broken nose, it won't make him any prettier."

A laugh bursts from Frank's throat. "I know but Ward has more support than I do. The youngsters like him."

"You're a lone wolf. You don't need others to fight your corner. I checked their website. You have to *apply* and there wasn't a limit on the age of the members. It's fucking weird. They even have the gall to ask for donations. Whatever it is, he's got others to fall back on and continue his work. Remember when he went on Good Morning Britain?"

Frank titters again. "Oh yeah, it was awful, like watching a car explode. He shouted at the hosts, it's not the right way to conduct yourself when you're getting a point across. Piers Morgan wiped the floor with him."

"He made himself look like a right tit, you're not like that," I say. "Look at how happy he was when he heard about Ian and Earl. The guy's a fucking dickhead, and a sick one at that. Who laughs when they hear about people dying? And he's meant to be standing up for noble purposes!" I stare at Frank, eager to drill some encouragement into my friend. "People *do* like you. The Sea Life Centre staff were in awe, as if they were meeting David Bowie."

Frank takes another sip of his coffee, his hand's still trembling. "It's because I respect what they do."

"And you listen to people's views, even if they disagree with you." I pause, watching him. "Can I ask you a question about your speech?"

"Sure, go ahead."

"Is it true about mercury poisoning? Will you lose your sight and hearing?"

"It's a possibility."

"*Shit.* Do you think I should get tested?"

He purses his lips before taking another swig of his drink. "You've been eating whale meat since you were little. It's dangerous, especially to children and pregnant women. It wouldn't hurt to know, but you might have to make a hard decision if you receive the result you don't wanna hear."

"What?" I say. "Stop participating in the culling?"

"Yep and cut out the meat and blubber all together."

I don't want to.

"Why did Mike come along?" Frank asks.

"He wanted to help."

Frank shakes his head with contempt. "That doesn't sound like him. He probably wanted to see me suffer."

"That's not the reason at all. What's wrong with you? What happened between you two?"

"It's a long story, Jules. And honestly, it's none of your business."

I'm almost tempted to give him fire and brimstone but I don't want to lose another friend.

"I hope Shy gets a slap on the wrist," Frank says. "While we're sitting here, what happened at the Sea Life Centre?"

"Emily caught us kissing," I reply.

Frank chuckles deeply. "Are you serious?!"

"Yep, she thinks I'm forgetting about Hanna."

"Nah, you wouldn't. You and Hanna were a match made in heaven. Why would that make Shy moody?"

"Em… tried to hit her," I say, wincing inside.

Frank rubs his hand along his chin. "Oh God, what did Shy do?"

"Nothing. She blocked her blow and left."

"Christ, I'm sorry."

"No, it was my fault," I say. "I should've been careful and-"

"Mr Finch?" a voice asks.

We both jump to the commanding tone, any faster and Frank would've spilt his coffee.

Drew stands in the hallway, her hands stuffed into the pockets of her long overcoat. "I think we need to stop bumping into each other, don't you think?"

"I agree," I reply.

"How's my niece?" Frank asks.

"She's fine," Drew says. "She's finished making her statement."

"And you've arrested Geoff and his friend, right?" Frank presses. "They attacked me first!"

She smiles thinly. "Yes we have, Mr Blothio. They've been sent to hospital to have their injuries examined first. Shy's lucky she only has a cut or two."

"So, what happens now?" Frank asks.

Drew smiles again but I'm not sure why. "She was very honest and upset-" Frank moves to interject but she raises her hand, a signal she has the floor. "She complied, she told us what happened. We've put her in a cell to calm down as she was very distressed." Drew flips a notepad from her pocket. "Do you want to press charges against Mr Ward and Mr Sheridan?"

"Will it affect Shy?" Frank asks.

"I can't guarantee it. They may press charges against Miss Blothio as she did assault them."

Frank's eyes light up. "She was defending my honour!

There wouldn't've been a fight in the first place if Geoff and his stupid friend had left me alone. They were goading me, they wanted something to happen. Geoff hit out first."

"I'm aware, Mr Blothio," Drew answers. "So, do you want to press charges?"

"No," he replies.

"*No?!*" I stare at him in shock. "What do you mean no? They started it."

"If it's gonna make things worse for Shy, then I don't want to go any further. Geoff gets off on shit like this. He's had several allegations against him for pushing the envelope on human decency."

"I see," Drew replies, watching us. "Mr Finch, can you come with me please?"

"Me? Why?" I ask. "I'm only here to keep Frank company. I told your colleagues what I saw…"

Her expression doesn't change. "I need to speak with you in private."

Nausea aches in my stomach and Drew twists on her heel. I glance at Frank who's looking confused. I follow her reluctantly, walking past several officers who give me dagger eyes. Drew stops outside a room and beckons me to enter, inside there's a table with two single chairs. She closes the door behind her and I sit. This chair feels uncomfortable.

"The reason I want to speak with you in private is not about this case, Mr Finch." Drew sits opposite me and I feel like I'm being interrogated again. "A man in his mid-forties by the name of Keith Dench arrived at A&E. He said he'd been viciously attacked and gave the description of a woman. I don't know about you but I think Miss Blothio has a very…*unique* appearance and the description fits her perfectly."

I've just heard the real name of the man who preyed on my daughter. I'm fighting not to show my joy for his injuries.

"Do you know anything about Mr Dench?" Drew asks.

"What makes you think I know?"

"Because he said he was going to meet his friend, Hanna Finch in Yearling."

"*Shit*," I whisper. "That's my wife's name."

"And your wife is deceased?"

"Yes. I'm sorry, this past year's been awful for me and Emily. But this Keith Dench forgot to mention he was meeting up with a fourteen-year-old girl. Emily came clean about it. This Keith Dench said he was sixteen. Shy was with her and… she sorted it out."

"She broke his ribs, Mr Finch."

"Yes, I know that now! But I didn't know then. A grown man meeting up with a teenager… *nothing* good comes out of it. If Shy hadn't been there, think about what could've occurred."

Drew nods reflectively. "We ran a check of Mr Dench's history and he does have a criminal record. He's also a registered sex offender. He was going to press charges, when he realised we knew about his previous convictions, he retracted them. This Shy Blothio seems to be a knight in shining armour. She stands up for the people she cares about. But, she can't go around beating people up."

She can break every rib of every paedophile in the country for all I care. Keith Dench deserves worse. If I had my hands on him, he'd be lying in a morgue right now.

"I will drop the charges against Mr Ward and Mr Sheridan. On the grounds that if I ever see her in this police station again, she *will* go to prison," Drew says. "Is that clear?"

"Yes, I understand but I'm her friend. What power do I have?"

"I know you're not direct family but I'm hoping you will... perhaps, inspire your friend to change her ways. Miss Blothio will also be attending some anger management classes."

"Are they mandatory?" I ask.

"Yes, or she'll go to prison."

Bugger, this is deeply serious. "Okay, I'll talk to her. Geoff Ward and his snivelling friend won't enjoy it. They want to make Frank's life a misery, keeping his one and only living family member behind bars will be a great revenge tactic."

"I'll be able to handle any fallout, Mr Finch."

I believe her too.

~

A couple of painful hours pass, well it could've been minutes the way my mind's processing everything. I swear I've been in this sodding police station for days. After Drew's stern conversation, she takes Frank off and speaks to him. When he sits next to me, he's muttering about glugging a tankard of ginger wine to forget about the horrors of the day. I'm planning on doing the same later with a bottle of whiskey whenever I fucking get home. I didn't have to explain to Frank about Keith Dench. Drew had informed him along with the iron warning about Shy.

I text Em, wondering if she's home yet. I get a response straight away.

Jordan doesn't want me 2 be at home on my own. He said I can sleep round his.

Good thinking Jordan, you're always watching out for her. *Have you got a change of clothes?*

Nope, Jordan said I can wear sum of his pjs.

Okay, I'll see you in the morning.

Dad, what happened at the rally? It sounds really serious.

I tap the words I want to say, then I delete them. *I'll tell you tomorrow. Have a good night. Sleep well.*

Ok, love u.

Love you too.

I stuff my phone into my pocket. I don't wanna look at it for the rest of the night.

Drew walks out from the back of the station with Shy plodding in front of her. It's such a relief. Two purple sore lines streak across her lower lip. That Yearling head-kiss she gave Geoff must've been painful.

Frank runs up to her, pulling her into a loving hug. Drew watches with a stone expression, as if she's calculating and analysing every second.

"I meant what I said Mr Blothio," Drew warns. "I'm not joking around."

"Yes, Chief Inspector," he answers. "Thank you for everything you've done."

Drew throws me a scouring nod and I smile back. This woman makes me want to shit myself. I hope I never set foot in this place again.

We race to Frank's vehicle and shoot off, sitting in silence with the radio blaring on. My window's down, the fresh air's brushing against my face and the exhaustion's crashing like tidal waves within me.

I glance at Shy in the interior mirror, she's sitting in the back seat, her skin's glistening against the silhouetting sunset. She looks at me now and then, and I try to offer passive smiles. *You're okay*, I want to say. *You're out of there, you're safe* but she doesn't appear happy or relieved.

"*Shy*," Frank says after a while. "I really appreciate what you did but you made a big mistake today."

"Frank don't," I say sharply. "Not now."

There's pain and guilt in Shy's eyes. "I... just wanted to protect you," she says delicately.

"I don't need protecting. I'm a grown man," Frank hisses. "I made my bed. I can cope when things go wrong. You're not coming to anymore of my talks. I'm better off going alone. Do you understand?"

"Yes," she utters quietly.

"Frank's just pissed off, Shy. I think what you did earlier was amazing," I say. "It'll make Geoff think twice about approaching Frank."

"I'm more than pissed off and Jules, you shouldn't encourage her," Frank mutters, his grip on the steering wheel tightens.

"I'm not!" I bark back. "She didn't do anything wrong."

Frank shakes his head. "It goes against all of my principles. We don't act with violence, even if it's thrown in our path."

"*Frank*," I press, noticing the shine in Shy's gaze. "Stop it, that's enough."

He's glaring into the interior mirror. "Fighting is *not* the answer. We use our brains, we use our voices. Not our fists!"

"*Frank*," I growl. "*Shut up!* You're upsetting her!"

Shy lets out a piercing scream, it makes my ears ring. Frank swerves on the road, Shy unbuckles the seat-belt and smashes her foot against the window. She's crying passionately, striking out again with her foot. A crack breaks in the window pane.

"Frank, pull this cunting van over. *Now!*" I yell.

He pulls up on the left-hand side of the road, skidding over the grass.

Shy kicks angrily at the passenger door, hammering her fist against the handle. I'm out of the van when she leaps from her seat. I run as fast as I can, calling her name but Shy ignores me. She yanks off her jacket, it falls to the ground. She sprints in full speed towards the edge of the cliff. Over the horizon, Becks Hill boldly stands. The bright beam from the lighthouse cranks against the darkness of the evening tide.

Shy raises her arms, leaping off the edge, performing an elegant swan dive. I hurry to the verge as she plunges into the water. My heart's thumping rapidly like a speeding train.

21

Shy doesn't come up for air. I don't know how long I've been standing here. I've seen her dive off Becks Hill and she was lucky to be alive. Em saw her dive off Drake's Tooth, but that was during the day. The sun's already hiding behind the horizon.

Frank's stalking back to the van; he doesn't seem worried. He says she needs some space. What if she's injured? How on earth is this normal?

Okay, Shy's an adult. She can come and go as she pleases. She can handle herself in a physical confrontation but her emotions… are all over the place. She's a hurricane in human form.

Frank drops me home. I offer to stay with him but he says he needs to be alone to process the events of the day. I'm on the whiskey, gulping from the lip of the bottle. Weariness and alcohol consumption inspire me to black out on the sofa.

I wake up with a crunching headache. I'm still clutching Shy's jacket. Keira's nuzzled by my side just like old times. She flexes her razor paws when I stroke her head, she's so cute when she's sleeping. I check the clock, shit, it's one in the morning. I try to get back to sleep but my mind's shooting off in different directions like fireworks.

I can't shut it out.

I hate what my hometown has turned into. We're a

joke, the freaks in the circus. We were a little fishing community nobody batted an eyelid towards and now... we're the laughing stock of the country. All thanks to technology and idiots who don't understand us. I don't kill whales to inflict pain on others. I don't eat their meat to upset everyone. My family and so many others have been doing it for generations. If I stop participating in the culling, and quit fishing full stop, then my livelihood goes down the drain.

I twist and turn on the sofa while another hour trickles past. I'm exhausted. I've got work later on. I need my sleep.

~

Eventually, I lock up and go for a walk. Maybe the exercise will encourage my body and brain to shut the fuck up. Drake Cove's pleasantly quiet during the night, I hear the gentle waves riding against the sand. I walk along the beach thinking about Ian and Earl. A cold shiver creeps down my spine. They were found here, stabbed and drowned. Who was watching them? Was one of those balaclava wearing cretins waiting in the darkness? Will they make things worse if their crazy leader is stuck behind bars?

I spin in circles, wondering if I have unwelcomed company.

Well, *you fucking bastards.*

Come and get me.

You said I was next...

Here I am.

But nothing happens.

I don't hear flourishing footsteps racing to hurt me. I spin again, my feet create pictures in the sand. I'm getting dizzy; my ribcage is tight. I'm on my own, it's dark out here. I'm standing in plain sight. If I'm prey, the predator should use this time to destroy me. I'm the perfect target… but all I hear is the sea's heartbeat.

I regain my breathing. The faintest of light brews from Drake's Mouth. I journey over the cobbled stones and crawl on my belly. I feel a wash of relief when I see her, breathing and… intact.

She's asleep. Her body's curled up. Her knee nearly kissing the button of her nose. She's made a small fire by her head to keep warm.

"*Shy…*"

Her eyes open delicately. I try to keep my voice calm and gentle as I kneel next to her, my fingers pinching when I caress her head.

After a lot of persuasion, Shy comes back to the bungalow. I offer to take her to Frank's but she refused. Keira's asleep in Emily's bedroom when we arrive. Shy gets in the shower and I find her some suitable clothes; my old sports t-shirt and trackies. I wash her own clothes in the kitchen sink, wringing them out with my hands and hang them on the radiator.

"You look lovely," I say with a smile as she steps out in my old baggy clothes. That scar on her right arm still looks nasty.

I make two mugs of steaming hot chocolate and sit on the sofa. Shy scans the lounge, approaching the bookcase, catching sight of the family pictures. She strokes the blades of her fingers across Hanna's veiled face from our wedding. There's a hint of sadness in Shy's expression. It changes when she moves to Emily's toddler picture. My little girl's face bright and giggly after Hanna and I taught her how to clap.

"How are you in one piece after that plunge?" I ask, my question rising from the nosediving stillness.

"I've been swimming and diving all my life," Shy answers. "It's natural to me."

"Most people would've died from the sheer height." I offer her the mug, she gracefully takes it. "The cliff's higher than Drake's Tooth *and* Becks Hill and... you're still alive. It doesn't make any sense."

Shy sits next to me, delicately sipping her drink. "Does everything have to make sense to you, Julian?"

I'm stumped by the question. "Well...yes. How can we understand things if they don't make sense?"

She smiles. "I didn't mean to frighten you before. Frank wouldn't stop shouting."

"Don't worry, you were frustrated. Frank was upset about..." my stomach twists as a wave of anger rises within me, "that Keith Dench and Geoff and his stupid friend."

A deep smirk spreads across her face. "He'll think twice about adopting another dog."

"What do you mean?" I ask.

"Didn't you see his hand?"

"Shit, yes I did!" I say. "It was bandaged up."

"The dog bit him."

I almost choke on my hot chocolate. "Fuck off. You're pulling my leg!"

She shakes her head. "I did warn him."

"Was the dog talking to you?"

"Not directly. He was thinking...out loud. He was frustrated because his owner wasn't listening." She smiles to herself. "It's funny. If a person attacked or neglected their pet, they'd be in so much trouble. But when it comes to the open ocean, nobody makes the same connection..."

"You should be a vet," I reply, downing the mug. "Not

a painter."

Her eyes narrow with scrutiny. "I like painting."

"I know and your work's amazing but...just think," I feel stupid and uneasy when I hear what I'm saying, "with your *abilities*, you're the ideal candidate for that type of career."

"I don't want to be a vet, Julian."

"Fair enough but... it's still food for thought."

We stare at each other for a while. Shy awkwardly slurps her hot chocolate to fill up the empty words. Frown lines cushion the skin on her forehead.

"You need to stop worrying about Frank," I say. "He'll bounce back."

"He's disappointed with me. He's always taught me to turn the other cheek, even if I feel threatened."

"I'm sorry to say this but sometimes, Frank can be...*an idiot*. If someone's in your face, pushing you around, you have every right to defend yourself. Only fight if they hit you first. It's what I've taught Emily." I place my mug on the coffee table. "I... want to thank you for protecting her. Fuck what Frank said, and fuck what Drew said too. Dench has caused a lot of misery in his life, he deserved what you gave him. I'm proud of you, Shy."

"Really?" she asks softly.

"Of course," I say, curling a strand of ethereal green hair behind her ear.

She closes her eyes, stroking her cheek against my cupped palm. "Sometimes, I feel like I don't fit in at Drake Cove. As if I'm supposed to be somewhere else. No matter what I do, it's never gonna be enough."

"You're amazing," I utter. "Though you can be scary when you want to be." She smiles briefly when I say this. "Above all things, I'm in total awe of you...I think a lot of people are."

Tears shadow Shy's gaze before I lean in and kiss her.

We hold each other as we kiss, her tears dampening my skin. Her hands race to the back of my neck, pulling me deeper into her embrace. She kisses me across my jaw. My pulse kicks up a notch. I hook my arm under Shy's knees and heave her off the carpet. We knock into the walls as I navigate our hunger across the lounge. My hands greedily pull at her t-shirt. It comes off, falling by our feet. My fingers glide up her back, relishing her soft skin.

Shy crashes against the duvet of my bed and we undress each other. She shakes underneath me as every piece of material's ripped away. I whisper against her skin and place loving kisses on her belly and the top of her thighs. I tell her not to be afraid, that she's safe with me. When our heartbeats unite, we become one and sleep engulfs me like a lover's caress.

In my dreams, I'm swimming in the deep blue sea, it's a beautiful endless space. Under my feet, a cluster of dark specks soar from the ocean pit. I recognise them instantly. Leading the sea tribe is the dark-haired woman from before, River, the menace who killed first.

We reach the shore, crawling to our feet across the sand. Droplets of water drip from our limbs. We're back at Drake Cove; the sea tribe race up the hill to the huts where brick houses should be standing. River clicks her tongue, lurching forward with a feline strength. Several men and women clutching swords guard the entrance to the village. The sea tribe move fast, cutting and slicing their tender throats. I'm witnessing the hunt of my ancestors.

After they slaughter the guards, they gain entry to the village. Sitting in the centre of the courtyard, Octavia, the

Sea Queen sits in a slumped position. There's rope lashed around her neck, wrists and ankles. She's breathing hoarsely, her skin's dry and it peels like she's been asleep in the sandy desert. She whimpers from fear when she sees River. They click their tongues at one another. Hang on, this is how Shy communicated with the calf...

I don't understand what they're saying, if it's what you call talking. Octavia's cut free and she flops into River's arms. There's no strength left in her anymore. She weakly reaches up, touching her sister's cheek, her crown falling through her fingers. Her other hand splays up River's arm, touching the seaweed covered lump by her chest. Her son is sleeping. I watch Octavia die in River's arms, the shells crunch and shatter in her palm.

~

Now, I'm standing in front of the blonde-haired warrior, Ursula the Usurper. She's sleeping soundlessly with her limbs wrapped in furs. A shadow crawls across the hut walls, dancing in the firelight.

Ursula wakes in a fright, searching for a weapon. River leaps on top of the bed, hissing like Keira when she's tracking birds. The most sinister point about this is... River's teeth... they're razor sharp. I swear they weren't before. She moves too quickly. The tip of the stone dagger swishes across Ursula's neck. A red line erupts on her throat, spurting life across the hut walls, casting River in a blanket of blood.

~

My surroundings swirl around me. Erik's tied to a wooden pole. He's been savagely beaten. River stands before him, covered in Ursula's blood. She kneels in front of Erik and he looks up, staring at her. Tears are in his eyes when he sees his son resting against her chest.

River spits an ear at his knees, I don't want to know who it belongs to. She breaks his shackles and he falls to the ground. Erik coughs, his limbs trembling from the strain. River crawls over to him, he cowers back, shielding his face as her sharp stained teeth nearly come in contact with his neck. River clicks her tongue, a deep growl escaping her throat. The baby boy cries from her embrace. She scoots back, rising to her feet. Erik uncoils himself, staring fearfully. There's a look of pure disdain in River's eye as she extracts something from her palm. The crushed shells trickle and fall through her fingers, hitting the hard ground. Erik stares, his eyes soften as the realisation kicks in with a grief-stricken agony.

The scenes of war and death wash away and I'm back on the beach. An old man sits at the edge of the shore playing Erik's whistle. Time and bad luck have consumed his soul, only a withered husk remains. After a couple of beats, a head pops up from the surface of the water, startling the old man to his feet.

Wearing a shell crown, a young man dressed in seaweed steps out from the waves. He walks towards the old man, a brief smile lighting his expression. There's a kinship between the two, they have a similar build and shaped face. The old man staggers back in shock as the younger one catches him...

They stare at each other for the longest time. In his final moments, Erik's wizened hand lovingly cups his son's cheek. *The Sea King.*

22

The morning sunlight splits through the wooden panelling of the broken window. I squint through the haze. I'm spooning Shy, my arms are draped around her hips. I sweep a strand of her hair off her shoulder, leaning over to peer into her face. She hasn't looked this calm before. I smile to myself, then I hear a click in the lock of my front door.

Shit.

Emily's back and she's early. Why do I have a morning bird for a child?

I haul on my clothes, signalling to a tired, now awake and confused Shy to keep her voice down. I tiptoe out of my room. The floorboards creak under my feet.

"Morning Dad," she says, taking white buds out of her ears.

"Morning hunnie," I reply. "You're home early. I thought you were coming back later."

She shrugs. "Jordan said I could stay for breakfast but I wanted to check on you."

"Oh, you didn't need to do that."

Now I feel even worse. I can tell she's nervous because she knows she's gonna hear unpleasant news. I walk to the kitchen to make coffee when my bedroom door screeches open, Shy stands in the doorway, wearing my clothes.

Em's eyes could've honestly bulged out of her head. I don't know where to look. Her gaze drops to my old t-shirt lying on the lounge floor. I'd whipped it off Shy's back, clutched in the mood of passion and completely forgotten about it.

"I guess… you had company after all then," Em utters.

Expressions as sharp as daggers pass between my daughter and my…friend, or my lover?

Shy takes her clothes delicately from the radiator and disappears into the bathroom.

"What's she doing here?" Em asks aggressively.

Prepare for a war, Jules. "Look, I know this must seem gross to you but…yesterday was horrendous and she needed a friend, so I invited her to sleepover."

"A sleepover?" Em asks. "And she stayed in your bedroom?"

"Yes…" I say, wanting the ground to swallow me up.

Em slams her phone on the kitchen work surface. "I'm not a kid anymore, Dad. And… I'm not stupid."

"I never said you were."

"I catch you two kissing and then she walks out of *your* bedroom wearing *your* clothes. It's pretty fucking obvious what you two have been up to."

"Don't swear at me!"

"Is that why you wanted me to stay at Jordan's?"

"No, not at all!"

Shy emerges from the bathroom back in her old gear. Her body stiffens, sensing the tension in the room. "I need to head back to Frank's and apologise."

"Yeah, you do that. And don't forget your jacket," Em sneers, taking it off the sofa, holding it out to her.

They glare at each other before Shy swipes it from her hands. She storms out the front door, banging it loudly as it shuts.

We eat breakfast in total silence. I don't know how to

handle this. Hanna always knew.

"So, what happened yesterday then?" Em asks, milk's dripping from her spoon.

Rather than protecting and hiding everything, I tell her the truth. I start with the rally, Frank's speech, Geoff spitting and Shy's arrest. Then I explain what happened at the police station. Em bursts into tears when I tell her about Keith Dench and what Shy did to him.

"Don't cry," I say.

She rubs her face into my chest. "I'm sorry, Dad."

I stroke my hand through her hair. "No, *I'm* sorry, Em. I should've been honest with you about my feelings for Shy. I understand why you said it, don't worry."

"Dad, I didn't know the guy was a…"

"He lied to you. He took advantage of your friendship."

"Shy was protecting me…" a tear drips down her cheek. "But why? She barely knows me."

"She's your friend."

"Or she must have really strong feelings for you…."

A small smile itches at the corner of my mouth. "I don't know, maybe. But I know she cares about you."

"I should apologise to her."

"I'm sure Shy will be fine."

"No, she was hurt. I could tell. Oh God, I didn't mean to hit her." Her eyes surge with energy as she thinks. "I can buy her a gift, you know… ease the pain a bit?"

When I think about it, getting a present for Frank would probably be a good idea too. We didn't exactly leave things on good terms. Em and I make plans to go shopping in the town square after she finishes sailing school.

~

Work pretty much plods by except Lance constantly points out my "cheeky grin" all day.

"Have you had sex?" Dan asks, resting his feet on the coffee table in the staff room.

"*No!*" I exclaim.

"Yes, you have!" Damien laughs. "You've got the afterglow!"

"The afterglow? What's that?" I ask.

"It's when you've come after making passionate sweet love and you bask in the sexy sensations," Lance crows. "You normally have a great sleep afterwards."

Shit, I slept like a baby last night. Except, for the gruesome murder dream.

Lance grins at me. "So, who's your mystery shagger?"

"I'm not shagging anyone," I say. "Can we have enough of this please?!"

He titters. "That's exactly what someone with a secret shag pal would say."

"I haven't got a secret shag pal, alright!"

"Come on, Jules," Damien teases. "Who's the lucky lady?"

I groan.

"Is it a bloke?" Dan asks.

Lance and Damien laugh at me and from the corner of my eye, Mike grins as he types. It's his first smile of the day.

I meet Em and we head into town. The podium and metal fences have miraculously disappeared. The heart of Drake Cove is suspiciously clean. However, the harsh reality is plastered all over the front page of the Yearling Echo. There's hideous pictures of Drake Covians pummelling the daylights out of the FAAC and the activists using their banners as lucky shields. We look like a gathering of headcases who are nothing but a bunch of angry, brutal beasts…

Not all of us are like this.

Em buys a pot of brushes, an A4 sketch pad and a tin of paints. I get a bottle of ginger wine, it's Frank's favourite. I debate whether to get something for Shy.

I ping Frank a little text that we're on our way but I don't receive a reply, maybe he's working or he's still pissed off. Here's hoping my ginger wine acts as an acceptable gift.

We arrive at Frank's. The front door's ajar, this isn't normal for him.

"Frank!" I knock on the door.

It swings open. The sofa's overturned.

"*Frank, Shy!* Are you there?"

Em runs past me and heads to the back of the house. I check Shy's room, her paintings are gone and the drawers are empty.

"*Dad, Dad!*" Em shouts. "Come here!"

I race to her voice. She's kneeling next to Frank who's lying on the floor of his study. His computer chair's toppled over. A red mark's blossoming across his cheek. Thank fuck, he's breathing.

"We need to put him in the recovery position," Em says, curling her arms around his hips.

I grab hold of his shoulders. We count to three and heave him onto his side. He's certainly put on the pounds. I thought vegetarians were meant to be slimmer than us carnivores.

"Frank. *Frank*," I say, clicking my fingers in his face.

His eyes flutter and he breathes out as if he's held a lung full of air.

"Frank, can you hear me?" I ask.

His voice breaks slightly. "Ugh. *My fucking head*, what happened?"

"I was gonna ask you the same question," I say. "We found you like this. What's the last thing you remember?"

Frank blinks several times. "I'm not sure. I was sitting at my desk and then I blacked out. Next thing I know, Emily's talking at me."

"What's happened here?" I ask. "The house is a tip. All of Shy's belongings are gone."

"I...don't know," Frank utters.

~

I call for an ambulance and the paramedics arrive. They test his breathing and blood pressure. Everything's normal and they give him the all-clear. They must have found the state of the house just as puzzling as we did. Frank says he had an argument with Shy. I don't believe him for one minute. It's camouflage to hide the truth. Shy has a wildness but it's not so unhinged that she'd flip out like this and take her belongings.

Frank has a mild concussion, he says he must've fainted and fallen, another story I don't believe. The paramedics inform me to keep an eye on Frank, he needs to take it easy, no heavy lifting, operating machinery, including driving or sailing. If he feels dizzy or nauseous, he needs to go to hospital straight away.

After they leave, I help Frank to the lounge and sit him in his armchair. "Frank, what really happened here? Where's Shy?"

He looks at me guiltily. "I can't tell you, Jules."

"And why not?" I flip the sofa back and crash onto the cushions. "You didn't have an argument, did you? She didn't trash the house. What's going on here?"

Frank watches me with this new meekness. He's normally a strong-willed guy and now he's a shadow of himself. I can't see the strength that was beaming from his eyes when he made that amazing speech.

I've had enough of people dismissing me. I'm tired of treading on egg shells. "Frank. *What* is she?"

"She's just like us, Jules. Stop it."

"*No, she's not!*" I say. "She's not like us. At all. I've been racking my head for ages. It's been driving me crazy!"

He sighs with defeat. "Em, can you get my phone and reading glasses? They're on my desk."

My daughter nods and returns with the items. Frank slides the glasses on and squints as he dials the number. He's shaking his head, sighing under his breath, rambling to himself. "Yeah, it's me. Well, I've been better." Frank stares at me, speaking to whoever's on the other end. "Can you come over? Yeah, I need you right now. Jules and Emily know about Shy."

~

I'm so freaked out I open Frank's gift, letting the feverish heat of the ginger liquid sooth my throat. Em's had a drop too, a little splash won't hurt her.

Later, there's a knock at the door and Frank twitches nervously.

"Stay there," I bark. "I'll answer it. They said you need to take it easy." I open the door and my heart pumps into overdrive. "What the hell are you two doing here?!"

Herb and Derek gawk back in horror then they catch sight of Frank and hurry past me, racing to comfort him. I shake my head and slam the front door; the loud impact makes Frank jump. "Stop glaring at me, Jules," he winces.

"*What's going on, Frank?*" I let the shock edge in my voice.

"Dad's right." Em doesn't look impressed either. "You need to start talking, Uncle Frank."

"Maybe you should sit down," Herb utters faintly, avoiding my gaze.

"I'll decide that," I say. "Who is she? *What is she?*"

"This story will take a while," Derek adds and then he eyes the sofa.

I sit reluctantly. "There better be a good reason, because I don't know how much more of this I can take."

Frank rubs his hands together, licking his lips before he speaks.

"It's okay," Derek whispers to him. "Take your time."

Frank breathes in and out, closing his eyes momentarily. "I vowed to keep Shy safe from harm but clearly... I failed." He looks at me. "You're right, Jules. She isn't like us."

"Okay, then what is she?" I ask.

23

Frank: 30 Years Before

He steered Olivia firmly across the water. The current was more aggressive than usual. His best friend and colleague, Michael peered over the side of the boat and turned to the mini crane. Frank flicked his gaze between the rear-view mirror and the open ocean, keeping Olivia steady. He watched his friend work the controls as he lowered the large net into the ocean.

"This is the last catch of the night!" Mike yelled.

"I agree!" Frank shouted back, his fingers fiddling with the steering.

After Mike had dealt with the net, he walked into the cockpit and sat next to Frank. They needed to give it time for the fish to wander into the net. His friend sparked up his pipe, a silver-encrusted token from his dad. The smoke curled from Mike's lips and his teeth crunched on the bridge of the pipe.

They watched the horizon together, revelling in the silence. Since they'd signed their first commercial contract, they'd received several slimy letters about the abomination of their fisherie. Animal activists were a fierce voice in their careers but with whaling, the actions and temperaments were constantly backed by an emotional, spiteful essence.

Frank and Mike heard the crane tick which meant the net was gradually getting to maximum capacity. Frank tapped the controls to steady Olivia. Any sudden swift movements would cause the net to dislodge and tear, plunging their income to the ocean seabed. Mike licked the ends of his forefingers, diminishing the flame in the well of the pipe and chucked it on the table, before downing the final dregs of his cold tea.

The crane ticked manically, quicker than it normally did.

"That doesn't sound healthy," Mike uttered, marching outside. "Something else is in the net!"

"Are you sure?" Frank turned his head when the boat shunted to port. "Shit, I think you're right! What do we do?"

Mike pressed the button on the crane to winch the net back onboard. It made a groaning sound; the rope was straining.

"It'll snap if you keep doing that!" Frank shouted.

And if he kept adding pressure, Olivia was going to play a vital role in a makeshift catapult, sending him and his friend hurtling into the sea.

"Well, fucking help me then!" Mike bellowed.

Frank wasn't supposed to leave the helm unless the boat was docked or someone else was there to take up his position. He didn't want to break protocol but he had no choice. He moved from the controls, grabbed the thick strings from the net and began to pull. Whatever was in there, was really heavy.

"Give it here!" Mike mumbled, clutching the other sides of the thick strings. "Ready?"

Frank nodded.

"One, two, three!"

Frank pressed his foot on the edge of the boat for added leverage. He dragged with all of his might, pain pulsed in his chest and the rope burned his palms. Mike pulled several ugly faces as they tried to help the crane. Frank pressed his other foot against the edge, so he was levitating. The arm of the crane whirred on and the net dropped onto the boat, plonking several discarded wriggling fish between the holes. Frank and Mike fell backwards, their bodies smacking against the decking floor.

"*Shit!*" Mike grunted. "That's gonna hurt in the morning."

Frank laughed and sat up, rubbing the burning twinge in the nape of his back. He stopped massaging when he saw something in the net.

"*Mike...*" Frank muttered.

"*What?*" Mike coughed, catching sight of the contents of the net. "Wow. I didn't go fishing for that."

Inside the net, was a dark-haired, pale skinned woman with heavy eyelids and piercing dark brown eyes.

Frank shuffled on his hands and knees as other fish jumped and jolted around him, gasping their final breaths. "How on earth did you get in there?" he asked the woman. "What were you doing in the water?"

The woman shivered, pulling her knees up to her chin, water dripped from her hair. When Frank nudged forwards, the woman edged back with fear.

"Hey," Frank whispered. "There's nothing to be scared of. I'm going to get you out, okay?"

She didn't respond.

Frank got to his feet and untied the strings from the crane's claw. Mike watched their new shipmate cautiously. Frank unravelled the net, a small mound of fish slid off her feet. He moved closer, offering his hand. "You're okay now."

The woman scrutinised him, her intoxicating gaze scorched into his. Damp smooth fingers slid across his marked and scarred palm, warmth brewed from within and Frank felt a spread of calmness.

"Do you not talk?!" Mike asked with irritation. "Where the fuck are your clothes?" Then he picked up a rock from a mound of dying fish. "What's this?"

Frank stared at the object; it was large enough to rest in his best friend's palm. It had a circular based handle and a curved blade at the top. It looked like a weapon chiselled from the materials of the coral reef.

"Were you trying to cut our net?" Mike barked.

She didn't reply.

"*Answer me!*"

"Stop it," Frank said. "You're scaring her."

"I don't care!" he exclaimed. "She could be a fucking activist trying to cause us grief."

"I don't think so," Frank smiled nervously.

They grew immediately uncomfortable as they saw the fish, the net and her coal black hair had been hiding her nakedness. Frank grabbed a blanket from the cockpit, threw it around her shoulders and helped her inside.

Mike sat at the wheel and started to sail Olivia back to Drake Cove whilst Frank made tea.

"Here," he said, handing the mug to her. "Taste this. It'll warm you up." He gestured to it, cupping his hands together, mimicking slurping up soup.

The woman nodded slightly and imitated him, taking a tiny sip from the mug.

"I don't want to frighten you," he said. "My name's Frank and this is my friend, Michael." He made a gesture to his colleague who didn't turn around. "This is our boat, Olivia. We're fishermen. We're taking you back to Drake Cove, our home. Have you heard of it?"

The woman blinked several times, her eyes twitching

frantically between Frank and Mike.

"What's your name?" Frank asked softly.

She didn't respond and he was starting to feel helpless.

"Can you understand me?" Frank asked again.

She nodded and his heart leapt with joy.

"Okay, that's good." Frank smiled. "Can you tell me what your name is?"

The woman stared at him anxiously. She shook her head.

"Why can't you tell me?"

"Maybe she's one of those mutes who's born without a voice box," Mike uttered.

Frank thought about it. He'd heard of mutism; he wasn't sure if it was a condition a person was born with or they developed it from a tumultuous upbringing or trauma. With the way the woman was looking at him, he favoured the latter.

"Do-you-have-a-name?" Frank asked.

The woman nodded.

"But you can't tell me?"

She nodded again. Mike was right, she was a mute. At least Frank was getting somewhere.

He fished a clipboard from the desk and scribbled letters on the paper. "Can you point to a letter for me and spell out your name?"

The woman nodded and gingerly began to point. Frank read the letters as she did so. He noticed her hands were trembling.

S...H...A...E

"Shae?" he asked.

She nodded.

"You have a beautiful name."

A spark of a smile gleamed on her mouth and Frank felt

a tug in his chest. "Okay Shae, where are you from?"

She leaned forwards, pointing again.

S...E...A

"She's crackers," Mike replied.

"She can hear you," Frank uttered, turning back to Shae. "I love the sea too. What is it to you?"

H...O...M...E

"I told you so," Mike sung, keeping his attention fixed on the horizon.

Frank didn't know what to think of the situation. They'd found a remarkably attractive naked silent woman in their net. They were far out to sea when they found her, there were no boats or mini-islands around for miles. They'd been fishing over an unfathomable part of the sea, it was as if she'd swam up from the depths.

Frank held up the dagger. "Shae, what is this?"

T...O...O...L

"A tool?" Frank frowned. "It looks more like a weapon to me. I bet this thing can do some serious damage. What were you trying to do?"

F...R...E...E

"I told you she was an activist," Mike replied. "She was letting the fucking fish out."

"Why would you want to do that, Shae?" Frank whispered. "Why do you care about the fish so much?"

Shae leaned forwards again, a seriousness growing in her eyes.

F...R...I...E...N...D...S

When they brought Olivia to dock at the quay, Mike phoned the authorities. After he hung up, he sat with Frank who was speaking to Shae. She hadn't said a word.

"Police are coming for you love," Mike said. "They

won't wanna arrest you looking like that. They'll throw you in the loonie bin."

Mike left the boat and headed to the office, on the hunt for some clothes. Frank was alone with the woman.

H...E...S...C...A...R...Y

Frank laughed. "He's not really, he's a big baby on the inside. Discovering you has left him in shock, for the both of us actually. What were you doing out there? Nobody's hurt you, have they?"

Shae shook her head.

"Because if someone has, you can tell us. The police will want to know."

She shook her head again.

Mike returned with a jumper and a pair of old jeans. "Well, it's better than nothing."

He handed them to Shae and she peered down at the clothing, unsure of what to do.

"Seriously?" Mike asked with bemusement. "Don't you know how to put clothes on?"

Shae stared at him timidly, shaking her head.

"*Jesus fucking Christ*," Mike uttered, rolling his eyes.

"When are the police coming?" Frank asked.

"Said they'd be here as soon as they can. Told us to stay put. They'll come and find us." Mike acknowledged Shae, breathing out a sigh of derision. "Okay, I'll help you change."

Shae blinked, standing in front of him. She nodded after a beat or two.

Mike knelt on the floor, folding the trousers out. "Step forward," he said.

Frank watched as Shae took his hand, Mike looked up at her slowly.

She stepped into the trousers; her hand still conjoined

with Mike's. His friend shook his head as if he had a niggling thought and stroked the trousers up her legs, fastening up her belt buckle. Mike was standing over Shae, significantly taller. She peered into his face, as if she was examining every facial hair and wrinkle on his skin.

"Arms up," Mike commanded.

Shae did as she was told.

Mike hiked the jumper over her head. Frank saw the outline of Shae's muscles. There wasn't an ounce of fat on her. She had broad shoulders, strong arms to pierce the water and skin-tight thighs, the perfect swimmer's body. The towel which had been covering most of her modesty dropped to the ground, revealing her pert breasts. Frank's cheeks bloomed crimson and he turned his head, trying to be a courteous gentleman. Shae seemed comfortable being naked, especially in the company of others.

After she was dressed, they sat in silence. Even his best friend was acting more nervous than usual; his knee was constantly shaking as tension filled the cockpit.

Red and blue lights finally flashed in the background.

Frank headed outside, offering his hand to Shae. "It's okay, they'll take care of you."

She stood up boldly, her eyes filled with panic and she legged past Mike, diving off the back of Olivia, splashing into the water.

"*Shit!*" Mike shouted. "Frank, why didn't you stop her?!"

"I don't know, she moved too fast!"

Mike leapt off Olivia and onto the jetty which was swamped in darkness. Frank grabbed a flashlight, scanning the waters but he couldn't see her. Where had she gone?

The mysterious shipmate had vanished into thin air. Had

Frank conjured her up from his subconscious?

The police weren't happy with him and Mike after the incident. They assumed their call was a ruse to waste time. If they called about the mysterious, naked woman from the water again, they'd be slapped with a handsome fine.

How understanding.

Since starting the fisherie, Frank had taught at the local sailing school. He'd cut his hours down significantly but helped out on Saturdays, especially if another tutor couldn't attend. On one particular day, he was teaching in the afternoon so he had time to grab a bite to eat. He packed his bag, fished some post from the office and hopped onto Olivia, untying the rope from the mast. He steered Olivia out of the quay and kept her at a slow speed until Becks Hill was up close and personal, then he ripped at the stack of letters. He groaned inwardly when he read another rivalrous threat from a ridiculous man called Geoffrey Ward. He sent dozens of them each month.

"Stupid twat," Frank muttered, scrunching the paper into his palm before flinging it into the water. "Don't tell me what to fucking do."

He sunk his teeth into the juicy sandwich, freshly made from the Crest Café. He loved the tanginess of the tomato and the luscious cream of the mayonnaise. He felt something wet and soggy smack his cheek and he dropped his succulent lunch. Frank noticed the letter in a splodge on the decking.

"I thought I'd dreamt you up," he uttered fearfully.

Shae was paddling in the water, her eyes burning into Frank's. She crawled onto the vessel, dirtying the wooden decking. She pointed aggressively at the white lump of paper and then back at the sea, shaking her head.

"I... shouldn't be throwing stuff in the water?" he

asked.

She nodded, pointing to the water again then she placed her hand on the centre of her chest. He thought about what she said the other night.

"Home?" Frank asked.

Shae smiled and walked towards him. Water dripped from her skin, she was getting too close, he thought she was going to kiss him.

"W-What are you doing?" he asked, backing up, terror aching from his throat.

Shae smiled, a sweet genuine motion of acknowledgment. Her fingers framed his face as if they were acting out a romantic tragedy. She placed her thumbs over his eyelids and thousands of images surged into his mind, some burning, some searing, others scarring him forever.

Looking back, Frank should've called the police, no matter how much they'd threatened him. He'd still be a perfect strip in the wallpaper of Drake Cove's traditions, a meat eater and a culling supporter if he'd done so.

Frank hauled the rucksack over his shoulder, his face gradually becoming sticky from the splatters of blood and sand. He unlocked the door of Olivia, wanting time on his own. He stored the meat in the fridge, sometimes he and Mike snacked on the blubber when they were out for a long time. It kept them going when their energy depleted, it was better than the dirtiest of coffees. He was glad their boat had a cabin with a built-in shower, even though it wasn't very big. He heard the hum of the bathroom light and flicked on the water. He held out his fingers, waiting for the warmth of the wet to stroke his fingertips. He undressed, wrenching every watery red drop from his clothes and placed them on the rails to dry before stepping into the shower.

Suddenly, the door of the bathroom closed and the slam made his eyes snap open. She was standing before him, staring with intention.

"*Shae?!*" Frank placed his hands over his private parts. "For fuck's sake, what are you doing here?!"

He squinted as the droplets stung his eyes. His confidence shrank when Shae yanked off her clothes, stepping into the shower. "What are you doing here?" he asked again, more aggressively this time.

Her hand whipped out, smacking him clean and hard across the face. His cheek burned from the aftermath. "*Ow!*" he growled, massaging the sting. "*Why'd you do that?!*"

His voice trailed off when Shae began to cry. They weren't little tears; they were huge and hysterical.

"Oh God," Frank uttered, realising what was behind her actions. "I'm so sorry, Shae."

Her fingers slid up his chest, the whale blood and water spray spilled over her skin. She stared at the remnants of the blood, some of it had clotted under her fingernails.

"*My friends,*" she whispered.

Frank had never heard her speak before and he was expecting some sort of deep, seductive tone. But instead, he heard a light croak as if she hadn't used the muscles in her voice box.

"I'm sorry," Frank said sincerely.

"*My...friends,*" she whispered again, the tears continued to spill.

He pulled her into a hug and she cried against his shoulder. He held her, tight in his embrace as the water spray from the shower drenched their skin. She began to fight him, anger welling from inside. She hit out at his chest, Frank took the knocks and the bashes. He wrapped his arms around her, pinning her arms to her side. He held her face in his hands as she sobbed tiredly, an overwhelming sensation of desire bubbling within him.

Shae's cries diminished as Frank pressed his lips against hers. After a couple of moments, she responded. He hooked his arms around her waist, twisting her so her back was up against the shower wall. A delightful moan rumbled in her throat when he slipped his tongue into the crevice of her mouth. He didn't know how long they had kissed for; he didn't care right now. Having her in his arms was all that mattered.

After informing Shae to stay on Olivia, he headed home, packing several plastic containers with sandwiches, crisps, fruit, chocolate and cereal bars. He didn't intend for Shae to see him in a bloody mess but that was the harsh reality of the culling. Possession of the meat came at a bloody price.

It was late when he returned to the quay, Frank was one of the few who enjoyed being out at sea late at night. He noticed the main light was on inside the cabin and he thought the worst. He'd had several uncomfortable surprises by animal activists who'd been sending him and Mike horrible letters. They'd plastered Olivia in violent pictures of dead whales and dolphins. One revolting individual who should've been in a mental hospital thought they'd make a radical point by leaving a bloody tampon on the decking. Frank didn't understand the sickening motives behind their bizarre actions. He knew there were people out there who didn't agree with his lifestyle. He welcomed their opinions if they wanted to talk to him but...vandalising his property, stalking his whereabouts – they were crossing a line.

Frank stepped onto Olivia; his fists clenched ready for a brawling. Then he heard the sounds, and then their shapes bled into view.

Mike's thick bare back tightened with every thrust, he moved swiftly between Shae's legs. Her neck arched; her lips parted as the sweet sounds of enjoyment rolled from her throat. Their eyes burned into each other as if the whole world around them had melted away.

Pain erupted in Frank's chest and he didn't know why. The emotions were gripping him like an invisible rope, pulling him to the ground. The plastic bag and the boxes slipped from his fingers, making a horrendous thundering sound as they crashed against the decking.

The animosity between Frank and Mike had been brewing and bubbling for several months after what he witnessed. They didn't talk about the event and kept things strictly formal. They never broached the subject of their mutual water friend. But as the months continued, Frank's resentment and jealousy deepened and darkened. Every time the office door chimed and Mike ambled in, Frank felt a dagger cutting along his spine. Maybe he should've just taken Shae and had his way with her. But every time he looked in his best friend's face, he was reminded of that awful memory, that Shae wanted Mike more.

To clear his overflowing head, Frank decided to take Olivia out. He hadn't seen Shae since...the incident, so he'd filed the wonderful shower kiss as a mistake or a blip. All of the conflicting thoughts were swirling around his head when he saw her treading in the water by the boat.

"What do you want?" Frank asked bitterly.

Shae stared at him, flinching from his anger as if he'd sent out vicious telepathic spikes to stab and prick at her skin. She was a succubus, preying on the emotions of two best friends, causing them to hate each other.

"Is this what you do?" Frank continued, staring her down. "Tease us… and break our hearts?"

Shae cautiously climbed on-board, edging towards Frank like a frightened little puppy. She placed her hands on either side of his face. The images and words shuddered through him.

"*No…*" Frank said, trying to shield his mind from the torment.

He glanced to her midriff and lifted her dripping jumper, exposing her skin. Shae placed his hand on her blooming belly. Underneath her fingertips, Frank felt the beat in the centre of her abdomen, the unborn imprint of a tiny hand.

Several months later, Shae gave birth to a baby girl. Frank had been by her side when she was shrieking from the painful contractions. The baby, a precious angel with two different colour eyes and small twigs of dark green hair. He'd only been gone for a couple of hours to buy additional baby clothes and blankets. He knew something was wrong when he heard tiny screams vibrating from Drake's Mouth, the desolate cave Shae used as her sanctuary.

Frank dropped everything when he saw the baby's face streaked with blood. Shae wasn't anywhere in sight. He gathered the infant in his arms, wrapping her in blankets. Tears blurred his vision when he wiped the blood from her skin. The child squeezed his finger, resting her little fist in the palm of his large hand.

He never found out what happened to Shae, although

his dreams and nightmares never ceased to plague him with sinister possibilities. Frank vowed to protect the child with every second of his life and... named her Shy, a tribute to her mother.

24

Julian: Present Day

There's a great stream of silence after Frank stops speaking. I let all of the new information wash over me, I can't believe what's been going on in Drake Cove all this bloody time.

"*Mike…*" I utter.

Frank nods. "Where do you think Shy gets her blue eye from?"

I've lost count how many glasses of wine I've drank but it doesn't stop me reaching for another. "Does he know about Shy?"

I see a shine in Frank's eyes, I'm not sure if it's guilt or something else. "I don't think Mike's the paternal type," he says. "He never asked about Shae, he didn't seem concerned she was missing. He wouldn't believe me if I told him the truth."

"Mike's a private guy, he rarely shows his vulnerabilities. All of his focus is on the business," I say.

"You didn't know him back then," Frank cuts in. "He was very different."

"You've robbed him of one of the best things in life. Mike deserves to know Shy is his. I asked him about Shae and he dismissed my question. He didn't want to talk about her, that could be because there's pain burning somewhere. Is this why you don't talk anymore? Because Shae slept with Mike and not with you?"

"Dad, stop it!" Em says. "That's not fair."

Anger flares in Frank's face. I instantly regret my words and how I said them. I brace myself for a rightful punch.

"Mike never loved Shae," Frank utters, glaring at me. "Regardless of her DNA, deep down, Shy's my daughter. I've raised her. Shae confided in me about her pregnancy because she knew I could take care of her."

I shake my head. "I think you're being unfair, Frank."

His decision was fuelled by jealousy and bitterness. He merely assumed Mike would be a bad father.

Frank continues, his eyes don't part from mine. "If she'd been under Mike's arm, she wouldn't have an identity, she'd be locked in some asylum. I didn't want her to be a mute like her mother. Her paintings, her articulate mind is because I taught her everything. I can't tame her personality. She should be allowed to be who she is. Just like the whales out there."

"Did you ever find out what happened to Shae?" Em asks.

"I've been looking for her ever since," Frank says. "I don't know if somebody got to her, or she was sick and she left Shy in Drake's Mouth to keep her safe."

"None of us know," Herb utters sadly.

Frank glances at my friends. "Derek and Herb have been helping me with research."

I look at them. "And what were your roles in this?"

Derek scowls at me as if I've just slapped him across the face. "We're not idiots, Jules. Frank was walking around the town with a new-born child. He had no partner or family supporting him. We could tell he was struggling."

Herb pats Frank on his shoulders. "We had to step in."

"You two saved my sanity," Frank replies.

"Mike said Frank was living with a woman," I say.

"That was Olga, Frank's au pair," Derek utters. "It was our decision to get her in. She helped around the house and looked after Shy."

"Why haven't we seen Shy before that?" I ask.

"We kept her a secret," Herb says.

"Until she was ready to branch out of her own accord," Derek adds.

That was another bad decision.

"So, you *don't* have a step brother?" I stare at Frank, my lips are quivering. "The car accident. It wasn't true, was it?"

"We lied to protect Shy," Derek whispers.

Frank watches me sullenly. "I'm sorry, Jules. I know it's not ethical but I had no choice."

"We needed a cover in case anyone picked up on Shy's behaviour. A trauma story normally works for a feasible reason behind someone's quirks," Herb says.

Em frowns at her uncles. "Hang on, you knew her all along? Even when I brought her to the shop?"

They both nod.

"Sorry Em," Derek states.

There's upset in my daughter's eyes. "But I would've kept her secret. You didn't need to lie to me."

"We couldn't risk it," Herb says.

"Un-fucking-believable," I sneer, staring at Frank. "What is she then?"

Derek pauses pensively before he speaks. "We reckon… she's some kind of… well… mermaid."

I've been swimming and diving all my life, I remember her saying. *It's natural to me.*

"Really?" Em asks.

"You can't be serious!" I chuckle. "Guys, they don't exist. They're just mythical creatures from fairy tales."

"Laugh all you want," Frank shrugs. "Why did you buy that Alice Green book if you weren't intrigued?"

Em gazes at me with captivation. "Yeah, Frank's right. You were reading about Davy Jones' Locker…and look at how Shy dives, the reason why she doesn't come up for air. She's made to live in the water… this makes so much sense now!"

Shit, they've infected my kid with this otherworldly romantic crap.

Herb smiles. "We had an inkling you'd find out when you bought the book."

No wonder they were staring at me so weirdly that day. "What is Davy Jones' Locker anyway?" I ask.

Frank wipes his forehead. "It's a refuge for dead sailors and shipwrecks, at the bottom of the ocean. It's metaphorical about death."

"Like an afterlife?" I ask.

Frank nods.

"It was to frighten sailors, a stern lesson to keep an eye on the waves and the weather," Derek replies. "If a ship sails into a storm, the sea will swallow them whole. The souls and ships are condemned to the bottom of the deepest pits forever."

I laugh nervously. "But it's a *story*, Derek. Like the Icarus myth about the boy who flew too close to the sun and his wax wings melted. He didn't listen to his father's instructions and perished as a consequence. Those stories were warnings, a moral to keep people safe. Davy Jones' Locker doesn't *actually* exist."

"We don't know for sure," Derek says.

Frank smiles wearily. "There's hundreds of folk stories about mermaids breeding with humans. Maybe they did and evolved into unusual people like Shae and Shy."

I laugh with unease again, but it sounds more like a snort of mockery.

"Jules, why is this idea such an alien concept to you?" Herb asks curiously.

"I'm a realist," I reply. "Things are black and white. They either make sense or they don't."

"So am I," Frank utters, "and I believe it."

I watch them. "So you're insinuating there are people walking around right now who could be a fucking mermaid or merman, but they don't know it?"

"Possibly. They could possess an element of Shy's heritage," Herb utters.

"They could be fantastic swimmers," Derek says.

"Or deep-sea divers, marine biologists," Frank adds.

"Therefore… Michael Phelps, the Olympic gold medallist, could genetically be a mermaid?" I ask disdainfully.

All three of them chuckle.

Derek smirks, his eyes seem brighter. "Jules, you're funny. It's a lovely thought but as we said, we don't know for sure."

"And what about mermaids *eating* sailors and sinking ships?" I ask.

"It's gruesome but it probably happened." Frank leans forward, resting his chin on his fist. "I want to ask you a question. When Shy touched you, did you *see* anything?"

My heart freezes and a bead of sweat trickles down my back. "What do you mean?"

"I want to know," he says. "Did you see any pictures or… have any dreams?"

I stare at them all, blood's pumping in my ears.

"Answer the question Dad," Em mutters, sounding annoyed with me.

"Yeah, I did. I saw the calf, the one you took to the Sea Life Centre. Then I started having dreams about these strange people from the ocean."

"Shy showed you her history," Frank utters. "Drake Cove in its early years, back when the Vikings invaded England somewhere around 800 AD."

"How did you know it was her history for sure?" I ask.

"We've clearly had the same dreams. Erik fell in love with Octavia, the queen of the sea. Ursula the Usurper took over because Erik fathered a child with a mermaid, an enemy of their village."

"River attacked after Ursula captured Octavia," I say, watching Frank.

He nods slowly. "Ursula was going to execute the queen as a warning."

"But she died anyway," I sigh.

"Suffocated." Frank glances down at his feet. "Octavia needed water to live. Ursula was cunning enough to keep her dry, and the queen perished. In despair, River executed Ursula, and her people slaughtered the rest of the village."

"*Fucking hell.*" I slump against the sofa, my brain wants to explode.

Frank smiles at me. "That's the thing especially with human history, it can be altered. Things are forgotten, secrets erased and falsehoods followed. Shy's can't be."

"You're right," Derek says. "The appearance of Queen Cleopatra is still being widely debated. We'll never know what she truly looked like."

Herb nods. "Exactly, the ancient Egyptians didn't write their history down. We only know accounts written *about* Cleopatra. They can put their own spin on it."

"Why did River have sharp teeth?" Em asks.

My heart jumps in my chest. "You've had the dreams

too?!"

"Yeah but I didn't think anything of it, Dad."

Frank smirks gleefully as if he's enjoying this. "Well, you both saw what horror she achieved. She sharpened them. For combat. Another handy weapon."

Em grimaces. "River spitting out Ursula's ear was grizzly. What happened to Erik?"

"River set him free, but only just," Frank says. "The Drake Covians imprisoned him on Ursula's orders. Njor, Octavia and Erik's son, became king when he was of age."

"Erik died in Njor's arms on the beach," Em answers. "I found that part really sad."

Another deep smile spreads across Frank's face. "Shy showed both of you by touch. Her mother did the same with me. It's one of their many gifts, a form of communication. I felt sick after the first dream, just like you did, Jules."

This made so much sense why Octavia touched Erik in the first place. She was *speaking* to him. It was how Shy extracted my past from her fingertips. She was "talking" to that octopus and the fucking flowers in the garden. This is ridiculous.

"To share her unknown history, Shy must really like you," Frank says.

Em and I glance at each other, we don't know what to do with these invisible mementos of honour.

"The artwork in her room," Em says. "Is she painting her ancestry?"

Frank, Derek and Herb nod in agreement.

I rub my temples, trying to process my words. "Okay, if this whole thing *is* true. How come Shy seems to be the only one? Why aren't there more mermaids?"

"Like all living creatures. They could've died out,"

Herb replies.

"But their blood line kept going," I say. "Shae and Shy wouldn't exist if they'd gone extinct, so what happened to the rest of them?"

"Shae and Shy only saw pockets of their family tree. Shae never spoke about her parents," Frank sighs. "She was very lonely. Living a hermit's life in the ocean. It wouldn't surprise me if she was the product of a short-lived romance, placed in a basket like Moses and nature looked after her."

"You're losing me Frank with the starry-eyed shit…" I say.

"What he means is the mermaids would've *bred* with humans, diluting the gene pool," Herb adds. "Evolving into Shae and Shy."

"I haven't gone on trips just to research animal rights. I've been looking for Shae ever since she vanished," Frank says.

"Have you had any leads?" Em asks.

He shakes his head. "I just wish I knew what happened."

"I want to help," Em whispers.

Frank taps my daughter's cheek. "You're a sweet girl, but it's my duty. I owe it to Shae."

"And where is Shy now?" I ask.

"I don't know," Frank sighs.

"I need to help," Em demands. "Shy protected me from that creep. I owe her my life."

Herb and Derek glance at one another in alarm. "*What creep?!*"

Crikey, here we go.

After several additional glasses of wine, Em and I recite the dreadful story of the vile Keith Dench and Shy's heroic intervention. Derek and Herb nearly choke on their drinks. The number of words spoken this evening has left me in a state of bewilderment. The threads of fresh truth have overloaded my brain.

I join Frank on a walk and leave a sleepy Em at his house; Herb and Derek are keeping an eye on her. We stroll along the beach. The fresh air and spinning waves offer some kind of relief for everything I've heard.

"I'm sorry I lashed out at you," I say.

"I know you have a great deal of respect for Mike but...what I said about his feelings for Shae are true. I wish I was wrong. I didn't keep Shy to myself to get one up on him."

"Frank, if I'd fathered a kid and my best friend knew about it and didn't tell me. I'd be livid."

"How would you feel if you caught Hanna making love to another man? And what if that man had been your best friend?"

I think about it. "I'd be confused and upset."

"There you go," he says.

"I just think it's sad you let it break your relationship. I heard you two were really close, like brothers."

"We were."

"What if she's dead, Frank?" I ask. "In my first dream, Shae was covered in blood. You found blood in Drake's Mouth, what if it was hers?"

Wrinkles form around Frank's eyes. "If she's dead, then I'll feel even worse about Shy. Her mother was so much like Octavia, enchanting and gentle. But Shy...she's so fiery and wild, just like River. Mother and daughter turned out to be such different people but they shared the responsibility to protect nature from being destroyed."

I see a father in agony. I know the pain too well.

"Shy is a queen, Jules. It's in her blood." Frank points to the ocean. "She belongs here, and out there. When she's on land, the sea and life underneath call out to her. Earth and water are constantly at war in her heart."

I look out, her words swirling around my head. *Sometimes, I feel like I don't fit in at Drake Cove. As if I'm supposed to be somewhere else. No matter what I do, it's never gonna be enough.*

Where are you, Shy? What happened to you?

25

Julian: Two Months Later

If anyone's up there, I want a better fucking year for my family. With everything that's materialised, I don't like how all of this new information has played with my thoughts. I'm questioning the ethics of my hometown and people I've known my entire life. I haven't been thinking about Ian and Earl or the window incident as much either. The cases are still open and the police haven't found anything. It's as if the events of this summer have been swept under the rug, lost and forgotten.

Derek said nothing is private in Drake Cove: he's wrong. My town nurtures many dark secrets. It was the birth place of another race. I thought the FAAC were bad, but Shy's lineage, the "mermaids" she's descended from are even worse. My ancestors participated in the culling for one sole purpose, to survive. Not because they loved clotting the blue sea water into a violent red. I understand why it upset the mermaids because they communicated with the whales on some level, but they didn't need to kill us because of that.

Shy hasn't made an appearance since everything was laid out. Frank's checking online every day and he rang the police. Drew wasn't impressed, she thinks the reason Shy disappeared is because of the incident at the rally and dealing with Keith Dench. Every couple of days we go for a walk around town, investigating. Herb and Derek make

2

posters and plaster Shy's face all over the place. I check Drake's Mouth all the time. We even spent a weekend in Yearling handing out flyers, but nobody's recognised her. This might sound stupid, maybe I'm overthinking it but…did Shy leave because of me?

Her vanishing hasn't felt right from the beginning. We were in bed together that morning. The passionate act of sex was not her forte. She was nervous, I had to calm her down and take control. But then… on the same day, she takes her paintings, her clothes and we find Frank unconscious with the house in complete disarray. She didn't leave a note and she didn't own a mobile.

Emily's deeply engrossed in the whole situation, announcing herself as head researcher and spends most of her time investigating mermaids online, and she's stole my Alice Green mythology book. I've found her asleep with it lying by her head. She's asked constantly if she can tell Jordan about everything and we've said no, not until we've found more information… or Shy shows up. I just hope its soon.

Em's staying at Frank's, then Herb and Derek's on alternative weeks while I'm out at sea. I hope nobody gives her grief about this summer and her drunk fuck-up for a father.

It's an early wakeup call on my first day. I tiptoe into Em's room and give her a hug; she pops a kiss on my cheek and warns me to be careful. I'm available by text and phone so she can contact me anytime she wants. Most people think once you're out on the waves, it's no man's land. As long as you have a good signal and you're tapped into the ship's network, it's fine.

I meet Mike and the others at the office. We catch a

bus to Yearling and grab a greasy breakfast before boarding my new workplace. I completely underestimate Matthew Waldemar's ship, The Molly. She's a big girl, much larger than I thought. She reminds me of the Mission Ark, the whaling ship on YouTube. I wasn't expecting Waldemar to be on the ship with us. He doesn't seem to be the type to get his hands dirty. He's too clean, not enough scars and dirt marks to convince me.

We sit in the bridge as Waldemar introduces us to his team, the main ones anyway.

Captain Jim Nielson is around the same age as Frank and Mike. He has the same large barrel chest and strong arms. He's kind, friendly and doesn't seem to have any barriers up. It shows in his honeycomb eyes.

Molly's first mate and the only female on the ship is Connie Mulvehill. Her blonde hair's lashed up in a pony tail and she stands with an energetic strength. She shakes our hands confidently, joking about being the resident dogsbody who flushes the spiders when the boys are too scared to do it themselves.

"You wouldn't do well in the olden days," Mike replies, smiling from ear to ear. "It was bad luck to have a woman on-board for a long voyage."

"I know, glad things are better now," Connie replies. "If I receive any lip from anybody, they'll be thrown over."

"She's not joking," Jim says proudly. "One of my seamen found out the hard way."

"He should've kept his trap shut," Connie shrugs.

I like her even more.

Craig O'Connor seems to act more as a bodyguard for Waldemar than a shipmate. His job title is Project Supervisor, a fancy term for keeping an eye on us and reporting back to Waldemar. This doesn't surprise me, seeing as he's made us sign a confidentiality statement. Craig says he's been working on the Molly for a long time, craning his way up from the bottom. He's a large muscly man who clearly takes care of himself. I wouldn't want to make eye contact with him at the pub.

After the initial introductions are made, Waldemar thanks us and excuses himself with Craig trailing after him. We're all given walkie talkies and Connie shows us around the Molly. She takes us to the main deck, the bow, the mast and so forth. The ship is composed of four decks. The second deck, just beneath us is the kitchen, accommodation and staff lounge. The engine room is on the third deck along with Waldemar's quarters which is prohibited unless presence has been requested. Then she takes us to the fourth deck, this is the area where all of the catches will be stored.

This isn't my first rodeo; we've all worked on ships and boats before. We've spent more time out at sea than we have driving on the road. There are fifteen other people working on the Molly, they all have their separate roles which Waldemar made clear is for one purpose, to keep the ship running smoothly.

Connie shows us to our rooms and hands over the keys. The staff quarters are tiny, a narrow space with metallic single beds reminding me of the military. I share a room with Lance. Damien's with Mike and Dan has one by himself. There's a communal shower. Great, this is gonna be fun to coordinate.

Afterwards, I stand on the main deck watching the shore float away. I feel an incredible ache in my chest. I hate being torn from Emily. I know she's a tough cookie but she doesn't have her mum with her, not this time around. Frank, Herb and Derek are amazing people but they can't replace Hanna.

"Mayday, mayday," Lance jokes into his walkie talkie.

I'm about to respond when Connie's scornful voice crackles through the speaker.

"*Fancy a walk along the plank?*" she asks. "*I'm happy to give you a crash course.*"

"Nope!" Lance replies.

"*Keep the channels clear for essentials and emergencies. Okay?*"

"Sure thing," Lance squeaks. "Sorry."

"Sounds like a ball breaker," Damien utters.

"She's the only female," I say. "She's had to be tough."

I close my eyes, breathing in and out, feeling the ship purr beneath me. I repeat the actions several times, thinking about Davy Jones' Locker and how many souls may have perished, doomed forever to the depths. Is it real? Are the lingering spirits of the Titanic trapped at the bottom of the ocean? Would mermaids really devour sailors?

I lean up against the railings and glance at the other end of the deck. I spot the harpoon guns. They look just as lethal as the ones on the Mission Ark.

Mike stands with his arms crossed; he's talking to Connie. I don't know where Dan's scarpered off to. When I think about it, I'm glad I'm not sharing a bunk with Mike. Every time I see him, I'm reminded of what I know. He's one of my closest friends and I have to keep it a secret. I hate this.

In the evening, we all have dinner in the lounge. It's dark outside, the outline of the moonlight shimmers on the water. I meet Bran, the ship's cook. He's young, in his mid-twenties and a former marine. He's been working for

Waldemar for about a year after he came out of the navy. He's made us spaghetti bolognaise; it smells wonderful. I meet some of the other crew. Connie introduces us as "our fishermen" and one of them is Tony, the chief engineer. I'd seen him in the engine room earlier in the day.

The others ask about the culling and our "killing methods", none of them have eaten whale blubber or witnessed whaling before. Then they start speculating about the FAAC. That's when Ian and Earl bleed into the conversation. My heart aches when I hear their names. In a fucked-up kind of way, I feel like I'm famous.

~

After eating and socialising, I retire to bed. I always have complications on the first night of sleeping in a brand-new place, it's the same whenever I go on holiday. Lance snores like a window rattler and I listen to music on my phone. My thoughts race to Shy and my dreams engulf me.

I'm walking along the ocean bed. Old wooden ships lie dotted about, drowned and tattered from the waves. Above my head is a pod of whales swimming and circling, singing their hauntingly beautiful songs. I reckon I'm about six hundred fathoms from the surface. In front of me, there's a congregation. Several lines of shadows face outwards. My steps are slow as the water and sand cushion my feet. My mum used to say walking in dreams was similar to wading through treacle. Skeletons and rotten corpses with gnarled flesh crouch on one knee, their heads stooped in a religious bow. Then I realise who they're worshipping...

She sits on a stone carved throne. Her green hair's waving weightlessly the way seaweed sways with the direction of the current. The same shell crown Octavia wore is around her head, she's clutching a long stone spear in her right hand.

I walk through the aisle of lost souls, stepping up to the throne.

Shy...

My voice echoes around me. Some of the skeletons are watching.

Shy...

I touch the bottom of her chin; her eyes open softly. Shae's dark sultry eye and Mike's watery blue shine back.

Are you okay?

She stares at me blankly.

Where are you?

Electricity sparks in her eyes and she grimaces before letting out a raw, harrowing ear-piercing scream.

I jolt awake, her voice is still vibrating in my ears. Sweat's pouring off me.

26

Emily

It feels weird having breakfast on my own now Dad's gone off on this fishing job. When Mum was around, she used to eat with me and sometimes, she walked me to school when she felt up to it. My uncles have offered but I'm nearly fifteen, I don't really need a chaperone anymore. Herb and Derek are already up when I stay at theirs. They seem frantic to get the shop open. It must be hard to run a business. Frank's up early too, I can hear him clattering around in the kitchen, switching on the kettle to make his coffee. I appreciate my uncles looking after me, but I prefer being in my own home, in my own bed with Keira wrapped around my feet. I just feel like a burden right now.

I can't wait for Dad to come back. We've videocalled a couple of times where his fuzzy face pixelates like he's composed of puzzle pieces. He seems cheerier though, maybe being away from Drake Cove is finally doing him some good. It makes sense, a different setting, a new crew to befriend, it's probably a massive breath of fresh air after everything that's happened. It must be strange being around Uncle Mike.

If Mum was still alive, she would've loved the idea of mermaids living beneath our little town. She was the one who introduced me to the fantastical world of movies and books. She used to tell me about those old Greek myths, like the tale Dad mentioned of Icarus flying too close to the sun.

On the weekends, I'm trying to do as much research as I can to find Shy. I've digested the Alice Green book and I've concluded that whatever species of mermaid Shy is, Green hasn't recorded it. There are several legends about people who came from the sea and they differ from culture to culture. Seriously, there are *hundreds* of videos about mermaid mythology on YouTube and I'm trying to sift through them. I've written several pages of notes, just from the videos.

Jordan and I passed our sailing exams which is pretty cool but we can't sail unsupervised until we're older. I can't tell him about Shy either which blows on a massive scale.

"What are we doing in here?" Jordan asks as we clamber into Drake's Mouth. "I thought we were going out on Henna for a bit. My dad said he'd accompany us."

"We are," I reply. "I want to do something in here first."

"What's to do in here?" Jordan's eyebrow rises suspiciously. "It's a shit hole."

I take my swimming costume from my bag. It's like a scuba diving outfit except I don't have any oxygen tanks. "I want to search the hole."

My best friend follows my eyeline and scowls in confusion. "But there's nothing there. It's just water."

"I need you," I reply hastily.

Jordan stares at me in shock.

"*Ew*. No, no, no, not in that way!" I take the rope from my bag. "I need you to tie this around my waist, so you can pull me out. I don't know how deep it goes."

"Em, why are you doing this in the first place?" he asks.

Think, come on, brain. "I'm… doing it for a project."

"What project?" Jordan asks sceptically.

"A poetry … project."

Jordan's scowl deepens even more. "You've started your blog again?! But your dad said you can't?!"

"*Photography!*" I blurt. "It's a photography project okay!"

"Did you bring a camera?"

Shit, I really didn't think this through. "No, I'm just doing some scouting. I really want to get into photography though. Underwater photos look really cool."

Jordan squints as if he's mulling over what I've said. He has a really good nose for sniffing out bullshit. "Okay, fine but we could've done this somewhere else," he says. "I'm scared you're gonna get stuck."

"I won't. I'm just having a look. I'm not swimming around. Just lower me up and down."

"I don't know, Em," he utters. "I don't like it."

"Come on, just a little dip. You can time me if you want."

"Fine, you've got two minutes. Then I'm pulling you out."

Bugger, I was hoping for longer but he's bought my little white lie so I won't complain.

"Can you hold your breath for two minutes?" he asks.

"No, probably not. I'll yank on the rope and you can pull me out. Can you look away?"

He turns his back, covering his face with embarrassment.

I pull off my clothes and shimmy into my swimming costume. "Can you zip me up?"

Jordan does so and laces the rope around my waist. "It's like you're on a leash, this is weird."

I chuckle nervously as his big hands squeeze the rope into a tight knot. He's done it pretty snug. "Are you ready?" he asks.

I snap on my goggles. "Yep, I'm ready."

Jordan takes out his phone, clicking the timer. "Okay, your two minutes start... *now.*"

The green from his phone lights up in the innards of the cave and the white numbers twitch. I lower myself into the water, the coldness nibbles at my bare feet. I switch on my waterproof flashlight. I take in a huge gulf of oxygen. Hundreds of pins and needles nip the side of my face when I'm fully submerged. I scan the flashlight against the rocks around me. It looks like a gloomy bottomless pit. I don't see how Shy thought protecting the whale calf in this awful place was a good idea. It's bleak and - there's no light with the exception of my torch. There's no other life signs either, not even any seaweed. It's a wall of rock, no wonder the poor thing got sick. *And*, there's no room in here. Baby whales are fucking huge, she would've been cramped like sardines in a crushed tin.

I push myself forwards with my other arm, navigating my way, spinning in a circle as I conduct my inspection. Something twinkles up in the corner of my view and I edge closer. It's lodged between the crevices in the rocks, it's flickering against the glare of the flashlight. I move over and yank at whatever's in there.

Damn.

It's really wedged in.

I pull again, using my legs as leverage, tensing the muscles in my thighs. Whatever it is, snaps from the wall and falls into my palm. The tightness of the rope burns into my belly. It's tugging. My body drifts to the surface. Jordan's arms loop around my waist and he yanks me out of the water. We fall into a tumble and I cough, gazing up at him.

"For fuck's sake, Emily!" he yells. His hoodie's soaking, the dampness is bleeding up the fabric to his shoulders. "I thought you weren't coming up! Are you okay?!"

I cough again, spluttering from the water. "I'm f-fine. H-honestly."

"What's that?" Jordan asks, eyeing what's gripped between my slippery fingers.

Shit. I don't know what to do or what to say.

"*Em*," Jordan presses, his eyes are darkening. "What the hell is it?!"

I'm sorry, Dad.

I have to tell someone.

I can't keep this to myself.

27

Julian

It's the big day.

After a flush of coffee and toast, Mike and Jim spot a pod of blue whales looming nearby. The water's slightly choppy, the clouds are grey but on the whole, it's good working conditions. The day before, Craig trained us on the two gigantic harpoons. They're even more intimidating up close and the bolts... are fucking menacing.

We change into uniforms, donning thick protective crash helmets. I've been paired with Damien to man one gun; Lance and Dan are on the other. For some reason, Mike isn't with us, he's up on the bridge with Jim. I'm not sure why. This gruesome job is why we were hired, maybe it's to keep an eye on the pod or to see if there are any others lingering around.

Our unusual work's drawn attention and up on the top deck, Connie, Bran, Tony and the other crew members lean on the railings, watching us. I don't have a surge of adrenaline like I normally do when I'm at the culling. The added pressure of everyone's eyes on us isn't helping either.

Molly dips and sways as her nose pierces the water. We ride along with the pod. Whales are solitary creatures; they glide slowly through the sea and they aren't afraid of juggernauts like massive ships swaying past.

"*Right, steady...*" Craig utters, his hand's up like an army sergeant.

For the first catch, I'm positioned behind the harpoon. Damien's by my side, holding on. Seeing the blue whales in real time takes my breath away for a few moments and a swell of nausea brews inside me. I point the barrel at the waves, feeling like I'm heading into battle, waiting for the command to unleash our weaponry on the enemy. The largest whale cranes its speckled head, looking straight at me. I aim the harpoon right at its face. The whale glares back, it must know what I'm about to do.

"*Now!*" Craig shouts.

I press the trigger, so does Dan and the vibration of the harpoon rumbles in my palm. We're engulfed in silence as we watch the bolt fly through the air, causing water spray to shower us. The bolt pierces the whales face and a pain erupts in my jaw. I'm losing my footing and I stumble onto the deck.

"Jesus Christ, Jules!" Damien blurts, holding onto the harpoon.

I'm kneeling on all fours, trying to breathe through streams as the pain intensifies in my face. I hear the strain of the rope. Damien and Craig are pulling on the harpoon, trying to make sure the impaled whale doesn't swim off.

A scream jets through my ears, piercing the inside of my head. I'm howling like a squealing pig at a slaughter house.

"Keep going!" Lance shouts. "*Someone help Julian for fuck's sake!*"

Hectic voices crackle through the walkie talkies. I hear the flapping tails of the whales. Agony intensifies in my chest, as if someone's prying my ribcage apart. I flip onto my back, eyes I don't recognise circle me, different voices spill over one another. I can't understand them.

Over their shoulders, Waldemar watches from the top

deck.

He's smirking.

The bastard's actually *enjoying* my agony.

Mike's face seeps into view, his eyes filled with worry. He tries to touch me but I flinch. My body's convulsing. Red and black mist swarm around my eyesight. The pain's electrifying now. My voice croaks as I try to shout that I'm gonna pass out. On the last syllable, the darkness swallows me whole and I fall.

I keep falling.

I'm wading in water, swamped in pure painless silence. I thought I'd perished on the Molly. Then I realise below me whales circle, their songs don't sound beautiful anymore. Gloomy shapes grow from the ocean bed.

River pops up from the surface, her eyes darken as she stares at me. Several other heads emerge, fuck, it's more of the sea tribe. River shouts and they charge forwards. I paddle in the other direction with urgency, my limbs creating white froth in the water. One of the sea people slams into my shoulder, knocking me underneath - another cracks my leg, yanking me deeper into the darkness. My chest's getting tighter. My air supply's diminishing.

River bucks her legs, performing powerful butterfly kicks. She's got a fucking dagger in her hand. I scream and the last remaining life bubbles escape my lips.

Green hair bleeds into my vision. Shy grabs me by the collar, pulling me across the waves and heaves me out onto the shore. Oxygen fills my lungs as I retch. Shy sits me up, water's dripping from her hair. She doesn't look well. She's thinner with dark purple rings sitting under her different colour eyes. I try to say her name but instead, she presses her lips against mine, breathing life back into me.

"*He's awake*," someone says.

The tips of the waves gleam and dance across the ceiling of my room. Shy's face slowly fades away and my body jolts. I blink, staring up at greyish the drab, the old scent of paint drifts under my nose.

"Don't get up just yet mate," Mike says.

"W-What happened?" I groan.

"You fainted. Thank fuck for first aid training," Connie replies. "You worried us sick! Four of us had to carry you in here. I'm glad we didn't have to use the defibrillator."

I sit up in bed. "I'm sorry, I…"

"Are you in any pain?" Mike stands by the door.

"No, I'm fine."

"Bran made you some chicken soup," Connie says gently.

My stomach rumbles when she hands me a bowl of creamy froth and broken pieces of bread. I rip into them like I hadn't eaten in weeks.

"Are the whales dead?" I ask.

Mike nods. "The meat's already chopped up. It's stored in the hull. Some of the staff had to help hose the deck down."

"I didn't realise there'd be so much blood," Connie utters.

Mike rubs the back of his neck. "The messy clean-up's a part of the job sadly."

"I better head back to work," she states.

Connie disappears out of the room and Mike sits on Lance's bed.

"Do you want to go home?" he asks.

"What?" I crunch my bread. "No, I'm here to work."

"Jules, I can't have you pass out on us again. Matthew

228

hired us by the skin of our teeth. He hasn't paid you to come on a fishing holiday."

"He seemed to enjoy watching my torment earlier."

Shock pinches at his face and then he laughs uncomfortably. "*What?*"

"He was smiling! I'm serious, Mike. The guy gives me the creeps."

"Well, don't say that in front of him. That's all I fucking need. Anyway, he wants to see you later."

"What about?" I ask.

Mike shrugs. "No idea, he didn't say. I'm just worried he's gonna sack you."

"Fucking wonderful," I mutter.

Mike watches me for a moment. "Shy Blothio is Frank's niece, isn't she? The woman with the green hair? The one who's gone missing?"

I cough, taking the bread out of my mouth. "What do you mean?"

"I was just wondering. You were saying her name in your sleep."

Shit. "Oh, was I? That's weird?"

"Lance and Damien were right - you do have a love interest floating around. It's her, isn't it?"

A lump forms in my throat as he stares at me. "Yeah... well, we kissed a couple of months back but... I don't think it was serious."

"What makes you say that?" he asks.

I hold up my hand so he can see my gold wedding band.

Mike acknowledges it, scratching the back of his neck as if he wanted to say something but has second thoughts. "Again, do you wanna go home? I'm sure Matthew will understand. Jim can telephone for someone to pick you up?"

"And what would I do?" I ask.

"Look after the office. You could do some admin work. I've got a load of filing that needs sorting out. Heck, having you there might help."

"Nah, me and the office don't mix."

"You could guard it so the FAAC don't burn it down." Mike irons the creases of his jeans with his fingers. "Are you *sure* you wanna stay?"

"I need to be out here, Mike. I need the money. I don't know why I fainted. Maybe it was the harpoon gun... it freaked me out. I didn't like everyone watching us. I thought Waldemar would've hired people who'd seen all this shit before."

"He hires who he wants. That's how professional whaling's done, with big fuck-off harpoon guns." Mike gets up from the bed, staring at me worryingly. "Alright, mate. You can stay, just no more fainting, okay?"

I grin at him. "I'm fine now. I promise."

"Good, we need you out here."

He nods tiredly and leaves the room. The appeal of the thick creamy soup soon evaporates. I don't understand why I was in so much pain. It happened the second I shot the whale. It knew its time was up.

~

Sleep drifts in and out like the tide. I twist and turn, trying to get comfortable but I can't. I don't want to let my team down but...the pain and that scream, it was impossible to shut out. My phone buzzes by my head, it's Frank on video call. I wonder what he wants.

"Jules, are you alright?" he asks. *"You look awful."*

"Thanks Frank." I rub my eyes and yawn. "I've had a really rough day. It was my first attempt at professional whaling."

"*Oh, how'd it go?*"

"Terribly."

Frank smiles. "*Good, I hope the whales flee.*"

"No, we got them all. Sorry. They're sitting in cubes in the hull right now."

"*Then why did it go terribly?*"

"When I was manning the harpoon, I shot one of the whales and felt the worst pain I've ever experienced in my life. It was like someone was stabbing me in the face over and over again. More intense than being kicked in the bollocks." The screen shakes as I balance my phone in my other hand. "The rest of the crew thought I was having a cardiac arrest or something. I've been in my room most of the day. They'll probably think I'm skiving." I wait for a response but nothing arrives. "Frank? Is there something on your mind?"

He blinks several times, his eyes flickering off camera for a moment. "*No, why?*"

"You look anxious."

"*It's nothing. I'm just tired. The promo for my book launch's knackering me out. Did you tell Emily about what happened on the ship?*"

"Yeah, she knows. The sleep's helped but…I had a nightmare."

"*What did you see?*"

"I was in the ocean. River was after me, and her people were knocking me around."

"*They were trying to tire you out. It's a hunting technique. Orcas do it to kill their prey. Most predators hunt in packs like lionesses, wolves, hyenas, even ants.*"

"Fantastic, just what I wanted to be. Mermaid bait."

"*Anything else happen?*"

231

"I was about to drown but… Shy saved me. She didn't look good, Frank. She was unhealthy, like she hadn't eaten or slept in days."

Frank asks with concern. "*Did you see anything else?*"

"No, I woke up after that. Do you reckon it means anything?"

Frank shakes his head. "*I don't know. I hope it doesn't. Shy looking anaemic will just make me worry even more. You could be having these nightmares from the shock of finding out about all of this…plus, you're concerned for her. We all are. I had nightmares too when Shae disappeared, some of them were pretty horrific. Her screaming in the dark, pleading for me to help her. They stopped after a while, after I'd processed everything.*"

"Maybe I need to start thinking about other things," I answer. "I'm not saying I don't care about Shy's whereabouts because I do."

"*Don't worry, Jules. Focusing on something else is a good idea. Try to not think about those dreams. It's your brain unwinding in your sleep, sadly we can't control how our subconscious acts when we're counting sheep.*"

"Anyway, enough about me. Has Em been behaving herself?"

"*Well, your daughter's become quite the explorer,*" Frank replies.

My heart palpitates. "What do you mean?"

Em's fresh face slides into view of the camera. "*Oh reeelax, Dad. It's always doom and gloom with you. It's nothing to worry about. I was the one who asked Frank to call in the first place.*"

My mind's racing a million miles. "Okay, what does Frank mean about exploring?"

"*I found this in Drake's Mouth.*" Em holds up two

pieces of metal.

With closer inspection, it's something I've seen before but it's shinier and has a decorative pattern engraved on the side. "That's Erik's whistle."

Frank and Em nod.

"It can't be the same one," I utter. "His was made of wood."

Frank takes the broken whistle from Emily and turns them between his fingers as if it's on a rotating display. *"You're right about that. This one's a later model."*

"It looks fancier," I say. "Do you know who made it?"

"No, not right now. I reckon it was an ancestor of Drake Cove. It was how Erik communicated with Octavia and Njor. I might take it to a historian I know and get his take on it."

I wonder if Shy knew about the whistle. Drake's Mouth was an important place to her tribe, it made sense why Shy was so attached to it. She was born there, so was Njor.

Em turns to Frank. *"Why don't we write to Alice Green? She might know something?"*

"It wouldn't hurt," I reply.

"I reckon Shae and Shy's kind made them to speak to us." Em's eyes glow as she speaks. I'm happy to see her enjoying herself, no matter how much all of this mystical stuff is messing with my head. *"It just proves this whole time... mermaids do exist."*

I smirk at Frank. "I think you've turned her into a believer."

He laughs, glancing at Emily. *"You'd be proud of her, Jules. She's putting Lara Croft to shame."*

There's an awkward silence when I walk into the lounge for dinner. Everyone's judging me. Dan and Lance are the first ones to mock my "little spin." I laugh it off the best I can. I wish they'd shut the fuck up and talk about something else. Bran's shepherd's pie is mouth-watering, probably one of the best pies I've ever tasted. For a nightcap, we have hot chocolate and brandy, which tastes glorious but it doesn't do my subconscious any good. In fact, it cranks my nightmares up a notch. It's worse than the previous one.

~

The top deck of the Molly is plunged into chaos, people are running amok with terrified curdling screams. The sea people are crawling all over the place, hunting my friends and colleagues with stone spears. The same weapon Shy was holding when she was sitting on her throne.

Lance is running and screaming. River's close behind him; blood's smeared across her mouth, streaking her sharp teeth. She's not stalking Lance, she's playing with him, there's a childish skip to her step. She raises her spear, squinting with one eye and hurls it into the air. It flies soundlessly and slices through Lance's chest within seconds. He drops to his knees, slouching forward, dying instantly.

I shout at River, anger spitting out between my teeth. I want to kill her. I want her to experience the pain she's inflicted on others. Someone kicks me in the back of my knees and yanks my arms to the side. Two or three of the other sea people have my arms wrenched in a lock and they're twisting my skin. It's burning.

River hisses at me, making her way over to the top deck. She casts her spear to the ground, locking her gaze on mine and slides over the bars. She grabs someone out of my line of sight.

Em squeals in River's arms, the sea bitch is pressing her

dagger down on my kid's neck.

"Let her go," I say. "She's not involved in this."

River wraps herself around Em even more as if her limbs are made of locks and chains.

"Dad!" Em shrieks.

"It's okay, I'm gonna sort this out." I turn my attention back to River. "Let her go. You've won. You've made your fucking point. I won't whale anymore. I'll become a vegetarian. I'll do anything you ask. Please."

River watches me, her sadistic eyes leering. The sharp tip of her dagger's edging at the hollow of Emily's throat and my child's eyes well up with tears.

An eye for an eye, the scaly voice cuts into me, shivering down my spine. *A heart for a heart.*

"Please," I cry.

Another scream booms down on the deck and a foot collides with River's face. Em's hurled into my arms and the others release me. I pull Em to me, scurrying across the floor where I see Shy standing on the lower deck, glaring down at River. They hiss at each other; the members of the sea tribe congregate around them forming a weird fight ring.

Shy throws herself at River and the violence begins. I hope she rips her fucking head off.

River punches Shy square in the jaw and she goes down, smacking the deck. A member of the sea tribe throws River another stone spear and she catches it, wiping the blood from her nose. She turns to face us, squinting as she takes aim.

Em screams against my chest, burrowing into me. Shy grabs the other end of River's spear, pulling her around, smacking her up against the bars of the ship. She pushes the spear against River's cheek, gritting her teeth, grimacing from the strain. Her muscles flex and intensify, draining to keep her at bay.

That crazy smile stretches across River's mouth as her eyes lock with mine. She curls her arm around the back of Shy's head, slamming her face against the rails. I yell. Shy bounces off the metal, unconscious and River drives her razor teeth into her throat.

28

Emily

I wrap my hands around a mug of hot chocolate. I scared the living bejesus out of Jordan earlier, waking him up in such a fright. I tell him every detail of my dream. Well, it wasn't a fucking dream, it was a bloody nightmare. I know Dad and Frank are gonna be pissed that I've told Jordan but he won't tell a soul. Plus, he's met Shy before and he knows she's not ordinary. Since I've told him, he's expressed an interest in helping out and he's really concerned for her wellbeing. Shy's our friend, we want to know if she's okay.

"And Mike has no idea Shy's his daughter?" Jordan asks.

I shake my head. "No clue. Frank said we can't tell him either. It'll be too messy."

"Damn it. This whole thing's just...crackers," my best friend says. "I mean, it's fascinating but it's so fucked up at the same time. You're right about her eyes, that blue one of hers is similar to Mike's. What if he killed Shae?"

"No way," I say between sips.

"Why not?"

"Uncle Mike's not like that. He's not a violent person. He's faced a lot of shit in his time. He's had to deal with those horrible animal activists breathing down his neck for years and he's never raised a fist to them."

"True, he's not violent… *now*. But Shae went missing when Frank and Mike were younger, in their late twenties, he could've been aggressive back then."

"Nah, … I reckon Mike knows more than Frank lets on. He paints him in a really bad light. Regardless of his jealousy, Mike and Shae were *intimate*. I know people shag because they're horny but…Mike seems too guarded for a one-night stand. I think there's more behind that passionate night. Think about it. We've known Mike our whole lives and has he *ever* talked about a girlfriend or a romantic partner?"

"No, he keeps his cards close to his chest," Jordan replies.

"Exactly. I wish I could pick his brains. It might lead us to where's Shy scarpered off to."

"Or what happened to Shae…"

I roll my eyes. "Whatever."

"We should check out their office. There may be answers."

My temperature shoots up. "What do you mean? Break in? We can't do that! What if we get caught? What would the police say? *What were you two doing? Oh sorry Sir, we were looking for information about a missing mermaid.* They'll lock us up!"

"They can't, we're teenagers," Jordan says. "We're at an age where we can get away with pretty much anything we want. Remember that video I showed you from last year?"

"You show me *a lot* of videos, Jord."

"True but remember those kids riding their bikes in the supermarket and they were chucking food on the floor?"

"Oh yeah, those stupid dickheads. My dad would've made me apologise, pulling me by my hair if I'd behaved that way. What's your point?"

"We're not attention whores like those kids. We're doing this to help Shy." He leans back in his huge blue bean bag. "Come on, what else will you do? Go through more YouTube videos? This is perfect timing. Nobody's there. They're all out at sea."

"And what do we do if there's security cameras?"

Jordan laughs. "They don't have any, silly. It's an old bloody hut. Do you'd think I'd suggest it if they did?!"

"Forget it. We're not spies. It's too dangerous."

"Your dad must have a key."

"Maybe, I'm not sure. I don't think he locks up though. Uncle Mike and Dan do it."

"Because if he does, we can just let ourselves in."

"And what if someone sees us?! What if we run into the FAA bloody C?! They'll beat us up!"

Jordan rolls his eyes. "God, you've got no sense of adventure in you at all. I didn't see hesitation the other day."

"Shut up."

"Nothing is standing in your way. Look at what you found because you took the plunge."

"*Oh God. Fine then!*" I say. "We'll go to mine first and check if there's a key."

Jordan crawls over to his chest of drawers and chucks black t-shirts, jumpers, joggers and woolly hats at me.

I turn my back as he changes out of his pyjamas, my face is glowing red. "We're not ninjas!"

~

I think Dad's right about our friendship. I am a bad influence. Normally, I'm the devil creeping on someone's shoulder and Jordan's the angel offering reasonable advice. I'm the one who invited that creep to his birthday party. Now, I've upped my level when it comes to mischievousness. If I'd kept my mouth shut about Shy and all of this mess, I'd be lying on Jordan's bedroom floor, trying not to wake him, performing yogic breathing to relax my heartbeat.

After we change, we sneak out of the window. How his parents don't hear us, I don't know. Maybe lady luck's on our side. Jordan's an only child too, and he lives in a bungalow, his bedroom faces the sea. His home is up near Becks Hill, the beautiful view is like something out of one of Shy's paintings.

We check my home first and I find a jumble of keys. There are several rusty ones. I know some of their functions but sadly not the others so I bring them all with me. We have a plan if we get caught. As I'm the daughter of one of the workers – I will say I'm watching the office while they're away. I know it won't hold water for long. Jordan says I can abuse the sympathy card. Being motherless, I can switch on the tears. Well, if it works, then I'll use it. I've got plenty of shadowy crap floating around my head to tap into.

Dad's office is in darkness when we arrive. Sometimes when I walk past, I can see the outline of Uncle Mike typing at his computer or the others sitting on the sofa. Not this time. Jordan's right, they don't have security cameras. You'd think with the amount of daily hassle they receive from the FAAC; Mike and Dan would've given the place a shiny upgrade.

We try several keys I don't recognise, they don't do anything. Then I try a really rusty key, it's so old the copper skin flakes off onto my gloves. I put it in the lock and it fucking works too. Thanks, lady luck.

I expect a siren to start blaring when the door swings

open. But it's just an eerie creak of the hinges. We step over the threshold and... nothing happens. Thank fuck.

I close the door quietly behind us and lock it. Jordan suddenly crouches like he's in an action movie. I have to smother an escaping giggle. We must look like a pair of lunatics.

"*Hey!*" he whispers. "Dan's computer is still on."

"So?" I ask. "What's he got to do with this?"

"I dunno, it might help."

We click on our flashlights and get to work. The glare from the screen shines against Jordan's face. I'm worried the light reflection will be detectable from outside.

"The first and last letters of his name must be his login," Jordan says, pointing at the screen as it reads: *dlcs*

"It's password protected," I say. "You won't be able to get into it."

"I'm sure we can find something." He pulls the drawers open in Dan's desk, his gloved fingers flip through heaps of papers.

I search the desk opposite Dan's, it's orderly and tidy. Too clean in fact, which gets my back right up. It's gotta be Mike's. "Make sure you leave everything as it was or we'll be rumbled."

"Don't worry. I know!" A stillness creeps on my friend's face. "Can I ask you a question?"

"Sure."

"Was Vanishing Acts about anyone in particular?"

"Jord, this is really not the time." I frown. "But if you must know, no it's not. Did you think it was about my mum?"

He winces. "Well, yeah."

"I don't wanna write about her."

"It might help, Em. You know, get your emotions out

and stuff. Poetry's great for it."

"No, Jordan. Leave it alone," I say.

"Have you thought about the other thing?"

"What?" I parrot. "Getting tested for Huntington's?"

He nods.

"*No.* Stop fucking asking me!"

"Okay, sorry!"

My attention snaps back to Uncle Mike's desk. I flip through what's on top, glancing through a big red book. The light from my torch strokes the paper. It's not an interesting read, just endless pages of dates and times of shifts, how much fish was weighed, where they were shipped to and the profit made. Dad was on a shift with Damien and Dan, they'd caught a hundred and fifty kilograms worth of haddock. I skim each page, nothing juicy jumps out and I put the book back in its original place.

On Mike's computer screen, a neon yellow post-it note reads:

Matthew Waldemar, the Molly, Yearling pier 8am sharp.

I take out my phone and snap a picture of it. At least I have the name of Dad's temporary employer and the ship he's working on. He hasn't told me much about the job, it's just fishing. Then a thought lights up in my mind, can ships be tracked?

Unlike Dan's desk, all of Mike's drawers are locked. None of the keys I have work. I can't break it open. In a weird way, I'm glad Mike's used his noggin and secured everything. I check the filing cabinet, that's locked too. The keys don't work on it either. I guess Dad isn't allowed an all-access pass. He should, he's been working for Mike for most of his life.

"Do you still feel pissed about your dad and Shy…?"

242

Jordan asks.

I look up at him. "I dunno. Maybe. But...seeing them together, kissing and... *the other stuff*. It... hurt."

"Because of your mum?"

"Well yeah, of course. But also...I felt protective."

"It's been a year, Em. Maybe your dad needs to start moving on. I mean, do you want him to be alone for the rest of his life?"

The question hangs in the air like smoke.

I boot up Mike's computer, watching as it hums to life. I have a hunch, I don't have a clue if it's gonna work but, there's no harm in trying is there. After the machine loads, I'm welcomed by the musical jingle of the Windows login page.

I type in: *mlbe.*

What would Mike use for a password?

If I make two incorrect attempts, it'll lock the computer. If Mike's backed up the security, he'll receive a text message informing him of a breach of his systems and then we're truly fucked.

Think. You've known this guy your entire life. It's gotta be personal; most of my passwords are. It could be a phrase, a name, a location. It's gotta be something none of his colleagues would be able to figure out, especially my dad.

A name...nobody would think of.

A name nobody would know...

My fingers hover over the keyboard.

s...h... a...e

I hit enter and wait.

My heart's jumping and I feel fleetingly warm.

The Windows icon swims in a circle as it processes the information.

I pray to lady luck to be on our side.

Come on, come on.

We're doing this for Shy.

We need to know she's okay.

Please, please, please.

Please.

The musical sound jingles again and my eyes snap open. "*Oh my God, I'm in.*"

"Seriously?!" Jordan exclaims.

"You were right, Mike *does* keep his cards close to his chest."

"I fucking knew it." His eyes widen at the computer screen. "*I'm in too!*"

Now mine was just a lucky guess. "How'd you do that?"

Jordan holds up a pocket-sized notebook. "Dan wrote the password on the back cover. It was under all of these invoices. He must've thought it was safe." He laughs, a deep buzz webbing from his throat. "Adults aren't very smart."

I don't know Dan very well; he didn't give off a friendly vibe. Dad doesn't have a high regard for him. He's a trouble maker.

I turn back to the screen and filter through Mike's folders. There's acres of word documents and Excel sheets, some are locked. They're pretty non-descript, payroll numbers, tables of sales and tax numbers, all that boring shit I'll have to figure out when I'm older.

"*What a cunt,*" Jordan says.

"What?" I ask.

There's an urgency in his voice. "Em. You need to have a look at this."

"What is it?" I ask again, hurrying over to him.

"I'm so sorry."

"Get on with it, Jord. You're scaring me."

He taps the mouse. The screen changes, words trickle in hurried paragraphs. I wanna cry when I understand the nature of it all. It's answered a puzzle my dad and I have been cracking our heads over.

I take out my phone, tapping the camera to video mode. "Start from the beginning."

Jordan scrolls down to the bottom of the screen and I press record.

29

Julian

Craig leads the way to Waldemar's quarters. I don't know why I've been summoned; maybe it's from my wobbly moment. I felt fine today when we were fishing. No pain in my chest or red and black mist creeping around my eyes.

We arrive at a white painted door. Craig knocks, his large bulky arms remind me of a burly bouncer standing outside a club doorway. If he donned a tuxedo, he'd be the ideal bodyguard. He bashes his hammy fist on the door again and after a couple of minutes, it opens.

"Yes?" Waldemar's demanding voice says.

"Mr Finch is here to see you, Sir," Craig answers.

Sir? He's not fucking royalty. He's just a businessman.

The door opens and Waldemar stands in a pristine dark blue suit. We're out at sea, there's no posh soirees or dinner parties here. He smiles at me. This bastard is always smiling.

"It's lovely to see you." He clocks Craig, nodding at him. "Come in, Julian. Make yourself at home."

I step over the threshold, glancing at Craig who's wearing a stone expression. He moves behind me, shuffling me into the room. I stare at the interior of Waldemar's office. There's a large shiny wooden desk, on top is the latest white apple Mac laptop.

There are several framed photos on the walls, some are

yellow with age and the edges crinkle. Numerous decanters probably filled with whiskey or brandy sit on the cabinet behind his chair. There's a black and white picture of a gruff looking man holding a gigantic dead plaice. Fishing must be in his blood. I still reckon Waldemar's never fished before.

He indicates to the chair in front of me. "There's no need to stand on my account."

I sit down. "Mike said you wanted to see me?"

"Yes, I did," he replies, repositioning the penholder on his desk.

Craig closes the door and stands off to the side behind me. I thought this would be a private meeting.

"How are you feeling?" Waldemar asks.

Oh great, here we go. "I'm much better now, thanks. I honestly don't know what happened back there." I glance to my side; I don't like Craig hovering. "I think I just had a bad turn."

"Yes, you seemed to be in a lot of pain."

"I was, not sure what triggered it. My home life's been quite stressful so it wouldn't surprise me if that was the cause."

Shockingly, Waldemar's eyes soften. "I'm aware of your personal issues. Michael and Daniel informed me of any necessary background information before we had our meeting."

"You're not annoyed at me for being ill on the job?" I ask.

"No, not at all. We all have our episodes. Stress can play a toll on our physical and mental health. I understand why it would cause you to feel unwell." He smiles at Craig momentarily, his gaze returning to me. "Craig's given me great feedback on your recent shift so it seems like you've recovered brilliantly."

I glance over my shoulder, nodding. "Thanks Craig." Inside, I'm relieved… and slightly unnerved when I turn back to Waldemar. "Okay, so what do you need to speak to me about?"

That slimy smile reappears. "I want your advice on something. I'm working on a little project. It's top secret." He holds my gaze. "Would you like to see?"

"Um." Well, I can't say no, can I. No wonder he made us sign a confidentiality agreement. "Yeah, okay."

"Follow me," Waldemar says, getting up from his chair.

I stand up and my heart plummets into my stomach.

How could I fucking miss them?!

They're propped up against the filing cabinet partially wrapped in brown paper. I was too fucking busy drinking in the luxuriousness of this office. I've only seen them in one other place. *Her bedroom.*

"Mr Finch?" Waldemar asks. "Are you feeling well?"

"Yes. I'm fine."

"Please…" he utters, watching. "Follow me."

There's another door, behind his desk, off to the side when I entered the office. I didn't clock it till now. Waldemar opens it, something in his eyes change. He's scanning me, teasing my reaction. Did he catch me noticing the paintings?

I edge inside and he clocks Craig, waving him off. "Stay here."

I don't like the way Waldemar spoke to him, as if his colleague is a bad smell or something.

We leave Craig in the office and walk through a mini corridor. I'm welcomed by the fresh pungent scent of cleaning products. It stinks like the waiting room of the dentist in here. Then I see it as clear as day.

A water tank sits in the middle of the room. Not as big as the ones I saw in the Sea Life Centre, but it's large enough for someone of my size.

She's floating weightlessly. Her green hair sways just like it did in my dream. Her body's shed so much muscle. Bones peak out from the top of her shoulders. Her eyes are closed, a mask covers her nose and mouth. White and black tubes weave around her arms and legs like vine plants. A red shiny collar's looped around her neck, spider leg chains spear out to the four corners of the tank. She wouldn't be able to get out easily.

"What is this?" I gasp with horror. "*What have you done to her?*"

Waldemar holds up his hands in surrender. "Hey, I haven't harmed her. She has sedation drugs trickling around her system right now. I had to administer them myself. She's a roughneck, almost broke my nose when I tried to examine her."

"Why are you showing me?"

He crosses his arms over his chest, grinning at the floating Shy as if she's a golden prize. "I know you've had some sort of relationship with this...*woman.* I saw those missing posters around town. I just want to know more about her... and her kind."

"Her kind?"

Waldemar frowns, walking over to another desk not far from the tank. "Oh, don't play dumb with me, Julian. Mermaids of course." He picks up a tiny handheld camera from the desk and places it in the drawer below. "I've had a fascination since I was a kid. My old man reckons he saw one. A dark-haired woman swimming in the ocean, with no boat or deep-sea diving apparatus. You see, when I came to your little fishing town, it was purely for business.

I wanted to see all of you in your field. On the day of the culling, I saw her dive off Drake's Tooth, and I just had my suspicions. And…I was right."

I place my hand up against the glass of the tank.

I think about the dreams and nightmares, was it her way of communicating with me?

"What's with the mask?" I ask.

"Oh, that? It's just a precaution," Waldemar replies. "She doesn't actually need oxygen."

Shy…

Her eyes flicker.

Fear fizzes from my core and I bite a bursting scream within me. Strands of her hair glide up to the glass as if they've got a mind of their own. The hair forms into the shape of a human hand, mapping the cushions of my palm and fingertips.

"She's remarkable isn't she," Waldemar answers softly. "Her hair? It's like another limb, a human tentacle. It's only active when she's fully submerged. When she's out on dry land, her hair's completely lifeless." Then he smiles greedily again. "I want to show you something else." He claps his hands musically and the lights around us diminish.

My free fist balls up by my side. "What's going on?!"

"Just wait," Waldemar whispers, "and see for yourself."

Seconds tick by until I notice something in the tank. A birth of green light beams from the centre of my palm. It starts off small, like a hovering firefly. The glow of light crawls along the strands of Shy's hair, growing in strength until it reaches her roots, cascading her body and my face in this beautiful, entrancing emerald blaze.

Oh my God.

Her hair.

It's alive.

"She's absolutely stunning," Waldemar says. "The deep-sea anglerfish light up in the dark as a way to entice their prey *and* warn off predators. Again, this only happens when she's fully in water." There's a beat of silence before he speaks. "She's never been this calm before. You seem to have a magnificent effect on her."

Can you hear me, Shy?

Her eyes flutter rapidly. Is she answering?

I'm sorry I doubted you and Frank. I'm gonna get you out of here. I promise.

Waldemar claps his hands, returning the lighting of the room to its original state. It stings my eyelids and Shy's luminous hair recoils from the side of the tank, fading like a flame.

"I found Frank knocked out when she'd gone missing," I say. "What happened to him?"

Waldemar smiles, his stare searching. "Well, I had to make sure my little enterprise wouldn't be compromised." He shrugs casually. "Craig dealt with Mr Blothio as he had to, by any means necessary."

I grab the leach by the shoulders, shoving his weight against the wall. Waldemar yelps loudly for Craig as I crunch my palm down on his throat. I glare right in his face. "You're nothing but a snivelling weasel!!"

30

Emily

Frank sits in his chair, leaning his head in his hands as we speak. His reading glasses are falling down the bridge of his nose. There's a heartbeat of peace before he lets rip.

"I told you with *every* nuance of seriousness that you were *not* to tell *anyone* about this, *Emily Finch!*"

"She didn't tell me," Jordan cuts in. "I kinda made her come clean about the whole thing. Em's behaviour's been off ever since and I had a feeling with Shy. She's pretty unique."

"You don't want to get involved, Jordan," Frank mutters.

"But I insist!" my best friend says. "Shy didn't just save Emily's life, she saved mine too. I want to help. I won't tell my parents, or my other friends. I promise."

I'm a little scared. Well, that's a lie, I'm shitting myself right now. "So, what do you think?" I ask.

"I think what you're saying is absolutely ridiculous," Frank retorts. "Do you have any idea how much trouble you could've been in if you'd got caught?"

"They'll never know we were there. We left everything in its original place," I say.

Frank points at me, stabbing his finger in the air. "You're hanging off by the skin of your teeth, my love. When your dad comes back, I'm telling him what you did."

"I'm not causing trouble to get attention. I'm trying to help my friend and we've discovered something horrible. Truth I wasn't looking for in the first place." I take out my phone and shove it in Frank's hands. "Press play. We're not bloody lying!"

We wait as Frank watches the video.

"So, what do you think?" I ask again, not masking my irritation. "Still think I'm overreacting?"

Frank looks up, his expression's a wash of shock and horror. "Have you told your dad?"

"I've tried but I can't get through," I reply. "His number keeps going to answerphone."

Frank gets to his feet, his eyes darkening and hardening. "What about Damien and Lance?"

"I don't have their numbers," I say.

"Mike's?"

I shake my head. "What are you thinking?"

Frank looks at me and Jordan. "We need to move quickly."

31

Julian

Grogginess fills my head as I regain consciousness. I was seconds away from throttling that piece of shit when everything went black. Craig knocked me out when his master was squealing for help.

I get to my feet, rather shakily. I'm in a room I don't recognise, it has white walls and a spotless floor. There are two black widescreen televisions hooked on the wall. I kick the door and pull at the handle. It's locked from the other side. Where's that pale-skinned freak? What's he doing to Shy?

Voices emerge from behind the door. There's a crank of a key in the lock and the door swings open. The chuckles of Lance, Damien, Mike and Dan are cut short when they see me in my anguished mess.

"Are you okay, mate?" Damien asks.

Waldemar walks in with that shit eating grin. I launch myself at him, spitting venom and curses. Lance and Damien grab me, prising me apart from the little mouse.

"Hold him back please!" Waldemar hisses, his eyes burning into mine. "Attempt to assault me again, Mr Finch and I will make sure Craig does ten times worse to you...and your girlfriend. Do you understand?"

Damien and Lance push me against the wall, their faces crumbled in confusion.

"What's going on here, Matthew?" Mike bellows. "You

don't speak to my staff like that!"

"Be quiet, Mr Blocksidge. You're in my domain and what I say goes." He wipes his suit, dusting off any creases. "Now, if you can all calm down. I have some information I'd like to disclose to you. It will make sense why Julian is so upset." Waldemar turns to the televisions on the wall and the screens spring to life. "I'm a business man as you all know, but I also have a little side hobby. I'm a bit of a detective."

"What the hell are you on about?" Mike asks.

"Do you believe in mermaids, Michael?" Waldemar teases, smirking at the corner of his mouth.

Mike doesn't respond but the blood drains from his skin.

Waldemar shrugs. "Well, I do. And I believe there's one living in Drake Cove. She's been there for quite a while, right under your very noses."

Damien and Lance look at each another nervously.

"She's done terrible things." Waldemar stares at me. "She's not who you think she is."

"Get to the fucking point," Dan sneers.

"Have patience, Mr Cripps." Waldemar pulls a phone from his pocket and uses one finger with precision to tap the screen.

The two screens change, twitching into grainy videos of a sandy sea shore.

"I know what happened to your colleagues," Waldemar warns. "This won't be pleasant viewing."

The images begin to move and we watch in silence. I recognise Drake Cove beach immediately from the curve of the neck to the tone of its skin. Ian's fishing with Serenity, he looks frustrated and tired. On the next screen, Earl is perched on the edge of a bunch of rocks, there's a can of cider next to him. He's fishing too, probably fetching tea for his family. There's no sound. It makes the footage even more sinister.

Something jumps out of the water and grabs Ian's rod, the same happens to Earl. There's a struggle and then they're pulled into the sea. Horrified gasps escape from my friends, and myself. Earl's legs flail as he tries to escape. I switch to the next screen and see Ian's legs jolt. Both of them twitch and flop, their bodies wade towards the shore... and I notice something. Long wavy feminine hair, a pair of eyes watching...

"*That fucking bitch!*" Damien yells, smacking his hand into the wall.

Lance begins to retch. Mike and Dan turn their heads, their glares silently accusing me.

No, no, no, no.

It can't be her. I saw her distress when she was watching the culling. I saw how emotional she got when Frank was attacked, she wouldn't do this. She wouldn't hurt anyone...

But...

Keith Dench...

Geoff Ward and Megaphone...

Oh God...

"You seem shocked, Mr Finch?" Waldemar asks. "I assume you didn't believe me?"

"Where did you get this footage?" Mike hisses. "Why hasn't this been sent to the police?!"

"I have my resources."

What the fuck does that mean? Who was filming? Why didn't they intervene and save my friends?

Waldemar switches off the televisions and stands perfectly still. "Now, I have two options I'd like to discuss.

I can tell you're all visibly distressed." He scans the room, judging and watching us. "The first option is... I send the videos to the police and they will deal with the woman accordingly..."

We all look at each other, searching for answers.

"And what's the second?" Lance asks.

He smiles unpleasantly. "The second option is my favourite. This little project of mine's been going on for a while, and the woman on the tape is incredibly valuable to me. Having her rotting behind bars will not be beneficial to my work. I will leave the room, and you can deal with her as you please. However, you cannot kill her. I need her alive. If you choose this option, you cannot tell anyone what you saw, *who* you saw and what you have done." Beats of silence swim past as he scans us all, his hands clasped in front of him as if he's making a pitch at a meeting. "So... what will it be?"

We stare at each other in confusion. I wish I knew what they were thinking.

"Option two," Dan answers.

"*What?*" I say out of dismay.

"Me too," Damien says.

"I'm with them," Lance utters.

"Guys, you can't be serious?" I say. "This is a mistake. It's not Shy Blothio. It's a set-up."

Damien glares at me. "Go fuck yourself, Jules. You stayed with that bitch and she was responsible for this!"

"I didn't know anything about it!" I yell back.

"I bet Frank did, the sneaky prick," Dan sneers.

"Eat shit!" I spit at him. "He'd hand her straight over to the police if he knew. He's not that type of person."

"Michael?" Waldemar asks.

We watch Mike. He looks at the others and then back

257

at me with defeat. "Option two," he utters. "I'm sorry, Jules."

Waldemar acknowledges me. "And you, Mr Finch?"

I hate the way everyone's staring at me. "Option one. If she's guilty of killing Ian and Earl, then she should be punished by the law."

Dan's eyes narrow. "Fuck the law."

"That's four to one, sorry Mr Finch. Option two it is then. Wonderful." Waldemar smiles again and I have the urge to wipe it off. He dials a number on his phone. "Craig. Please bring her in. Thank you."

We wait in tormented silence when the dragging of shackles scrape against the door. It's kicked open and Shy's pushed through. Her body's wrapped in chains. Craig's got a tight grip on her like an owner walking their dog. If she tries to run, he could break her neck.

Waldemar watches us carefully as his henchman chains Shy to the walls below the television screens. "Right, gentlemen. You have thirty minutes to do with her as you please." He holds up his finger like a teacher cautioning a classroom full of children. "You must *not* kill her, under any circumstances. Any loss of life will result in dire consequences, for all of you." He turns to Craig. "Let's leave them to it."

Craig ignores us and leaves the room. Waldemar gives me a final cheerful smile before closing the door.

I look around, the angry faces of my colleagues stare back. Shy's slumped forwards as if she's given up on life.

"Guys, let's think this through," I say, helplessness is sinking me in quick sand. "You're not really gonna hurt her, are you? I won't standby and witness it!"

"Fuck that. She deserves everything she gets," Dan

growls, running at Shy. He lifts his knee, sending his foot into her stomach. Shy squeals, crashing to the shiny floor.

I run forwards, yelling but Damien and Lance catch me.

Dan grabs her by the back of her head, pulling on the chains, yanking on her hair, forcing her to look at him. "I bet it felt good killing my friends, didn't it?" He scrapes the green strands from her eyes, scrutinising her face. She's staring back at Dan. "The guys were right. You do have a pretty face. I'm gonna have fun messing it up." He hurls his fist into her cheekbone and she goes down again.

"*Fucking bastard!*" I scream.

"Somebody, deal with that cunt or I'll rip his tongue out!" Dan barks.

Damien knees me in the abdomen, just above my groin. I fall onto my hands and knees, panting through the fire. He sits on my back, pushing me to the ground, pinning my arms behind my hips, adding pressure to my joints.

"Why doesn't this bitch say anything?!" Dan hisses as he punches her again, doling out another kick.

I scream from the intense pressure in my body.

"Shut him up!" Dan shouts.

"Don't Damien," Lance says. "Hold him down. We'll take it in shifts."

What the fuck is wrong with everyone?! Mike's letting it happen. How can he stand by and watch this?

My friends have lost their minds.

If Dan comes anywhere near me, I'll tear an organ out.

Damien pulls my head back, twisting it painfully, forcing me to watch. Shy is curled up in a ball by the wall, wincing and wheezing. Dan looms over her, slapping and beating her. I shriek from the pain in my head, thrashing to get free. Damien presses the side of my face even harder into the floor, pushing his elbow into the valley between my shoulder blades.

Dan staggers from an injured Shy and turns to Mike. "She's all yours, pal."

"Mike. Don't do this." I struggle. "You're making a big mistake."

"Don't listen to him." Dan glares at me. "He's just pissed because he can't handle the harsh reality that his girlfriend's a psycho bitch."

I glare at Dan, sending every malicious thought and urge I've ever had. I hope it bites his skin, scurrying into his veins. "Please, Mike!" I lick my lips. My throat's dry like the sand in the desert. "*Please don't do it!*"

Mike squats in front of Shy, watching her with a stillness. He's studying every pore and line on her skin. Does he recognise her? Does she remind him of Shae? *Does he know?*

Shy squints, observing him, her eyes fluttering like they did back in the water tank.

"*Don't hurt her, Mike!*" I yell. "*You have no idea!*"

Dan turns to me, foam boiling from the corner of his mouth, muttering that I need to be quiet. Mike stands to his feet, his fists clenching and flushing. Shy produces a raw, painful scream and in unison, so does Mike. Even their voices, in these horrible circumstances sound similar. Dan's boot cracks against the side of my head as I wail like a banshee. Then, every single light in the world goes out again.

32

Emily

My hands are shaking as we wait in the police station for Chief Inspector Drew. She's in a briefing at the moment. We've been waiting for five minutes. I've told Jordan to go home but he doesn't want to leave, he said he's a part of this now. He's right, we wouldn't have found this nuclear bomb if it weren't for him.

I still can't get through to Dad. I hope he's alright. He'll go absolutely bonkers when he hears what I have to tell him. He said if I can't get through, it'll be because he's working, in a meeting or sleeping but I've been ringing every hour and he's not fucking answering. He's not safe. He needs to come home.

Drew finally comes out, her long black cardigan sways behind her. She walks behind the reception whispering to the officer, repositioning her dark blue lanyard. The officer on the front desk indicates to us, making her aware of our presence.

"Mr Blothio, Miss Finch, it's lovely to see you again." She clocks Jordan. "It seems you have company?"

He leans forward, offering his hand. "I'm Jordan McKeefe."

"Nice to meet you," she says, shaking his hand. "I've been informed by my colleague that you have some information for me?"

"Yes we do," Frank answers.

"Where's Mr Finch?" Drew asks.

"He's out at sea working," I reply.

"And who's looking after you?"

I indicate to Frank. "I'm staying with my uncle part time and my other uncles for the rest of his absence."

Drew nods, her expression's blank. "Follow me," she says, leading us through a labyrinth of corridors. We sit in a cold void of a room.

I wonder how many criminals and witnesses have been interviewed in here. I grab Jordan's knee when Drew's probing eyes slowly scan over us. I swear this woman can stop crowds with just the power of her peepers.

"And you haven't seen your niece since the day she was arrested?" Drew asks Frank.

"No," he replies.

Frank gives her the low-down, delicately cutting out the part about being bashed in the head.

"So, you two *broke* into the Blocksidge and Cripps offices?" Drew asks.

"No, I have a key," I reply. "Dad and his friends have had some run-ins with the FAAC so I wanted to keep an eye on the place."

"Were you asked to do this?" Drew asks.

"Yes."

She smirks. "You're only fourteen, Miss Finch. I find it hard to believe that adults would leave such a huge responsibility in the hands of a teenager."

I smirk at her. "But if I was asked to look after someone's pet it'd be fine, wouldn't it?"

She smiles briefly, as if she likes my response. "Okay then. What did you find out?"

I slide my phone over to her. "Press play."

Drew watches the footage silently. I can't decipher her reaction. She's good at concealing it. I guess when you're a police officer, you have to wear a social mask.

Drew places my phone back on the table. She's completely calm. "I'm sorry you had to see this, Miss Finch. It should've been us discovering this information."

"What will you do?" I ask. "I'm really worried about my dad. He's on that ship with *them*. He can't be safe."

"I'll get straight onto it," Drew says. "Have you tried contacting your father?"

"Several times but he's not picking up."

"Keep trying."

As we make our way out of the station, I feel the tiniest fraction better after talking to Drew. She's taken a copy of the video and will update me of any progress. I dial Dad's number again on the way to Frank's van. It goes straight to answerphone and my heart sinks. He's never set a voicemail announcement. The computerized speech advises me to leave a message after the beep.

I really don't want to tell him what I recorded on my phone but... he hasn't really left me a choice. I hold my breath as I hear the melodic bell. I count to three before I start to speak and... I let it pour out.

33

Julian

The darkness unravels me from its hold. The light stings my eyes. The tears have dried, I'm too tired to do it anymore. Blood streaks the white walls, the knuckles of my colleagues are smudged as if they've been finger painting. Shy's lying on the floor, her face now a crimson bruised mess.

Lance releases me, blood caking on his fingers. I rise to my feet, shaking off his grip, ignoring his pathetic apologies. Damien shouldn't stand so close; he's not ready for it. I shunt my fist into his nether regions and he goes down, cupping his testicles, groaning like a little tart. He deserves so much worse. They're all disgusting.

Dan's smirking at me.

"If I'm alone in a room with you," I whisper angrily. "I can't promise what I'll do."

"You haven't got the balls," he sneers.

"I've got a child, dickhead. What have you got? Oh yeah, *nothing*. You might as well not exist. I bet you were the one filming whoever killed Ian and Earl."

"Whatever, Jules." Dan scoffs, rolling his eyes. "You're just upset. Get some panty pads from your girlfriend. She's bloody enough as it is."

I point my finger in his face. "It should've been you they took out. Nobody would miss you. Nobody likes you anyway."

Dan's lip twitches and he steps forward.

Mike stands in between us. "Oi. Stop this. You've hurt each other enough." He turns to Dan. "*Leave it.*"

There's a standoff for the next couple of seconds. The way we're staring at each other reminds me of a wild pack of hyenas, ready to rip each other apart. Dan's eyes narrow like daggers. I ignore the pain in my head and turn on my heel to observe Shy. She's still breathing, but only just.

"*Shy.*" I kneel down next to her and she flinches when I touch her head. I take in the degree of her wounds. One of her eyes is so swollen, she can't open it. She has cuts on her face. Her body's riddled with fresh bruises. I wished I could've stopped this. Her blue eye is blood shot. I reckon it won't be very long till she'll lose her sight completely. "I'm so sorry."

Waldemar must have been mistaken. The tape wasn't clear enough; it was out of focus most of the time. He said he had plenty of connections, maybe he arranged the whole thing. He's been stalking Shy for a while - he could've paid someone to dress up as her. Green wigs can be purchased from shops or the internet. But...

She's the only person I know who has that type of strength. She's the only person I know who can swim that well...

I think about everyone who knew Ian and Earl. I remember their funerals, hating the atmosphere and the sheer agony of their loss. They were hard working men; they didn't deserve it.

Fuck.

I've been accusing the wrong people. Oh, God. Em's gonna be so disappointed.

In Shy, in Mike...

And me...

I pull Shy up to her feet, anger trembling in every fibre of my being. I smash her up against the wall, the muscles tensing in my arms. "*Why?*" My throat's aching. "I let you in, I let you see everything." I run my finger over the scar on her arm. "*Why did you murder my friends?*"

Shy watches me, her bloody blue eye's welling up with tears. "Because… they killed mine."

34

The sunrays crown from behind the clouds in the early dawn. A navy of seagulls' glide past the Molly as if they're bouncing on the wind. I haven't been to bed yet. I'd just hear those shouts, her whimpers and the thud of bone against skin if I try to sleep.

I'm feeling dizzy, probably riddled with a concussion from being knocked out. I should be scared but for some reason, I don't feel any concern; the numbness in my head is nothing compared to the horror I had to witness.

I didn't touch Shy after I asked her the question, I was too distraught. There's an ache in my chest, it's been scorching since Craig dragged her away from me when Waldemar's horrendous arrangement ticked over. Frank's right, she's not like us. Shy belongs on land and out at sea, she's from two completely different worlds with their own laws and functions.

My back stiffens as I hear his boots on the decking and my palms tighten around the rails. "What d'you want, Mike?"

"To see how you are," he replies.

I sigh, hearing my jaw click. "I'm fine."

"You're not fine, Jules. I've never seen you this upset before."

When I look in his face, in those blue eyes, I'm reminded of the past. "When we get back to Drake Cove, this is it. My last shift. I'm done."

His eyes widen in shock. "You can't leave, you've been

with us forever."

"I can't do this anymore."

"Where will you go?"

"I'll figure it out. Yearling has plenty of fishing opportunities. I can't stay silent about what I saw back there. All of you attacked her when she was restrained. Fucking cowards. Waldemar's had her locked up and drugged like a junkie. And I can't believe you all turned on me. Damien, Lance and Dan beat me up and you did *nothing* about it. How can I trust you after this?"

"I know you're mad at me and I know you bonded with that woman but...she killed our friends. You saw the footage, it was definitely her. You can't shove it under the rug."

"I'm telling everyone what happened on this ship when we go home. Including the police."

"Be cautious. Waldemar will sue you if you do. I hope you don't take offence but he knows more about the law than you."

"I don't care, I'll get a bloody solicitor. I have plenty of crap on him," I scoff. "He's a monster."

A flare of irritation erupts in Mike's eyes. "Think about what it would do to Emily if he takes you down the legal route. It'd destroy her and she's been through enough!"

"Em will understand. She wouldn't want me working alongside people like you. She'd want me to stand up for what's right."

He sighs tiredly, his large hand rubbing through his red grey beard. "You're being really immature about this, Jules. You're backing that woman up and you barely know her. Two of your friends are lying in the ground because of her actions!"

"Do you even know who that woman is?" I ask bitterly.

"Frank's niece."

"She's your daughter, Mike."

His expression drops and he steps back, his hand racing to his chest. There's a quietness on his face, a brief moment of pain. Then something changes, his gaze darkens. He's watching me, the way a lion does when they stalk their prey. "*I don't believe you.*"

"Frank's been bringing up your child."

"Rubbish. He's filled your skull with fairy stories to make you hate me."

"Hate you?" I say. "No, you've done all of that on your own. Frank told me everything, he told me the truth. He saw you and Shae shagging each other's brains out and then nine months later, she disappears after giving birth to *your child.*"

"He's lying. Shae left Drake Cove. I thought it was because Frank caught us and she didn't know how to deal with the situation. Our relationship was one of those short-lived romances, you know… ships in the night. Frank's always been jealous because Shae wanted me. I wanted more than what we had. It's not my fault."

A deep smile spreads across my lips. "Then why did she confide in Frank about her pregnancy and not you? Why did she want Frank bringing up her baby? If she preferred you, surely she would've told you about it…"

"Stop this!"

"Did you know Frank and Shae kissed before you slept with her?"

"*Enough!*" he barks.

"I'm stating the facts, Mike." I step towards him, keeping a tight grip on the rails. "What? Don't like the truth? How does it feel to physically abuse your own child?"

Mike's fist and jaw tightens. "Watch it, Jules."

"Or what?" I chuckle. "You'll hit me?"

"I'm trying really hard not to."

I edge closer, our noses nearly meeting. "I admired you. You were one of my best friends. You know how I feel about Dan and yet you let him have his way. And it's not just me who'll lose respect for you, Emily will too."

"I didn't hurt-" Mike closes his eyes; his lips begin to tremble. "I...I didn't hurt that woman."

"Her name is Shy."

"I didn't know, Jules. *Please believe me...*"

I turn my back. "I'm sorry, Mike. I hate that it's come to this but...don't speak to me again."

35

Matthew Waldemar flicks through his emails. He finished a conference call with a potential buyer for the whale meat. They'd proposed a handsome quantity of money but his instinct was telling him to see what the next client could pitch to him in the morning. The tiredness from the day aches at his shoulders, cramping in his back muscles. He stretches his arms in the air, bending to the side when his bones give a gratifying crack. He closes all of the apps, shutting his laptop down.

He grabs the decanter from the filing cabinet, pouring a rare single malt into a glass. He walks over to the window, gazing outside.

Night is on the way. There's a storm coming.

It's Matthew's favourite time of the day. Everyone's true identity emerges in the evening, when they think nobody's watching. He takes a delicate sip of his drink, the sturdy taste swirls around his tongue before it performs the adrenaline kick to his core.

Matthew glances at the paintings by the wall. Even he was shocked at the behaviour of his new workers, he didn't think they'd hurt her as severely as they did.

They didn't know it, but there was a hidden camera recording *everything*. He'd watched the whole debacle from the start to its ugly finish. If they blabbed to anyone, the video will be automatically uploaded to YouTube. Their names leaked to the press. Their reputations and families tarnished for life. That Julian Finch was certainly going to snap under the pressure. Nobody would grab someone by the throat, threatening to hurt them if they weren't serious about it. But this isn't Matthew's first dance with blackmail.

There's a knock at his door.

"Sir, can I come in?" Craig's muffled voice asks.

"Please do," Matthew answers.

Craig enters the office, agitated.

"Is everything running smoothly?" Matthew leans off the wall, walking towards him.

"I've received a call from Yearling Police. The Chief Inspector said she needs to talk to you concerning a very serious matter. She wants you to return to Yearling immediately. And she says if you don't, she has the authority to come and arrest you."

"She can't do anything," Matthew laughs. "It's nothing. Ignore it."

"What does this all mean, Sir?"

Matthew takes another gulp of his whiskey; his throat tightens momentarily. "*Nothing* you need to worry about."

Craig backs down, shrinking by the second. "Sorry, I didn't mean to interfere."

"You can finish early tonight." Matthew plucks a crisp fifty-pound note from his trouser pocket. "I'm going to check on our special guest." He holds the money, maintaining his gaze, remembering the knife on his desk, hiding discreetly in the pen pot.

Craig gingerly picks the note from his stern fingers. "Thank you. Have a pleasant evening, Sir."

Matthew raises his glass as Craig scurries from the office like a bug. Of course, he didn't like the idea of actually attacking his assistant. Craig is a good, loyal worker but if it comes to drastic measures, there would be no thought behind Matthew's decision. Craig's a big man; he'd need a couple of hits to go down but Matthew could do it. He's done it before. Plus, Craig would be a decent sized meal for the sharks. If it wasn't for the beauty next door, Matthew would've ordered Craig to throw that Julian Finch overboard for strangling him. Finch was a big man too. The ocean would be appreciative of his generosity.

Matthew downs his whiskey, placing the glass on the table before lathering his hands with sanitizer. Craig has spent all day working with the cargo in the hull and he doesn't want any contaminated remnants to spoil his expensive suit. When it comes to business, clean appearances is key. Matthew waits for the disinfectant to dry and yanks the knife from the pen pot. "Just in case."

He ceremoniously removes his suit jacket, loosening the buttons from his shirt. He opens the door situated behind his desk and walks through to the other office, sliding the knife into his pocket. He walks towards the figure lying in the middle of the room.

"How are you feeling?" he asks softly, stroking the top of her head.

Shy murmurs in her sleep, grimacing from the pain in her face.

"I know, I know it hurts," Matthew whispers. "I wish I could make it disappear. I would've got in there sooner if I'd known how they were going to treat you." He strokes his fingertips along her slender jawline. "Don't be scared. I've put painkillers and vitamins in your drip. You're responding brilliantly to them. You'll be back on your feet in no time." He looms over her, placing a soft kiss on her forehead. "I'm so glad I found you."

Her blue eye opens fully, taking him in; they watch each other for a while until she starts to mutter.

Matthew leans down, listening to her words.

"You're a...you're a bad man."

Anger erupts inside Matthew like a volcano. He grips Shy's arms tightly and grins when she moans from the sudden pinch of pain. The chains looped around her arms scrape against the table. "I think you've got me mixed up with someone else, darling. It's okay. I understand why you're upset." Matthew holds her face firmly between the palms of his hands like a vice. She stops making noise when he does this. "I'm so sorry but... I don't think Mr Finch loves you anymore."

Tears stream from her eyes at the sound of the fisherman's name. A pang of jealousy erupts in Matthew's heart. He didn't have this effect on her like that dumb fat bastard did. "It's okay, you're safe with me," he utters. "I'll never let you go again. I'll make it all better."

Matthew delicately kisses her chapped lips. Shy whimpers, her body aching from his touch, even when his tongue slips into her mouth, probing her rigid teeth. He grabs the back of her head, shoving her into the curve of his arm so he can kiss her more deeply. She winces from the cuts on her lips, crying loudly, thrashing against him. He grows as hard as a rock at the sound of her distress. It electrifies his blood.

He hops onto the table, pushing her back, his lips racing along the curves of her body, tasting and savouring every inch of her skin. Matthew senses her hands slide down his stomach, gripping his belt buckle, stroking his nether regions.

Matthew slowly pulls away from the kiss, staring into her eyes. *She wants this.* He fiddles with his zipper, pulling her underwear to the side. When he enters her, Shy's neck arches, letting out the most amazing cry of pleasure he's ever heard in his life.

He cups her thigh, relishing the fullness of her power in his grasp and commences to move in and out of her. Matthew grabs the sides of the table, giving him plenty of momentum to thrust. Desire ripples from his abdomen, shooting down his legs. He rocks his hips back and forth, staring into her face. Their bodies nudge up and down the table. The back of Shy's head wobbles over the edge.

"It feels good doesn't it," he whispers.

He grows angry when she doesn't respond and grabs her by the throat. Her one eye bulges as he cuts off her airway, the blood rushes to her already injured face.

"*It feels good, yes?!*" Matthew growls.

More tears stream from her face as she manages to nod underneath him. He releases her throat, continuing to buck his hips. Investing in her beauty and power was a great move for Matthew's welfare. People will be in awe of her and curse him with the green-eyed demon. He'll be the hot topic of the ball. People would claw and fight each other to get at him. They'd pay through the nose to see her. Double, or perhaps triple for a private viewing. If their relationship continues at this swift rate, Matthew thinks about impregnating his ethereal concubine. Their mixed-race spawn will have a lot to offer.

"Get on top of me," he utters, fishing a key from his trouser pocket, frantically unlocking her arms from the chains.

An energy lights up in Shy's eyes as the shackles fall away. Matthew yanks her from beneath him, twirling her over, his back hitting the table surface. The tubes feeding her those drugs drape from her arms like a make-shift cloak. Matthew grabs her hips, stirring below her as the pleasure throbs from their intertwined legs. She begins to take over the rhythm, gliding her hips back and forth along his body.

Shy's exactly like Matthew imagined. A hungry, seductive creature from the blue depths. She's making love to him with such desperation, her hips bucking and grinding against his bones, her face twisted in lust. He wishes he'd done this before instead of fucking her in the tank, drugged to the eyeballs, barely conscious so he had to do all the work.

Shy curves her back, her thighs rousing in rhythmic movement, getting faster and faster each time. The pleasure wells up within Matthew, groans roll from the back of his throat. He surrenders to the sensation when he takes note of something concealed in her hand.

"How did you-?" he asks.

She slams the knife into his chest. The blinding pain explodes from the bands of his sternum. Matthew yells out, anguish emanating from his throat. Shy smiles darkly, his dick's shrinking inside of her. She yanks the blade from his chest. Blood gushes like a fountain, staining his expensive blue shirt. His heartbeat's careening out of control.

Shy wraps the rope of her green hair around his throat. She pulls on it, pushing pressure on Matthew's windpipe, causing the blood to rush to his head. He struggles to move but Shy's body fixes him to the table. She scowls from the strain, the veins in her muscles are pulsing. He tries to shout for Craig but his voice is hoarse and croaky. The oxygen is depleting.

Matthew Waldemar is losing consciousness.

36

I'm in the middle of a dream, a peaceful one too when I'm thrown from my bed. My back hits the wall. I shout and swear from the discomfort. Molly's performing a rapid U-turn. The force of the gravitational pull is like being trapped in the mouth of a beast and its trying to crush my bones. The ship howls, she shouldn't be executing an acrobatic twirl for such a big girl. I hold on, pain erupts in my knuckles as the ship suddenly pulls up to her original stance, revealing the waves outside my room. Rain droplets drift down the window pane.

I grab my phone from the floor, the vibrant light hurts my eyes. The screen spurts with tons of notifications, missed calls and text messages. They're from Emily, Herb, Derek, Frank *and* Chief Inspector Drew. What does she want?

I pull myself up, holding on to the rails of my bunkbed to keep myself steady. I listen to the voicemail messages. There are five from Em demanding I call her back, she doesn't sound good. I flick to the next one and my heart's in my mouth when I hear her voice:

"Dad, I didn't want to tell you over the phone but I can't get hold of you and I'm exhausted. Don't be angry but...Jordan and I broke into your office and we managed to hack into Dan's emails." She takes a deep breath. *"We thought it was the FAAC who broke my window, right? Well, we were wrong. It was Dan. That Waldemar guy paid him, it was a set-up. We've got email correspondence to prove it. I don't know what happened but Shy's disappearance is linked*

in some way. It was Frank's idea to tell Drew. She's on the case right now, she's gonna arrest them." Em takes another breath, trying to compose herself. *"Dad, I know how pissed off you're gonna be but… please stay away from Dan. Don't try to teach him a lesson. Stay safe. I love you. Come home, we need you here."*

The line goes dead.

There are no more messages.

I stand in utter shock.

Dan.

A dark rage is brewing.

My fists ball up. I hear my bones crack.

Fucking Dan.

It was him all along. He's the reason my daughter has nightmares. Dan's always carried a bad vibe. It's why he doesn't have friends or family. It's why he rejoices in the commotion and violence. He's in love with chaos. He was working with that creep this whole fucking time. Does Mike know about it? Does he know my deputy manager is a back stabbing, two-faced liar?

A piercing siren goes off above my head, accompanied by red lights matching the pace of the alarm. I clamp my hands down on my ears. Lance appears in the doorway; he's got this hyped look in his eye.

I wince from the noise. *"What?!"*

"She's escaped," Lance utters, twisting a crowbar in between his palms. "That green-haired bint. Your fucking girlfriend – she's killed Waldemar. We found him with his trousers around his ankles. His heart was practically hanging out of his chest. And Craig… she's gutted him like a pig."

"Waldemar's dead?"

He nods frantically, twirling the crowbar. "I'm gonna kill that bitch myself."

"Lance?"

"What?" he asks.

I yank my arm back, connecting my knuckles to his temple. He's knocked out instantly, his body dropping to the floor. The crowbar clatters with a loud clash. I pull Lance into the bedroom, picking up the crowbar. It feels good to have something lethal in my hands. I lock the door behind me. I can't have Lance acting stupid right now. He doesn't know what I know and he'll end up like Waldemar and Craig if he's not careful. He'll be furious when he wakes up. Call it pay back.

I stalk down the corridor, the red light of the alarm's flashing in my eyes. I know Em told me to keep a distance from Dan. I don't want her to be disappointed but... I can't promise anything right now.

I race to the main deck, reaching the bridge. The rainwater's already bleeding into my clothes. Jim's sitting, stooped over with one hand on the helm while the other rubs the back of his head. He's spouting directives into a walkie-talkie hanging from a wire above the steer. The reception's bad on the other end.

"*Mayday, mayday.* This is Captain Jim Nielson of the Molly," he shouts. "We are under attack. Crew have been injured. We need support urgently!"

"Jim, are you alright?" I ask.

He shakes his head; his knees are wobbling. "No, mate. Somebody hit me. When I woke up, somebody had fucked with the steering. I thought we were gonna sink but I managed to get her level again."

The receiver slips from his fingers and I grab him as he falls over.

"Just stay there," I say softly, rolling him into the recovery position. "You're gonna be okay."

"She…came out of nowhere. I, I've never seen her before."

"Waldemar's kept her hidden. This boss of yours has a lot of secrets." I inspect his head. He doesn't have any cuts, bruises or bleeds. He's probably in shock.

"Seriously?" Jim's eyes widen. "Is he hurt?"

"He's dead, so's Craig."

Jim winces. "Oh, shit. What the fuck's been happening?"

"A lot we don't know," I say. "Look, we can't stay out at sea any longer. We need to head back to Yearling as soon as possible."

"Absolutely," he says.

Bran and Connie race onto the bridge.

"What the fuck's going on?!" she barks. "I nearly threw up my dinner this ship flipped so fast!"

"It's a long story," I reply.

"What happened to Jim?" Bran asks, pointing at the crowbar resting by my leg.

"A woman knocked me out," Jim says. "Julian's done nothing wrong guys."

Connie flusters. "Dan's fighting someone on the lower deck. A green haired chick - I've never seen her before."

"That's the one who hit me!" Jim yells.

"Don't go anywhere near her," I say, getting up and grabbing the crowbar. "You don't know what you're getting yourself into."

"And I suppose you do?" Connie hisses angrily.

I glare at her. "Yes, as a matter of fact I do!"

"*Don't argue!*" Jim shouts. "This isn't the time. We've got two dead bodies onboard, I don't want anymore. Stay away from that woman. That's an order. Got it?"

They nod obediently.

"We're going home," Jim mutters. "I've had enough of this. Bran, put the hoses on. Connie, keep calling for help."

Connie races to the steer, grabbing the walkie-talkie as Bran legs it from the bridge. Jim nods at me, giving me the all-clear I can leave. I reach the lower deck, some of the other crew members observe the mayhem with confused fascination like they did when we were whaling.

Dan and Shy shout at each other, arguing in the middle of this harrowing monsoon. The hoses chug as the water spills out, emptying into the sea. The siren's whirling in the background. Damien watches from behind one of the lifeboats.

"Get away from here Damien!" I shout.

He turns his head, noticing me. "Are you crazy?!" he jeers. "*Fuck off!* That slut deserves everything she gets!"

Fine, so be it. I launch forward, kicking him in the chest, remembering how he punched and pinned me to the ground. The crowbar comes swinging, just missing his head. Damien dodges my next attack, calling me every conceivable swear word there is. I threaten him, bellowing like an animal. If he comes near this area again, I'll kill him. He knows I mean it too and he scuttles off to the stairwell with his tail between his legs.

I advance, whacking the crowbar against the rails. Dan and Shy snap apart, breaking their fight.

"Haven't you had enough of bullying women, Dan?" I ask, wiping the rain droplets from my vision.

Shy's face is a painting of bruises. Small puddles of blood trickle down her arms. The wounds are hideous. The jagged pipes from the intravenous tubes stick out of her like rows of teeth. She must've ripped them out.

"What the fuck are you on about?" Dan sneers.

"How much did Waldemar pay you to attack my home?"

Dan's lips curl viciously. His eyes slowly drift to the crowbar in my hand. "How'd you find out?"

"We hacked your emails."

There's a moment of contemplation on his face before his natural scowl returns.

"So, how much did you get?"

"More than I make from fishing," he utters.

"Does Mike know about it?"

"Of course he doesn't. He would never agree to it. He respects you too much."

"The police have been informed, Dan. The second you step off this ship, you're getting arrested." My knuckles click around the crowbar. "I know we didn't see eye-to-eye but you nearly killed my daughter. If you have a problem, you take it up with me. You *don't* bring my kid into the mix."

Dan rolls his eyes. "Oh my God, Jules. You're such a drama queen. I wasn't trying to kill her. It was just to frighten you. Waldemar wanted what Frank was hiding. Your bungalow was just camouflage."

I love how he says it so casually, as if it's not a big deal. "*That's a lie.* You've been in my home, you know the front room was Em's and you did it anyway. She saw you fleeing from the scene." I stare him down. "You're going to prison. I'll make fucking sure of it."

"Oh, yeah?" Dan says sarcastically. "And what if I don't go willingly?"

I tease the crowbar in my hand. "We'll have to do it some other way, won't we?"

Dan laughs to himself, shaking his head in denial.

"*Fuck you!*" he hisses, lunging forward.

He rugby tackles me into the column. The crow bar's knocked out of my grip. We're locked in a brawl on the decking with legs and arms squirming. My feet and hands slide on the slippery floor. Dan's fists crack against my jaw. He tries to shove my face into the column and I tense my back muscles. I ram my elbow into his throat, curling myself around him.

We fall back onto the decking, wrestling and cursing. The rain hails down on us. I grab Dan's arm, applying pressure to his joint. He's forgotten I can use my brawny size to my advantage.

I twist it backwards in an unnatural motion, squeezing every muscle in my body. I think about how frightened Emily was. I think about the paranoia his actions created within me. I remember every mean glance, every snidey comment. I remember his laid-back attitude at Waldemar's first meeting, and the lies spewing from that bastard's smug mouth as he shook my hand, grinning in my face, knowing he was tearing my world down.

Dan's screaming hysterically now. It's music to my ears. Mike, Connie and Bran plead at me to have mercy on him. I dive back into reality as I hear the satisfying *snap* of Dan's arm. I shove him off me when the crowbar swings into my sight, crashing against his back. Dan yells out, coughing and spluttering from the blow, falling onto his broken arm. He screams even louder, the sound shudders down my spine, electrifying my heart.

Shy stands over him with the crowbar sleeping in her hand, she's manically clicking her tongue.

"No, you're not killing anymore people!" I growl.

Shy winces as if I've just slapped her. "You don't know, do you?"

"Know what?" I stagger towards her. "Please, Shy. Give me the crowbar. He'll get the justice he deserves."

She presses her palm to my temple. Images I don't want to see flood my concentration. It's like I'm in a dream but I can feel everything around me. Another world's hanging over my eyes. "I saw it as soon as he touched me," Shy explains. "The final clue Frank and I have been hunting for all this time."

The truth hurts like a cut to the skin.

Shy pulls me back to normality, her hand slipping from my face. "What if it was Emily?!" she cries. "What would you do then? Just let him go?!"

Mike wouldn't have stood by him if he knew the truth, none of us would. I don't want to admit it but... she's right. What if it had been Emily? What if that voice had been Hanna screaming for help?

I step away from Dan.

He's not mine to take...

Not anymore.

Shy begins to batter him, smashing the crowbar down over and over on his back. Damien and Connie shout at her to stop. Mike stands behind them, staring at his child in disbelief. Shy clocks the audience and rams the crowbar into Dan's mouth. The blow shatters his nose. Blood and teeth spew like a fountain, transforming his face into a crimson canvas. She casts the crowbar to the ground; it clatters as it hits the decking. She wraps her arms around

Dan's neck, dragging him like a lump of meat towards the edge of the ship.

"*Shy*. I'm warning you," I say. "Don't do this."

She climbs over the railing, holding onto Dan's limp ragdoll body.

"Shy. *Please*."

She watches me cautiously. She looks beaten down and exhausted, as if this motion's the final draw to regather her power.

"*Listen to me!*"

Shy binds Dan to her chest, giving me a little smile. She tenses her back, kicking out at the bars with her feet. It's almost soothing watching her leap with such elegance.

I run towards the bars, leaning over the side of the ship. She plummets through the air. Their bodies hit the surface, causing a wave of eruption. I watch helplessly as neither Shy or Dan rise for breath. The water has swallowed them whole.

37

Frank stands at the kitchen window, holding the smoke in his lungs before blowing it out through his lips. The misty shapes drift, escaping outside. It'd been a long time since he smoked. He'd stashed the cigarette packet on top of the kitchen cupboards, behind a bunch of dusty wine glasses. The last time he'd done this was when Shae went missing. With the latest revelation, Frank forgave himself for indulging in the nicotine infusion.

Reporting the betrayal of Daniel Cripps to the police had hit him quite hard. He knew the man couldn't be trusted. Everyone tolerated his bad behaviour. Why? Because he was an original Drake Covian?

Maybe Frank shouldn't have sold half of the fisherie to Dan, perhaps the power acted as a catalyst. It swamped and rotted his mind, especially after the FAAC sprang into the mess. Frank had known Dan for most of his life, he remembered teaching him at sailing school. A skinny kid who mouthed off, playing to the crowd for praise and attention. Dan didn't have the best relationship with his family. His father, Brian was a bruiser, who was constantly out on the boats or getting drunk at The Sea Horse, dancing from woman to woman. His mother, Gladys, fled when Dan was little. If only she'd taken her son with her. He'd probably have a better life.

Since the visit from the station, Frank began meticulously researching this Matthew Waldemar. He hadn't found any incriminating information as of yet, it was hard to pinpoint where the obsession started.

Mr Blothio has something I want, he'd written to Dan.

Frank knew who Waldemar was referring to and he hated how he spoke about Shy like she was a possession. Waldemar must have been spying on Frank somehow, watching in plain sight. She hadn't left the house of her own free will, she was taken and Waldemar had got someone to steal her and knock him out. Who else was behind it? How many more dark secrets are being concealed in Drake Cove?

Frank hears the front door open and the burst of jovial squeals, disturbing him from his morose thoughts. He stubs the cigarette out in the sink to find Em bear hugging her father. Julian smiles tiredly against her, lifting her off the ground, continuing the hug.

"Hi Jules," Frank says, trying to compose himself.

Julian opens his eyes, looking pissed off. He lowers Em to the floor, stepping back.

"I'm so glad you're home," Em utters, lightly touching the new bruises on his face. "What happened?"

"Don't worry about it." Julian pulls an assuring smile and rubs her shoulders. "Em, I need to speak to Frank in private."

"Is everything alright?" she asks, her eyes are wide with concern.

"It's fine, but I really need to talk to Frank."

Em nods, glancing at Frank cautiously before disappearing upstairs.

"What happened to your face?" Frank asks after a beat.

Julian laughs lightly, it doesn't sound genuine. "Lance and I had an altercation. It's okay now, we've sorted it."

"Well, whatever happened, you should probably get it checked out," Frank says.

"I haven't got time."

"Come through to the kitchen." Frank turns his back, busily making tea. "I'm sorry Dan was behind the attack." He pushes the mug across the table. "I wish I could've seen it earlier."

"Don't worry about it. Nobody saw this shitstorm coming."

"What happened on that ship?" Frank asks, his throat itching for another cigarette.

Julian glares at Frank. "Shy ruined my life, that's what happened."

"I... don't understand."

"Shae wasn't the only reason you stopped whaling. There was another purpose. I didn't realise until I experienced it for myself. *The pain, the screams.* You stopped participating in the culling because you *physically can't.* It makes so much sense now."

"Damn it." Frank sighs under his breath. "It's the worst pain I've ever felt in my life. As if I was being broken from the inside out..."

"Why didn't you tell me?" Julian asks.

"I didn't see the signs but I guess I was wrong. You experienced the side effect of the mermaid's kiss. It's a scar, Jules. A transference of pain. It's a warning about our actions. We feel what the whales experience when we hunt them. Octavia did the same to Erik. I know you're upset and I know how much you care about the culling but, you need to let it go."

"I can't participate in my family tradition," Julian utters, his face painfully welling up. "She's robbed it from me."

"I'm sorry, I should've told you."

"Mike doesn't participate in the culling either, he never whaled on the Molly. He must've experienced the pain too." Julian's eyes narrow like razors. "I hate to break it to you but…his relationship with Shae was stronger, much more meaningful and significant than you think. He loved her. I could feel it."

"Not as much as I did," Frank hisses.

"You ruined Shy." Julian's knuckles stretch under his skin. He looks away, blinking several times as if he's knocking back tears. "You put a noose around her neck… by shielding her from the world." His eyes resume on Frank, a raging fire glowing from within. "Her life would be so much better. She could've been a famous artist, a vet, an Olympic swimmer or a diver."

"*Stop it*," Frank utters angrily. "I did what I had to…to protect her."

"And it got you nowhere!"

An emotional tremor thumps in the cave of Frank's chest. "You're scaring me, Jules. What happened to you?"

"Waldemar had her on the ship, locked and incarcerated in a water tank. He had her paintings in his office. He's been researching mermaids for years. Apparently, his dad saw one. A lonely, dark haired woman swimming in the ocean."

"*Shae…*" Frank says.

Julian nods. "Waldemar saw Shy dive off Drake's Tooth. He said he needed her for *his work*. I don't know what he meant but… it wasn't anything decent."

"Is she okay?"

"She escaped. I don't know where she is now but…she's done so much damage."

"You've lost me…"

"She's killed people, Frank."

"*What?*"

"You heard me. Waldemar, Dan, his bodyguard Craig *and*...she killed Ian and Earl. Waldemar was spying on her. I don't know how but I saw the footage with my own eyes. I know you raised her to be better than that but you can't control what she is. Torturing Shy was a tool Waldemar used to manipulate us, to hush us into silence," Julian utters. "I took no part in it."

"Did...did Mike touch her?"

"I don't know. Dan knocked me out."

"This can't be happening. I don't want to believe it."

"I'm sorry, Frank. I truly am."

"How can I make things right?"

"There's nothing you can do. This isn't your battle anymore." Julian rises to his feet and walks to the window, gazing out at the garden. "I've thought about it. I don't know if it's a good idea. I've gone over it many times but..." He plucks the knife from the wooden block; the silver blade glistens against the overhead light.

"You can't be serious..." Frank says, his voice breaking.

"There's only one way I can solve this." Julian's back tenses, his fingers strain around the handle of the knife. "I don't want her to rot in a prison cell... she won't survive. We both know Drew will send her down for a very long time. Doing something now is the best option for her *and* everyone else."

"You're not thinking clearly, Jules. Shy didn't kill anyone. It's not in her nature. That Waldemar guy must have framed her somehow."

"I don't know." Julian turns to face him. "But even if he did, it's more than that now. People have suffered because of her. She's crossed the line. Our world is not the open ocean. There's no law or moral mark out there."

"You can't do it, Jules. If she dies, then all of her history, all of the preserved knowledge about her people will perish," Frank says. "She might be the last of her kind. Remember what I said. She's a queen."

"It's too late. I really wish there was some other way."

Frank stood up, his hands racing to Julian's shoulders, clutching the material of his jacket. "Listen to me, Jules. *Listen.* Mike may have fathered her but I'm her dad. She's a Blothio through and through. I love Shy like you love Emily. Please. *Please* don't take her from me."

"I'm sorry, Frank but this is the way it has to be."

38

The dawn twinkles over the clouds when I reach the beach. It's so serene and quiet. I was honest about my injuries. Lance was furious when he regained consciousness and he tackled me to the ground. After we got prised apart by Mike, I informed him in the most calming way that knocking him out was for his own good. He stopped shouting at me when he heard about Dan's fate. That could've been him. He should've been fucking grateful...

I step over the rocks, a hunch pulling at my insides. I hated seeing Frank so upset, especially after I unrolled the truth direct from her touch. I don't know if I'm making the right decision but it's the only solution right now, even if it means hurting or excluding my friends to carry it out.

I crawl into Drake's Mouth, calling her name. My voice echoes, bouncing off the walls. The eerie sound of the wind whistles sending chills down my spine. I crawl on my hands on knees, groaning from the exertion, calling her name again.

Seeping out of the darkness, Shy whimpers by the wall, trembling from the cold, wincing from the pain in her body. I can't see Dan. Anywhere. She must've abandoned him. I didn't like the guy but that's three of us gone, fallen under her hand. Am I the next one to lose my life?

I edge towards her, crouching on my knees. She glares at me, clicking her tongue angrily like River did. Right now, she reminds me of a wild beast unsure of whether to fight or submit and if I get any closer, she could attack or close up.

"You don't need to be afraid..." I say.

"I'm not going back on that ship," she hisses.

"You don't have to. It's all over."

"He was hurting me."

"I know..."

"Why did they torture me?" she asks anxiously. "Why didn't you stop them?"

"What do you mean?"

"*Waldemar!*" she shouts, her voice vibrates painfully around the cave. "I was in that tank for weeks. He was drugging me, punishing me. He... *did* things." She winces again, craning her head, scrunching her eyes together as if the memory's too powerful to block out.

A fresh wave of rage brews within me, he was in my grasp and I should've broken his neck when I had the chance. "He was a bad man, Shy. You did the right thing. He won't hurt you again."

"And what about your friend?" she presses.

I stare at her.

"You still can't admit what he did, can you?" she asks. "Not just to me? But to *her* too!"

I sit back on my heels, watching her. There's a tightness in my chest. "I'm not taking you back to the ship. I want you to come home with me. I want you safe, I want you dry and in my arms. *I'm sorry, Shy.*"

She crumbles at my words, folding into my embrace. She starts to cry, hiding her face in my chest. I hold her for as long as I need to, resting my chin on her head. Tears bite at the corner of my eyes. Her sorrow's infecting me.

I think about what I have to do. I think about what Dan, Damien, Lance and Waldemar did to her. I gaze into her mesmerising eyes, holding her face delicately in my hands. I pull her into a deep kiss. Her tears spill onto my skin as she responds with desperation. I didn't realise how much I've missed her, until now.

~

Shy agrees to leave Drake's Mouth. I wrap my jacket around her and we walk hand in hand, past Becks Hill and stop at the top of Drake's Tooth. She stands in front of me, her arms are wrapped around my midriff. I think about the first time I saw her and how her threatening stare hypnotised me.

We watch the sky meet and greet the sealine. The colours blend into one another like old lovers at a reunion. I nuzzle my head into the slope of her neck, kissing her salty skin, drinking her in. My nerves cascade waves within me when I sense the steely cold blade of the knife resting against my back. Her body shakes in my embrace. I shut my eyes, my heart beating relentlessly, pulling her closer to me. I engrave every patch of her touch, every smile, every emotive word she's ever uttered to my memory. That's when I count down from ten.

Shy places a hand over mine. Images flash painfully across my mind like hundreds of lightbulbs exploding and shattering.

Eight.

She felt something when our eyes met at the culling. It scared her.

Six.

She loved watching me sleep.

Four.

She was fascinated, drunk with love when she tasted me for the first time.

Two.

She felt truly alone in that water tank. She heard *everything* going on around her. She felt the same agony when I skewered that blue whale's face. She was convulsing and screaming like she'd been electrocuted. Oh God. She *knew* I was on the ship. She heard me talking to Waldemar. She was trying to break out when I attacked him.

One.

I kiss the side of her head, extracting the knife from the back of my jeans. Shy shivers, her final moments resting on my shoulders.

I'm so sorry.

She turns her head, sensing a change in the wind. Her eyes widen when she catches sight of the knife.

I lunge forward. Something moves behind me. The energy's knocked out of me and my head slumps against the grass. Frank's face burns into mine, he's pinning me to the ground.

"What are you doing here?" I growl. "This isn't your decision to make!"

Emily stands in front of Shy, guarding her. "*No Dad,*" she utters. "If you want to kill Shy, you'll have to kill us too."

39

"Get out of here!" Em shouts at Shy. "Go now! You need to leave!"

I shove Frank off me, jumping to my feet, clutching the knife. "Go home you two. I'm warning you, Em. I don't want you to see this."

Frank pushes me in the chest. "You're not thinking clearly. I won't let you do this!"

I push him back. "I mean it, Frank. Stay the fuck away from me or I'll do something I'll regret."

Frank raises his hands, surrendering as if he's trying to tame me. "Look, I know you're hurt and you've seen some awful, upsetting things on that ship but... I can't let this happen. If it means my life is on the line then so be it!"

"I can't let you destroy yourself," Em adds.

"I won't!" I yell. "I'm putting the wrong things right!"

Frank rushes me again, his meaty hands grab at the knife. We struggle, wrestling with each other. My fingers brush against the blade as I try to heave him off me but I get nicked and it cuts into my skin.

"*STOP IT!*" Em shouts powerfully.

I pull my arm back, slamming it forward. My knuckles crunch into Frank's face and the impact sends him to the ground, blood spraying from his lower lip. Vengeance gleams in Shy's eyes and she moves too quickly, breaking into a sprint, bashing and knocking into me. There's a frantic rush of her shouts and her arms hitting my aching face. She's on top of me, resuming the wrestling of the knife. Frank's groaning, ordering Shy to stop.

I wriggle beneath her, releasing one hand off the knife, grabbing the back of her head. I roll on top of Shy, pushing my weight down, pinning her to the soil. Our hands are clammy and I nudge her fingers, tipping the knife at her throat. She needs to stop fighting me or with one big nudge, she's done for.

"Let her go, Dad." Em's standing by the edge of Drake's Tooth, her heels are licking the wind. "If you don't, I'll jump."

"Don't be stupid. Come away from there!"

"I mean it," she presses.

Shy whimpers, scratching at my fingers clutched around her throat.

"For fuck's sake listen to her Jules," Frank moans.

"*Let her go!*" Em opens her arms. "If you don't, I'm gone."

We stare at each other. Her voice is getting edgier. Even Shy has stopped struggling. Just when I think she's fucking bluffing, Em tips back, the ground disappearing from under her feet.

The only anchor to life disappears before my eyes. I'm locked in slow motion as a terrified scream bursts from my throat. Shy pushes herself off me and I'm propelled onto my back. The knife is chucked to the grass. She runs to the edge, leaping off, her arms arching into a dive.

I crawl desperately, peering over as Em hits the water, plunging to the depths. The vicious waves slam into her face, the shock will fill her lungs. Shy strikes the water just after and the current drags her underneath. Em doesn't have long.

Frank and I run to the beach; my throat's hurting I'm

screaming so much. My senses are overloaded. Pain eats at my chest. I can hear Hanna's accusations swirling around my head, that I'm a bad father and I'll pay for my actions.

Frank points at a tiny figure crawling from the waves, her clothes are soaking.

"*Emily!*" I howl, running up to her.

A dam of tears spills down my daughter's wet face and I heave her off the sand, wrapping my arms around her.

"What happened?" Frank asks. "Where's Shy?"

"She...she saved me," Em sobs, coughing. Several strands of green hair poke out from her closed fist. Sadness fills Frank's eyes. "Her head smashed against the rocks. I don't know where she went, the tide took her away."

40

Mike: 30 Years Before

He chugged the final cold dregs of his beer. The dramatic troubles of the day had left him in a state of exhaustion. It was getting rather raucous in The Sea Horse. Shifty side glances had already been shot across the pub like arrows. He didn't understand some of the people who opposed their tradition. Especially their behaviour. A group of "activists" were sat in the corner, sipping their drinks with lemon tight mouths. One or two of the locals eyeballed them like crazy, doubling the staring time with every ordered pint.

Mike paid his tab, thinking it was best to scarper before he'd have to dodge flying glass. It was going to happen sooner or later and he didn't want to spend the rest of the evening picking debris from his hair.

"Oi Charlie," he said to the landlord.

The elderly man turned, wiping a dirty glass.

"Have you seen Frank?"

"He only came for the one," he replied. "I think he's gone to the quay. Left after that Ward guy was here."

"Oh *him*, that makes sense. Thanks mate."

Mike staggered out of the pub. Maybe he should've stopped after the second tipple. He'd lost Frank in the crowd during the culling. They'd agreed to help each other in case of any emergencies. Even if it meant, fighting back-to-back. They didn't want to resort to self-defence but with the way these activists were carrying on, coming to blows was on the cards. The "peaceful" protestors had broken through the line, trying to steal fishing equipment. The whales were already on the sand, being gutted from the neck to the groin. It was a stupid attempt. They couldn't save them. About five or six police officers had to intervene.

Mike stopped his wobbly walk, checking that he wasn't being followed. He breathed in slowly so the fresh sea air curdled the storm in his mind. He sparked up a flame in the well of his white pipe, breathing in the smoky air.

He journeyed over to the quay, noticing the main cabin light of Olivia was on. There was movement inside, dark shadows danced. Frank must have been spending the night there. *Or those bastards are looting the boat, again.* Mike wanted to bite down on his paranoia but they'd already found the address to the office. They'd stuffed and crammed the post box and fax machine with threats - what's not to say they hadn't managed to fish for details on Olivia too.

Mike stepped onto the boat; his fists clenched at his side. "Frank?"

There was no answer.

"*Who's on my fucking boat?!*"

He heard a noise behind him and saw Shae sitting by the wall, shivering under a towel. Her dark gaze piercing his mind.

"What the hell are you doing here?!" Mike sneered, walking towards her. He saw the light glare from the bathroom door. "Have you been using my shower?"

Shae didn't respond, she just stared at him with guilt.

"You need to get out. I'm not a fucking charity," Mike

said. "That prank you played last time wasn't very funny."

Shae's eyes dipped, staring towards his feet.

She's not going to leave, is she?

He sighed with frustration, picking up on why she was feeling uncomfortable. "Do you want me to wash my hands?"

Shae nodded.

"Does the blood really bother you?"

She nodded again.

"*For fuck's sake.*" Mike rolled his eyes, stomping into the bathroom and tried his best to clear the red crap from beneath the bed of his nails.

When he came out, Shae was standing up, the towel bunched under her chin like a blanket. Her commanding stare was unsettling. Since her grand escape, he'd pondered who she was and where she'd come from. He'd read in the newspaper that a man was found half dead in the English Channel from a backfired gangster assassination. It had got him thinking, if Shae had witnessed something she wasn't meant to. Her silence and bizarre behaviour would make sense especially if she was psychologically damaged and why she fled when the police arrived.

Shamefully, Mike couldn't shut out her insane attraction. His heart was beating like the clappers when he helped her into those clothes. Her powerful gaze didn't move when she held his hand. Pictures he didn't ask for blazed through his mind, accompanied by something he couldn't explain. Faces from the past he didn't recognise yet they knew the veins of his homeland.

Mike opened his eyes to find Shae so close he could taste her breath on his lips. "You really are a strange wonder, aren't you?" he uttered delicately.

Her mouth instantly closed over his. The barrier Mike

had been trying to hold up dissolved like sand. With instinct, his fingers trickled along her skin, passing over the soft rounds of her buttocks and he massaged her shoulders. Shae's towel fell to the ground. Hunger pulled at Mike and he yanked her into his embrace, his hands racing to the back of her head. They kissed with fierce passion. Their bodies walked the space of the cabin, bashing into the walls, knocking objects to the floor. Shae's fingers pulled at Mike's belt, tenderly unzipping the denim. Mike crawled out of his clothes and their writhing bodies dropped to the ground. Olivia swayed but he wasn't concerned. She was a tough girl; she'd been out in the full gales and chaotic storms and *still* managed to return home.

Mike kissed Shae and she groaned, squirming beneath him. He took his time, nibbling at her neck, parting her legs. He stared into her eyes as he entered her. Shae let out a stifling cry, he wasn't sure if it was from pleasure or pain.

Shae tugged him into a kiss and Mike responded, kissing her back. He moved gently, her hips gliding back and forth, meeting his thrusts. They were climbing that ladder together. He pressed her deeper into the floor, curling his fingers around her wrists. Her body squeezed down on him. She twitched, twisting around his limbs like a snake. Mike moved faster and faster. Pleasure shot through them both. Shae clung on for dear life and they cried out at the same time.

Warmth trickled from Mike's chest, shuddering down his legs, plunging his mind into an ocean of ecstasy. He gazed down at Shae, sweat loomed on her forehead. They looked at each other for the longest time. Her lips quivered and trembled as if she wanted to communicate but she couldn't form the chain of words. Mike stroked the back of his hand against the curve of her face, trying his best to comfort her.

Say something…

He heard a clatter collapse behind him and his heart plummeted to the depths when he saw his face.

Oh God…

Frank was standing in the doorway of the cabin.

41

Frank: Present Day

When he saw Shy's fine green locks poking through Em's fingers, his soul shattered into a million pieces. If a magical device could erase the past fourty-eight hours, he would've gladly given up all of his savings to use it. After Emily's heroic leap of faith, they called the ambulance and Julian and Em sped off to the hospital. Frank retreated home in a depression, his lip stinging from Julian's punch. He didn't want to talk to anyone or see anybody.

I didn't even get to say goodbye.

Frank tries to sleep but insomnia refuses to release him. He throws off the bed covers, noticing the red numbers of the clock glaring back at him. It's six in the morning.

He pulls on his clothes and decides to go for a walk. He paces past Becks Hill, standing on the edge of Drake's Tooth, scanning the waters, searching for her. But only the beauty of daybreak stays with him. He doesn't want to think about her corpse bouncing around the ocean pits, her blood trickling, rousing the creatures to devour her flesh. She'd met the same watery grave as her mother. It should've been him floating out there. Frank would've willingly walked along the ocean bed with the other drowned spirits. *Fate chose the wrong soul to destroy.*

He clocks a presence on the beach, noticing something strewn amongst the rocks. He runs down, stumbling over his feet, anger quenching in his throat like a fierce thirst.

The tide must have pulled him in, destroying his body. *The sharp rocks would've acted as the final execution.*

Frank picks up a rock smothered from the sand and sits opposite the body, staring into his face. "*Why?*" he asks passionately.

Blood clots around his lips. Riding the harrowing waves and smashing into the rocks has dislocated his jaw. Bone pokes through his greying skin. The light has oozed from his eyes like a candle dwindling in the dark.

Frank shuffles the rock in his palm.

Why did you kill Shae?

He remembers what Julian saw from Shy's touch. Dan had caught sight of Shae swimming during one of his fishing trips. He'd followed her into Drake's Mouth, his curiosity and desire as sharp as a razor. Shae had crawled fearfully from his advances, trying to protect her child. The baby began to cry when Dan shoved his gutting knife into her mother's leg, his dirty fingers groping at her body. Shae had been screaming for Frank when her life was slowly squeezed from under Dan's palms. After he'd finished, he sneered as he did up his trousers, the green haired baby wailing as she stared at her dead mother lying a fraction away from her.

He left Drake's Mouth not caring about the infant inside, she'd probably die from the damp or be a handy snack for the seagulls, he thought. Dan sailed his boat out of Drake Cove so the town looked like a knot of levitating lanterns, he needed distance in his favour. He wrapped Shae in suffocating black binbags and weighed her down with rocks before chucking her overboard. He enjoyed watching the body melt into the depths. That hateful grin was poking at the corner of his mouth.

Frank's fingers tense around the rock, playing with a lethal idea. Death had already surpassed Dan, stealing the moment from Frank's grip but he could still reclaim the balance. He could smash Dan's head in right now, stuff his pockets full of stones and walk into the sea, never turning back. Dan's murder and his suicide would be memorable, exonerating Shy from all responsibility. His actions would upset the ones who were close to him and be a blessing in disguise for others. But he'd see Shae and Shy again, spending blissful eternity with the two loves of his life.

Not a bad way to go.

Then another thought slithers into his head, disrupting the flicker of happiness he's feeling. The continuation of the work he's sweated and fought hard for would cease; nobody would take up the mantel of Frank Blothio after his demise. Drake Cove would want it buried, never to resurface. Shae would be disappointed, and Shy would be furious with him. He couldn't let that happen.

Frank sighs tiredly, bowing his head, whispering a small prayer. He rises to his feet, hurling the rock aggressively into the ocean, allowing a wail of despair to spill from his lips.

He calls the authorities about the discovery of a body washed up on Drake Cove beach. The siren and bright lights of the ambulance disturb a handful of the locals.

Fifty minutes pass before Frank walks into the Crest Café. He's welcomed by the sight of Mike sitting at one of the booths. He's not reading the newspaper, instead, he's staring off into space. His latte's getting cold.

Frank orders his usual, eyeing his familiar spot. Mike shows no hostility when he sits opposite him, his whole face aches with exhaustion.

"Hi Mike," Frank says.

His former best friend blinks sluggishly in acknowledgment.

Even Dylan, the owner of the café is mystified when he brings over Frank's tea, particularly eyeing the cut on his lower lip. Frank glances around, taking time to examine the windows and their wooden framework.

"I didn't know she was mine…" Mike utters, his voice rising from the agonising silence.

Frank didn't want to cry in front of him. He'd done enough of that already. "I… didn't know how to tell you." He wipes the tea from his spoon and plops in two sugar cubes, trying to disguise the rickety train of his emotions.

"You've should've regardless," Mike replies. "I would've stepped up to the plate and supported Shy. You know I've always wanted a family. I know you hate me for sleeping with Shae but I was owed the truth." He turns his head slowly, his gaze finally meeting Frank's. Even in this moment, Frank could pick out his daughter's likeness in Mike's face, especially with those blue eyes of his.

"I know."

Mike's jaw tightens. "I wanted to talk after the night you caught us but you kept shutting me out."

"I did."

"*Why?*"

Frank thought about it, trying to piece his words together before speaking. "Bitterness." He laughs lightly, hearing his own words. "I know it's pathetic. But you always got the admirers. Women constantly looked your way. They never did with me."

Mike shakes his head in dissatisfaction. "I didn't steal her from you, Frank. I didn't know you felt the way you did. You should've told me."

"I know. You're right."

"I thought Shae and I had something, I felt it the *second* I touched her but… she disappeared. I put it down to one of those fleeting romances, like the stuff you only read in books. A love that was meant to happen but sadly never to last. I didn't mean for you to see us, Frank. I didn't know you'd been on the boat. I didn't want to hurt you."

Frank sucks in a breath, taking a delicate and shaky sip of his tea before putting it on the table. "I think she loved both of us, in her own way."

"What happened to her?"

"She's dead, most likely," Frank replies, tears nudging behind his eyes. "I've tried tracking her down but I could never trace her."

"And Shy?"

"She's probably dead too. Julian told me what happened on the ship. She…wouldn't have made it to shore with the extent of her injuries."

"What do you want, Frank?" Mike asks. "Why have you come here?"

The muscles in his arms harden as he forces the words out of his mouth. "I want to apologise for my behaviour over the years. I… should've been honest about Shae and Shy." He lets the words hang in the air. "I want the past to be in the past. I want us to parlay as the pirates say. I'd like us to try and forgive each other, if you'll let me."

42

Julian: Six Months Later

They say the scars will fade over time. I have one above my right eye and another in the shape of a crescent moon on my left cheekbone. The doctors said I had a concussion, wasn't as severe as I thought but they kept me on the ward for a couple of days for observation. Em was checked over, other than being cold and soaked through, she was given the all-clear. She visited every day, bringing Derek and Herb with her. Even Connie, Bran and Jim came along. I hate fucking hospitals; they remind me too much of Hanna. What made it worthwhile was that Frank and Mike had buried the hatchet of their problems. I don't know what occurred but seeing them chatting again by my bedside like old times was a beautiful sight to behold.

Mike doesn't know how Shae died. Frank's sworn me to secrecy and I agreed. I don't think he'd be able to live with himself…especially if he knew who was the root cause of it.

With the episode on the Molly, my little hometown didn't get a breather from the media. We received more attention we didn't want. Drew and her team ransacked the ship, finding footage on Waldemar's laptop of my colleagues beating up Shy along with Ian and Earl's murders. I had no idea there were cameras in that room. Drew also found vile videos of Waldemar assaulting Shy while she was unconscious. It was fucking disgusting. They were on that handheld camera; I saw him sliding it into his desk. I knew there was something wrong with him. He was too clean for a reason, scrubbing out the secrets and pain so we couldn't see him for the monster he really was.

Lance and Damien left Drake Cove without a single goodbye. We'd been friends for years and they just fucked off. The events must have tainted Drake Cove, living here was no longer a feasible option. Or, they scarpered to avoid a jail sentence. I reckon the latter.

With dwindling staff numbers and everything else going on, Mike was beyond stressed to keep the fisherie afloat. Dan hadn't drawn up a will and he had no next of kin. We had a good long chat with Mike's solicitor and it was his idea to give me Dan's share. I really didn't see myself as managerial material. Mike has this calculated professional way of dealing with all the administrative shenanigans. I don't. Frank offered to help and I was able to fill notepads of useful advice. Em encouraged me to take Mike's proposal, so I agreed.

We are now called Blocksidge and Finch.

I know. It still feels weird.

With this new responsibility comes the challenges of learning to do clerical work. I did bits and bobs before but now I'm spending more time in the office. We sold Dan's stuff and I bought a posh office chair with back support. It's really comfortable. I'm learning to type faster too but I still revert to plodding with my two meaty fingers. Mike's hands dance over the keyboard when he's typing. And he doesn't look down when he's doing it either!

We interviewed for three other positions. Herb and Derek did some advertising in the local paper and on social media. Frank sat in on the panel. We received more applications than I thought. It took a couple of days to figure out who we wanted. We chose David from Fishknot, an experienced fisherman looking for a new location. Oli from Yearling who was about five years younger than me. He was a chef and got sick of being stuck in a sweaty kitchen. For the third position, we went with Liam from Drake Cove who's our youngest worker yet; he's eighteen, ripe from school. It'll give him the experience he needs to start his career.

Mike and I agreed we wouldn't take up commercial whaling again. The big quids aren't worth burning our memories. I don't participate in the culling anymore. It's too painful. There hasn't been one since before everything happened. Pods haven't been spotted for a while and we're not sure why. I won't be in Drake Cove whenever it does start again. I'll have a trip to Valtern or drive to Fishknot and do a spot of shopping. I like it round there.

I worry about Frank but he seems more determined for change than ever. After Waldemar's death, the media didn't just drag Shy down as the introverted psychopath, they blamed Frank for her actions too. The FAAC loved it, lapping every burn and bone break chucked his way.

I think I would've buckled under that type of criticism. I don't know how he gets out of bed every morning. He's an exceptionally strong person and keeps himself busy whether it's writing his next book, appearing in documentaries or going travelling. Recently, he addressed Yearling City Council about environmental issues. It was televised and I found it really inspiring viewing. He's still searching for the existence of mermaids. I don't blame him. I want to know if there are more out there too. He took the broken whistle Emily found in Drake's Mouth to a historian and according to them, it dates back to the seventeenth century. It's crazy when I think about it.

Another world living behind the ordinary.

I'm not gonna lie. I think about Shy all the time.

Frank still has her paintings, he hasn't sold them, they're sitting in storage. I think it's too painful for him to let go. Em has her portrait of Octavia, the Sea Queen pinned up on her wall.

Learning to be a deputy manager and being a father tends to take up most of the day but the evenings are the hardest. I miss her terribly. And sometimes, I feel guilty for feeling that way because...

She's a killer. Or is she?

Fuck. I still don't know. I don't know if it was her on that tape or if it was someone else. I...don't want her to be a murderer. She saved Em from imminent death and there was no thought to it. The second Em fell, Shy flew off after her. *It was instinct.*

I dream about her a lot too. Sometimes we're happy to see one another and then she's sitting on her eerie throne, ordering the skeletons to execute me and I wake up soaked in sweat. Scary River hasn't made an appearance in my nightmares since being on the Molly. I hope I never see her sharp toothed vicious mug again.

I'm taking each day as it goes. I won't be hunting for love anytime soon.

I don't know what it is but when I'm out at sea, I feel Shy watching me. I swear I've seen her eyes in the water and when I look again, they're gone. It's probably wishful thinking on my part. But when we pull the net out, I hope I'll catch her... with her smouldering green hair draped around her shoulders.

Epilogue

She races through the blue abyss, kicking her legs, spearing her arms as she twists through the current, keeping up with the pace of the boat. She hears the frantic flapping of the large shoal of cod. There's a thundering crank and the net plunges into the water, engulfing a cluster of the fish. Shy dips under the net - her temper ripening as the caged cod frantically swim. She pulls at the strings of the net, the muscles in her arms toughen as she yanks with all of her might. Pain erupts in her ears. Their calls double and triple in heightened hysteria.

They don't want to die.

The horrible cranking sound starts again and the net suddenly rises, taking Shy with it. She pulls the carved dagger from the seaweed lashed around her leg and begins to tear into the rope, hearing the groan of the crane. The intensity knocks her backwards. She somersaults as the net breaks loose from the crane. The cod plummet back into the North Sea, some of them spin like tidal waves creating gigantic air bubbles before dispersing themselves.

A fisherman she doesn't recognise races out of the cabin. He's young, maybe Emily's age. She giggles as some of the cod stroke her thigh and arm as they escape, a thankful gesture for their rescue. The net floats on the ocean's coat and the fresh-faced fisherman pulls it back onboard.

Her stomach dips when Julian emerges from the cabin. The younger fisherman shows him a part of the net, Julian

313

scrutinizes the rip; his auburn stare darkening momentarily as if an idea has sprung to the surface. He leans over the boat, examining Olivia's paintwork, searching for something.

It's wonderful and frightening to see him again.

He tracks the water and his eyes meet hers, it's just for a second but it breaks her trail of thought. The memories come hurtling back, causing goosebumps to ripple along her pale skin.

Shy panics and dives, arching her arms, kicking her feet so the belly of Olivia resembles a mere grey speck. She hides in the blanket of darkness, fathoms below, willing and wanting for her wild pulse to slow.

~

After a while, Olivia sails off. Shy waits until she feels absolute reassurance the boat is gone. Her hair lights the way, causing emerald sparks to drift.

Large shadowy clouds coast towards her and she clicks her tongue, the tendons in her throat vibrate. Shy asks the pod where they're swimming to and the leader replies. She screeches at the sound of the dreadful place and warns them off. Members of the pod squeal when Shy recounts her story, expressing her worry of their possible bloody fate. She dips underneath the family, pleading for them to change course. The leader bows its speckled head, thanking her, heading the way they initially swam.

As the evening draws in, Shy returns to her spot in the coral reef. Seeing Julian again was like a dagger to the chest. She misses her father and her friends. She loves her garden, she yearns to paint again, to sleep in a bed with the gentle whistles of the wind outside her window. But she couldn't go back. Drake Cove isn't safe anymore.

Tiredness aches in her joints and strokes the chambers

of her mind. Her imagination tumbles into deep dreams of a better world. Her body floats weightlessly, her green hair curls around her limbs, encasing her in a protective cocoon. To any roaming outsiders, her body is merely a limb of seaweed swaying with the flow of the tide. A simple, natural fragment of the ocean's heart.

Kateri Stanley

Kateri Stanley is a pseudonym for the multi-genre fiction writer. Since being a child, Kateri has been inspired by the wondrous mediums of books, music, TV and film. After working in the healthcare industry for eight years and studying for an Arts and Humanities degree, she made the decision to move cities in the West Midlands and live with her ever-suffering partner and their two cats. Her debut novel *Forgive Me* was published by indie press house, Darkstroke Books in 2021 and it reached #1 in the US Horror Fiction charts on Amazon. She is currently working on her third novel, Bittersweet Injuries and would love to pursue a full-time career in writing.

Kateri can be found across social media and her website: http://www.kateristanley.com

Twitter: @sal_writes **Facebook**: @salwrites2

Instagram: @sal_writes

Also from Burton Mayers Books…

Renata Wakefield, a traumatised novelist on the brink of suicide, is drawn back to her childhood hometown following her mother's ritualistic murder.

£7.99 UK

A fast-paced blend of science fiction and historical fiction interwoven into an ancestral, time-travel mystery.

£7.99 UK

Lightning Source UK Ltd.
Milton Keynes UK
UKHW010637170522
403125UK00002B/312